THE BOY WHO KNEW THINGS

Martyn Croft

ISBN: 978-0-9559872-4-3

In this work of fiction, the characters, places and events are either the product of the author's imagination or they are used entirely fictitiously. Any resemblance to actual persons, living or dead, is purely coincidental.

For Shell, who encouraged me to keep writing.

'*I have seen the future, and it works*'.

Lincoln Steffens (1866-1936)

3

CONTENTS

1

Memories

Little Ed could see things; things that no one else could see; things that didn't even exist – in the real world. Ever since he had been a baby, he had had 'experiences', like the one he only had distant memories of – memories of his cot and seeing his 'Uncle Eddie' standing beside it and smiling at him. He had realised later, by the time he was about four that it couldn't have been his real Uncle Eddie, who *was no longer with us* to quote his mum, but it had left him with a strange feeling that he had met his mother's brother after he had *passed on*. There had been another occasion that had kept coming back to Ed – memories of a previous Christmas, shopping in Fenton-on-Sea with his grandma. Confused images of his uncle as Santa Claus in Woolworth's came to him in his dreams – recognised from the framed photograph that hung over the mantelpiece at home at 26 Acacia Avenue, Fenton-on-Sea, on the East Anglian coast.

Ed was five now and it was Monday, September the 8th 1975; his first day at Fenton Central Junior School – the school his Uncle Eddie had started at nineteen years previously; the uncle he had never met and the uncle that had disappeared in strange circumstances a few years before Ed had been born. His mum, Jenny Compton-Jones, didn't talk much about her brother and often used phrases like: '*God took him, dear*' and '*He's in a better place, Ed*', to explain his absence from her only son's life.

By the end of that first day in school, Ed had learned a little more about the disappearance of his Uncle Eddie and at tea-time he had questions for his mother.

"Mum?"

"Yes, love."

"Mum, how did Uncle Eddie die?"

His mum looked wistfully at her son and nervousness was etched on her face.

"Die? He's not dead, dear."

"Miss Sandbuck says he his. Says he ran away from home and he's in heaven now. You have to be dead to be in heaven, don't you, Mum?"

Ed's mum was getting tetchy. She had dreaded this moment.

"How did she come to tell you that, dear?"

"She's my teacher and she said I didn't look much like my uncle and I asked her if she'd known him and, Mum …?"

"What?"

"She taught him, Mum, and she said everyone at school had been sad when he just disappeared one day. Did he run away, Mum?"

"No, dear, he didn't run away. It was just one of those things. Nobody can explain it."

"But he must be somewhere, Mum."

Ed paused to munch on a fish finger while he considered his next question.

"Can you go to heaven without dying?"

"I don't know, Ed, dear – maybe."

It was clear to Ed, even at his young age, that his mum didn't want to talk anymore about her brother – just like she didn't like talking about his dad. That had been a taboo subject for as long as Ed could remember. He'd had to be satisfied with his mum's simple but challenging explanation for each oddity in his short life so far: '*It was just one of those things*'. He almost seemed to know when people would be upset if he mentioned certain things – so he didn't. Ed could not only see things, he understood things as well. He could recognise emotions and feelings that normally took people years to understand, with some people never acquiring that perceptive side of their nature.

By the end of that term at Fenton Central Junior School, Ed had gained a reputation for always being one of the first to put his hand up whenever Miss Sandbuck asked a question. However, his written work was nowhere near as good as his uncle's and his mathematical prowess was sadly lacking. But Ed had other skills. He could remember things – things that his classmates needed to be told several times before they stuck. Sometimes, it even seemed to Miss Sandbuck, he appeared to know the answer before she'd asked the question. On one or two other occasions, Gabriella Sandbuck was also convinced that she'd asked questions that she hadn't previously given the answer to. Ed Compton-Jones seemed to 'know' things – things he'd no right to know.

Apart from this trait, there were two other things that stood Ed out from his classmates. One of them was observed in a friendly and sensitive way; the other was used to make him the object of some mickey-taking. Almost from the day he had been born and christened Edward James, his mother and grandparents had decided not to shorten his name to Eddie, out of respect for his uncle. Consequently, in order to set him apart in conversation and to provide him with his own identity, he was always addressed as 'Little Ed'. In the weeks before he started at Fenton Central Junior School, his mum had begun to drop the adjective though, strangely, it had come to fit him to a tee. Though chubby in his early months, that puppy fat had left him by his fifth birthday and he was now small for his age – unlike his uncle Eddie who had been slim and fairly tall. It had not been long into that autumn term before one or two of his peers had, albeit kindly, renamed him 'Little Ed', if for no other reason than to distinguish him from Edward Morrison, also of form 1Sb.

The butt of the mickey-taking was Ed's surname. Jenny Compton had split from her husband, one Gary Jones, before Ed had reached his first birthday. This separation had been less than amicable, but Jenny had been determined that her former spouse should not be relieved of his responsibilities, whether in deed or name. Unfortunately, for Jenny, Gary Steven Jones was sorely lacking on the first front and his son's surname would be virtually the only and, indeed, tenuous connection between father and son. To avoid embarrassment for her son, Jennifer Compton became Mrs Jennifer Compton-Jones and Little Ed was re-christened with his double-barrelled surname before he reached his second birthday. As Jenny would often say to her parents, Fred and Ann Compton:

"I'm not going to let him forget that he has a son."

Apart from Mr Sempleton-Osgerby at Fenton Central Junior School, Ed was the only other person with such a type of surname and the children of Form 1Sb had been quick to pick up on it. Mr Sempleton-Osgerby was fortunate in that only the staff new his full name; he was always referred to as Mr Osgerby in the children's presence. Little Ed had had to put up with several insensitive quips ranging from '*posh boy*' to '*two-name squirt*'. Unlike boys of that age of a more sensitive nature, Ed seemed to cope with the mickey-taking with admirable ease, using the name-calling to his advantage, particularly when it was combined with his unusual talent for answering questions in class before his fellow pupils. In short, he was envied, yes, for his seemingly 'posh' surname, but he was also respected for his obvious talent in other areas and by the end of the autumn term, the mickey-taking had begun to wane as this other talent gained him respect from teachers and classmates alike. Little Ed had an inner confidence and even at that tender age he already knew he was different from other boys. This would stand him in good stead for many years to come.

Ed had begun to acquire a small circle of friends at school by the time the last day of the autumn term approached. Thursday, December the 18th turned out to be cold with a touch of frost in the air, the first such day after a relatively mild start to the Christmas month. Initially that term, Ed had formed a natural friendship with his other namesake in the class. Edward Morrison, or simply 'Big Ed', had also gravitated to his namesake at the start of the term for a similar reason as Ed himself. Not to put too fine a point on it, young Morrison was fat and, though not enormously so, he was also the tallest boy in the class. His mum would probably have said he was built solidly of good farming stock. Indeed, the Morrisons were local East Anglian farmers who lived to the north-west of Fenton-on-Sea where Bill Morrison ran a small dairy herd on the excellent grazing land below Peewit Hill. Too much butter, cheese and cream were readily available in the Morrison family for 'Minor' to have any chance of having a sylphlike figure – at least not until he took an interest in members of the opposite sex. Though the pupils of Form 1Sb had soon cruelly christened the farmer's son with the name that emphasized his size, Ed himself had just as quickly named his friend both subtly and aptly after a car his grandad had once owned and continually talked about as '*the best little car I ever owned*'. Even aged five, Ed could display some irony in his choice of a name for Edward Morrison.

As usual that break time, the two Edwards wandered to their special corner of the playground to chat about the forthcoming holiday and the excitement that that time of the year held for them both.

"What's Father Christmas bringing you, Minor?"

"Dunno – I want a dog, but Mum says we've already got two but they're only farm mongrels and aren't allowed inside. I want a spaniel that can lie on my bed at night."

Ed smiled at his friend. He knew he loved animals whereas he had never really taken to them and preferred inanimate toys that couldn't wreck each other.

"Oh – I want a Jaguar racing car," replied Ed.

"What – a 'lectric one?"

"No, just one you wind up and let go."

Ed paused and thought for a moment before he continued.

"Do you want to come to my birthday party?"

"Are you gonna be six?" asked Minor with some surprise in his voice.

"Yeah, next Monday."

"Who ya inviting?"

"Just you and maybe Ian and Greg. I haven't really asked my mum yet. I think Granny and Grandad are coming, but they won't mind."

Minor was silent for a while until he seemed to pluck up courage to say,

"I don't like Greg – he calls me names."

"Like what?"

Minor looked slightly embarrassed.

"Smelly and piggy. Do you think I smell, Ed?"

"Of course not. He says it because your dad's a farmer and he just jealous."

"Well, I don't like him – Ian Flower is alright though."

"I'll just invite him, then. He's good at football."

Minor appeared to want to change the subject.

"What ya doing tomorrow?"

"Nothing much – Grandad says I can go with him to the station sometime over Christmas and watch him in the booking office. He works there, you know."

"Yeah, I know. I'm helping my dad, too – on our farm. You wanna' come and play, Ed? We've loads of different animals: ducks, geese and cows. I can show you them all and you can have tea with us as well."

"I'm not sure, Minor," replied Ed. "I'll have to ask my mum and see if she'll bring me."

"My dad'll bring you back. Do you know where Peewit Farm is?"

"No – is it far?"

"It takes mum about ten minutes by car in the morning when she drops me off. From here you go down the big road to the roundabout and then go on that rough road – our farm is near Peewit Hill. You can't miss it."

"My mum'll know, I expect," said Ed.

Just then the bell sounded for the end of morning break and the two boys made their way back inside. They were going to be playing games for the rest of the morning and then there was Christmas lunch to look forward to. School was scheduled to end after a small carol service in the assembly hall after lunch. Ed had lots to tell and ask his mum when he got home that afternoon – he'd never had a birthday party before. Would she let him have some friends to it? Come to that, would she let him have a party? All she'd said was that Granny Ann and Grandad Fred were coming round. Would she let him go to the farm and play with Minor? He'd never before been allowed to go to someone else's house and play without her being there. He didn't know it at that time, but Jennifer Compton-Jones was far more watchful of what her son did than most parents of children of that age and in that era. As far as she was concerned, nothing was ever going to happen to her Little Ed – nothing like what had happened to her brother Eddie. Although it wasn't much, Little Ed's mum knew more than anyone else about 'Uncle' Eddie's disappearance, including, in addition, one or two secret visitations by her brother's ghost, both before her wedding day and on the day itself. Maybe, in some strange way, it had been an omen of the impending break-up of the marriage. No one knew anything about those occurrences and Jenny herself wasn't even sure that they had really happened. As time had gone by she had put them to the back of her mind where they resided as nothing more than half-remembered dreams or even just wishful thinking. Indeed, whatever power lay behind the extraordinary visitations had also ensured that their memory would fade with time and much more quickly than would be normal for such paranormal events. If nothing else, these fading memories had left Ed's mum with an acute sense that her son was in some way special – special in a way that had been inherited from her brother Eddie.

Jenny was waiting for her son outside Fenton Central Junior School at two-thirty, nearly an hour earlier than usual. Acacia Avenue was only a few hundred yards to the north of the primary school on a new housing development which backed onto the maze of cul-de-sacs and closes of mostly pre-war houses, known locally as the Garden Estate. As soon as Ed ran out to meet his mum, he was agog with questions.

"Mum, mum, can I go to Minor's farm tomorrow and can he come to my birthday party? Can he, Mum? Can you take me, Mum?"

The gabbled and muddled questions hardly registered with Ed's mum and, as she took his hand outside the school gates, she did her best to stop him jumping and skipping as they made initially for 38 Fir Tree Close for tea with her mum, Ann Compton. The sun was already low on the horizon and shining directly into Jenny's eyes, causing her some difficulty in absorbing the excitement written all over her son's face.

"Slow down, dear – one thing at a time. Now what's this about tomorrow?"

"Minor says I can go and play with him at his farm and stay for tea."

Ed's mum smiled knowingly.

"And has he asked his mum, Ed?"

Ed shrugged his little shoulders.

"Dunno."

"Well, I'll ring Mrs Morrison when we get home, but I'm not sure I want you outside in this weather, dear. We'll have to see. It might be O.K. – at least I'm not at work tomorrow."

Ed looked a little upset at this perceived setback. He seemed about to cry and said,

"Minor says his dad will bring me home, Mum. I'll wear my big coat and my wellies."

They had reached the entrance to Fir Tree Close by now and Ed was reminded of his second question.

"Are Granny and Grandad coming on Monday, Mum?"

"Yes, I hope so. Why?"

"I've invited Minor to come to my party."

"What party? We're only having some tea, love. You are naughty, Ed."

And then Ed's mum began to wonder how far the idea of a party had gone. She stopped walking outside number 38.

"Who else have you invited, Ed."

"Nobody, Mum. I was going to ask Ian Flower but I forgot. Anyway, he wouldn't be able to come."

"Why? What's he doing?"

Ed looked coy.

"He's going to be sick, Mum."

"Going to be?" queried Jenny, but as soon as she'd phrased her simple question she knew what her son's reply would be.

"Yeah, I just know he'll get a cold over the weekend"

And then to disguise his strange prediction, he hurriedly qualified his statement.

"He sneezed at lunchtime, Mum – I saw him."

Ed's mother smiled inwardly as they walked up the front path of 38 Fir Tree Close. There had been a certainty about her son's original remark; a certainty she had learnt over time to accept without question. Her son's 'guesses' had a strange habit of coming true. Seeing the pensive look in her son's eyes as they reached the front door, Jenny said,

"I'll ring Mrs Morrison when we get home, Ed. If it's alright with her you can go tomorrow and Minor can come on Monday – just try to remember to ask me first in future – alright?"

"O.K., Mum."

Warmth suddenly radiated into their faces as Ed's grandma opened the door and Ed ran forward into her arms.

Hi, Granny. I'm going to a farm tomorrow and …."

An uneasy feeling permeated Jenny's being as her son gabbled out the reality of her decision. The birthday tea wasn't a problem – her son would be in her care and sight the whole time, but the farm …. She began to regret at least one of her decisions.

2

Peewit Hill Farm

Ed and his mum stayed until just after five, just long enough for Fred Compton to get home from work at Fenton railway station and see his grandson. Fred was getting accustomed to leaving work earlier as he approached his retirement in about three years time. There was even the possibility that he might take early retirement the following summer to spend more time gardening. Ann Compton certainly wanted him to, particularly when she had to listen to her husband moan about how things had changed on the railways in recent years. She constantly reminded him that his assistant, Gordon White, was just about ready to take over the reins as the senior booking clerk.

Though it was dark and the pavements were getting icy, Jenny and Ed declined the offer from Grandad Fred to drive them the short distance home. When the new housing development had been completed on the north side of town, an alleyway had been conveniently constructed between numbers 48 and 50 Fir Tree Close which led directly into Acacia Avenue, and Mother and son were soon home at number 26. A surprise was waiting for Ed after he had walked through the front door.

"*That* came for you today in the morning post, Ed. Mrs Stanley brought it round after I got back from work at one."

Ed's mum pointed knowingly at the small package on the telephone table in the hall.

"Ooh – what is it, Mum?"

"I don't know what it is, but I think I know who it's from – I can recognise the writing."

"Who, Mum?"

"Daddy."

Ed's response said it all with regard to the almost non-existent relationship with his father, Gary Jones.

"My daddy, Mum?"

It had been over two years since his dad had even sent a card at Christmas or on Ed's birthday, let alone a present. Indeed, Jenny had also fallen out with Gary's parents over the issue and hadn't spoken to them since, thus depriving Ed of a full complement of grandparents.

"Ooh, can I open it?"

"Not till Monday," replied Ed's mum, even though she was quite curious to see what her former husband had sent her son. She had had virtually nothing off Gary for the last four years and she was still seeking child support from him, so this package was giving her some cause for thought and, possibly, concern. Ed held the package up to the light to see if he could make out what was inside but apart from it being quite a heavy parcel, he could determine nothing of its contents and he soon gave it to his mum and said in his innocence,

"I don't think it's a Jaguar, Mum," and then Ed turned to his mum and continued,

"What's he like, my dad? Is he big?"

It was a simple and naïve question from a soon-to-be six-year-old but it seemed to fluster his mum who hadn't kept a single photograph of her former husband. Indeed, she rarely talked about him apart from the odd occasion when her parents raised the issue of maintenance. She answered a little guiltily.

"No, not very big. He's quite handsome, though."

Those few words were more than she had said in quite a time to Ed about his father and she had found it almost painful to give the simple description to her son. Ed could tell it was not the time to persevere with his inquiry, natural enough though it was. Unlike the vast majority of boys of his age, or indeed, of any age, Ed didn't possess that instinct for a father figure in his life simply because he had never had one. He didn't know what it was like to have two parents. It would not be long, however, before he would realise that he *was* missing something that other boys had, but at that moment his mum was all he needed. He reached up and put his arms round her waist.

"I love you, Mum."

A tear or two began to well up in Jenny's eyes as she kissed her son lightly on his head. Part of her knew that she had been partly to blame for the lack of a relationship between father and son, but it was hard to put aside her own animosity towards Gary. Another part of her reminded her that he had never shown any interest in Ed almost from the day he had been born. Alcohol and other vices, and not fatherhood, had seemed more important to him. Secretly, she was, however, beginning to hope that the surprise gift might be the start of a relationship between Gary and Ed which could remain independent of hers with her son.

After the prolonged hug between mother and son, Jenny pushed him gently away from her and said quietly,

"C'mon, Ed, you can go and watch some television until bedtime. You can stay up till half past eight tonight with no school in the morning. I'll go and phone Mrs Morrison about tomorrow. Did you have enough to eat at Granny's?"

No reply was forthcoming as Ed had already disappeared into the lounge to curl up in his favourite position on the sofa. He would be fast asleep by seven, having relaxed in a good humour after his mum had confirmed the arrangements for his visit to Peewit Hill Farm at two o'clock on the following afternoon. It had been a long day with promise of much excitement over the next few days. His mum would not carry him to bed till after ten, reluctant, as she had been, to disturb his peaceful slumbers.

The following day turned out to be much milder than the previous one and, after the sea mist had lifted by mid-morning, Fenton-on-Sea became bathed in bright sunshine; as bright as it ever got so close to the winter solstice. The prospects for Ed's visit to Peewit Hill Farm looked good and by noon, he was impatient to make the short journey to see his friend and all the animals he had talked about. His mum had already lost count of the number of times he had asked the question: *'Are we going yet, Mum?'* Even replies like: *'After lunch, dear'* and *'only another few hours, Ed'*, did nothing to placate her son. Words like *'hours'* or *'after'* didn't really register much in her five-year-old's brain and by twenty past one with lunch over, she gave in to her son's urgings and dressed him in his black duffel coat, scarf, woolly hat, gloves and Wellington boots. By half past the hour they were already heading out of Fenton-on-Sea in Jenny's Austin 1300, bound for the 'rough road' to Peewit Hill Farm, if Ed's mum could locate it off the roundabout at the start of the A132. Find it she eventually did, but only after two complete circuits of said roundabout, having initially missed it for the most obvious of reasons – it wasn't a road, but just a grass-humped farm track. Minor's idea of a 'rough road' was based on his dad's negotiation of it in a tractor and not in an automobile with ordinary suspension! Fortunately, the nearer they got to their destination, marked by Peewit Hill itself, the track became easier to negotiate, having patches of tarmac that eventually joined into one even surface for the last quarter of a mile. The road widened out into a relatively clean and concreted farmyard surrounded on three sides by a series of barns and low outbuildings which were dominated in one corner by what looked to be a classic Victorian red-brick farmhouse. Green pasture rose up behind the house to the dominance of Peewit Hill. Ed caught a glimpse of several black and white cows slowly descending the lush-covered hill to the farm.

"Ooh, look, Mum – moo cows!"

Like his friend, Edward Morrison had also been excited by the prospect of having someone of his own age to play with. Farmhands Aaron and Ben were alright when they thought the gaffer's little son could offer them some help or when they just needed someone to tease, which they did on a regular basis, but Minor needed someone he could call his special friend. And he had decided that Edward Compton-Jones was indeed 'special' – at least as special as Nelson, the one-eyed black and white collie cross that followed him everywhere in the farmyard. 'Black-and-white' was also a fitting description of the two boys' hair colours. Unlike either his mother or father, Ed had eventually acquired a head of jet black hair, it having gone through several shades from ginger at birth to dark brown in his early months before settling on the darkest of shades. In complete contrast, Minor Morrison's was pure blond. Ed's strange hair transformation often caused people to comment that his mother had deliberately changed his hair colour with artificial dyes because it reminded her too much of her lost brother, Eddie. Nothing could be further from the truth and, though the process had been 'natural' enough, it seemed to mirror the development of his other strange talent. The two boys' skin colourings were again at different ends of the spectrum and not in keeping with the norm – Minor's was a deep ruddy brown, even in mid-winter, and Ed's was pale, made all the more colourless by the darkness of his hair. With the differences in their physiques and weights as well, their juxtaposition at school always struck an unusual sight to the casual observer – 'Little and Large' and 'Yogi Bear and Boo Boo' being the commonest and kindest appellations for the unlikely duo.

Minor had stationed himself at one of the dining room windows from almost exactly the same time that Ed and his mother had left their semi-detached house in Acacia Avenue. Bill Morrison was up on Peewit Hill with Ben Filsom, repairing a break in the old wooden fence in the upper pasture. Evelyn, his wife, was busy in the parlour-cum-office making Christmas decorations out of home-grown holly and flowers, suitably dried from that summer. The only other person at Peewit Hill Farm was seventeen-year-old Aaron Coppick, a local reformed tearaway ousted eighteen months previously from Fenton Secondary Modern School just prior to taking his CSEs. In the end, he failed to register a grade in a single subject which was hardly surprising since he also failed to attend on more than three out of the required ten occasions to sit the examinations in the first place. Mrs Coppick had pleaded with a couple of local farmers that Aaron was really a good boy and just needed to be given a chance. Kindly Bill Morrison had finally succumbed to Barbara Coppick's pleadings and took him on for a trial period for the month of August, 1974. After young Aaron had survived Bill's probationary period, his position was soon made permanent and he quickly blossomed into a strong, willing and surprisingly reliable worker. Though a bit rough and ready, he seemed to have a way with the animals and didn't even baulk at the less glamorous side of farm life – like mucking out the cow sheds; a task he was just finishing as Jenny pulled the pale yellow 1300 to a halt in the middle of the concrete apron. As Ed's mum made to open her door, a voice bellowed from a shed somewhere to her right.

"Hey – you can't park it there Missus! Farmer's gonna' bring them cows down soon for a-milkin'."

Jenny hastily pulled her door to and not only because of the unseen but unmistakable command.

"Phew, what a pong!" she said, restraining Ed from jumping out of the passenger door.

"Get back in. We'll drive right up to the farmhouse – might be less of a whiff there."

Ed's mum slipped the car into first and drove forward a further thirty yards or so, glancing in the rear view mirror as she did so to observe Aaron Coppick returning almost triumphantly to his mucking out. Jenny parked right adjacent to the window that Minor Morrison had just left. Another voice called out as Jenny opened her door for the second time. A dog was barking excitedly in the distance.

"Over here, Ed!"

Ed's mum peered over the car door to see Minor standing in the doorway of the main door to the farmhouse. Nelson seemed to be attached to him by remote control. Minor's excitement was there for all to see as he jumped up and down on alternate legs, waving almost as frantically, as if Jenny was suddenly going to jump back in her car and drive her charge away from Peewit Hill Farm forever. Nelson weaved in and out of Minor's legs desperately trying to avoid them on their downward stamp. Ed's mum leant back inside the car.

"Wow! He's a big lad. Are you really in the same class a school?"

"Yes, Mum. He's a nice boy and I like him. He's my friend"

Ed's extension and qualification to his affirmative response seemed to indicate that he had registered a veiled criticism of his friend in his mum's voice.

"I'm sure he is, dear. He looks pleased to see you. Let's go and see you inside."

By this time, Mrs Evelyn Morrison had also appeared in the doorway to greet Ed and his mum.

"Welcome, Mrs Compton-Jones," she said with some pleasure, as if she was gaining some satisfaction from being able to call someone by a double-barrelled name.

"Oh, call me Jenny, please. I'm sorry we're a bit early but Ed here wouldn't keep still at home," said Ed's mum as she approached the farmer's wife. Meanwhile, Ed said a quick goodbye to his mum and joined his friend, with Nelson displaying his own welcome by jumping up to lick his master's new friend's face. Ed's diminutive stature enabled said mutt to place a paw on each of the boy's shoulder with ease. The two women shook hands as Evelyn Morrison replied,

"Edward neither – he's been like a cat on a hot tin roof all morning. And please call me Evelyn."

The two mothers exchanged a few more pleasantries, including a mention of the two boys' identical first names. Evelyn Morrison put Jenny at her ease by saying,

"We don't mind him being called Minor. We started calling my husband Bill Senior as soon as Edward told us that's what he was nicknamed at school – better than some of the things he could be called ...,"

Minor's mum paused while the two boys, with Nelson in tow, made their way inside the farmhouse. She continued when they were out of earshot.

"... given his shape and size."

After Minor had taken Ed on the obligatory tour of the magnificent old farmhouse with the young visitor's eyes widening by the minute, they returned to the stone-floored kitchen to decide how to spend the time until teatime. Just then, with Minor unsure what to show his friend next, his mum popped her head into the kitchen; she had only just finished talking with Jenny.

"Why don't you take Ed to the lower field to watch your dad and Ben bringing the herd down for milking? You'll have to be quick, though; they're already leaving the top pasture."

Minor needed no second instruction and Ed trotted after his friend who had already made for a rear door at the back of a room that had all the hallmarks of a heavily-used laundry – *'farmers get dirty'*, as Mrs Morrison was prone to say. Down a narrow stony path the two boys scampered to a stile and gate which formed the entrance to the lower field. Ed had found it difficult to keep up with his friend who, despite his size, seemed to be very fit and surprisingly athletic as he clambered on top of the stile where, at last, he rested while Ed caught up. He peered between the bars of the gate and watched as the mainly black and white phalanx moved like a crocodile towards them.

"Ooh," remarked Ed. "There's a lot. Will they get out?"

"Not till my dad lets them. He'll open the gate and they'll go down the way we've just come," replied Minor proudly. "Sometimes Dad let's me help with the milking, but I'm not allowed on the path when they come down, so we'll have to go back when they reach the gate."

"How many cows are there?" whispered Ed.

"Don't know – thousands, I think."

Ed smiled at his friend. Could there be that many? He studied the advancing mass but said nothing. Five-year-old boys could exaggerate wildly and, in this case, Minor was out by twenty-fold or more. The noise of the cows was suddenly getting quite frightening for the two boys and, after a final look, they quickly ran the short distance back to the farmhouse. This time, Minor led Ed round the left-hand side of the building through what appeared to be a small herb garden to reach the concrete apron in front of the house. Nelson was there to greet them; he clearly wasn't allowed near the cows and had stayed behind. Minor shooed him to the front door where he trotted obligingly and disappeared inside. The two boys took up a position on the edge of the apron furthest from the cowsheds.

Ben appeared first and, with Minor's dad in the rear, the cows were swiftly and efficiently ushered into the milking sheds. Minor shouted a greeting to Ben and received a cheery wave in response. When Bill Morrison finally arrived and had checked all the cows home one-by-one, Minor then, and only then, ran up to him and clutched at his sleeve. It seemed a well-rehearsed ritual designed for the safety of all, whether animal or human.

"Dad – this is my friend. He's called Edward like me, Dad, but everyone calls him Ed."

"Hello, young Ed," said Minor's dad as he ruffled Ed's shiny black hair. He laughed and continued. "Quite the little magpie, aren't we?"

Ed looked blank and had visions of his mum's apple pie until Minor said,

"What's an 'agpie, Dad?"

"Oh, just a bird – I've shown you one lots of times."

Whether it recalled anything in Minor's memory was irrelevant, since the comparison was totally lost on its intended recipient and Ed would spend the rest of the afternoon wondering why Farmer Morrison had called him an apple pie.

For the next half an hour or so, the two boys were allowed to stand quite close to the cows as they were milked, Ed gasping in astonishment at the amount of liquid that a cow could contain, both white and pale orange in colour. When they got bored, Minor took Ed on a tour down a short farm track to a pond where they spent some time feeding the ducks with bread and scraps brought out to them by Minor's mum. Before long they heard Mrs Morrison calling them in for tea. Time seemed to have flown by that afternoon and eventually, with the light fading fast and an icy nip in the air, they returned to the cowsheds where they joined up with Minor's dad who led them back into the warmth of the farmhouse kitchen before he disappeared into the back. The table was set for four; Ben and Aaron had made their way back to their own homes.

"You sit there, Ed," said minor's mum warmly. "Just help yourself. There's ham and fresh cheese with cakes afterwards. Bread and butter is in the middle. You like orange squash to drink, don't you?"

"Yes, Mrs Morrison."

Ed looked nervously about him and didn't pick up his knife and fork. Minor's mum sensed something was wrong.

"What's the matter, dear? Don't you like ham and cheese?"

"Oh no, I like them both, but …."

And then Evelyn Morrison knew what the problem was.

"Here – let me get it for you and cut it up."

Ed's little shoulders relaxed and he murmured,

"Thank you, Mrs Morrison."

Minor's dad soon returned, clearly washed and changed into fresh clean clothes. Ed still couldn't pluck up the courage to ask him why he looked like one of his mum's pies and the lavish tea passed off without further alarm or embarrassment. At the end of the feast, Ed was beginning to understand why members of the farming fraternity seemed to be larger-than-life people in more ways than one! The conversation had covered nearly every aspect of farming life and while a lot of it was way above Ed's head, the final part sparked some interest in him. A chance remark by Minor jogged something in his special memory.

"Dad?"

"Yes, son."

"Dad – how many cows have we got?"

Bill Morrison smiled. He knew precisely how many he had, but he liked to have his fun with his son.

"Well, let me see now – you saw them all this afternoon. Didn't you count them? How many would you say?"

Minor screwed up his face – his dad knew he wouldn't have a sensible answer as he was sure his son couldn't count much beyond forty or so. But Minor had *an* answer.

"Well, I say we've got thousands, Dad, but Ed laughed at me."

Bill Morrison grinned widely.

"Thousands, eh? That would make me a millionaire, son, I think."

"What about you, young Ed. How many do you say?"

Ed appeared to close his eyes as though he was trying to remember some forgotten dream. A few silent seconds passed and even Minor's mum paused from clearing the plates away. Then, Ed's eyes opened wide and he looked directly at Bill Morrison, fixing him with a glazed stare.

"You have fifty-seven cows today, Mr Morrison."

Bill Morrison's jaw dropped ever so slightly.

"Well how did you come up with that figure, son? What a fantastic guess. Do you know you're only one out? I actually have fifty-six. I'm amazed – did you count them?"

"No – I just saw them and I know there are fifty-seven."

The kitchen went silent for a moment and it appeared that Minor's dad was about to get angry with the five-year-old who was contradicting him so adamantly, but soon a broad smile reappeared on his face and he relieved the strange tension.

"Well what a clever boy you are. What's one cow anyway? You're a very good counter – I shall have to employ you next time I count them in. Fifty-seven, eh? Well that is good news, mother."

Bill Morrison winked at his wife who returned in kind. Minor also seemed pleased that, as far as he was concerned, his own estimate hadn't been too far out.

"Well that's nearly a thousand, isn't it, Mum."

"Course it is, love. You were nearly right."

More winks were exchanged between wife and husband. Ed said nothing further and no one seemed to want to discuss the matter further.

The rest of Ed's stay at Peewit Hill farm was spent mostly playing with Minor's wooden replica farm until at seven o'clock Bill Morrison broke up the boys' fun by announcing,

"Your mum's phoned, young Ed. She wonders when you're coming home. What time did she tell you?"

"I forget – I think she said about six but I don't have a watch and I can't tell the time."

Half an hour later, Ed was back home courtesy of a bumpy and somewhat smelly ride in Bill Morrison's battered Land Rover. He didn't receive even the mildest telling off for being late – his mother just seemed to be relieved that he had arrived home safely and in one piece, despite the lingering odours that still clung to his clothes. A hot bath and a warm cuddle on the sofa restored some sort of normality after the excitement of an exhausting afternoon – exhausting for both son and mother.

It was mostly a peaceful evening too at Peewit Hill Farm, particularly after Mrs Morrison packed her son off to bed shortly before nine, though he actually didn't need much persuading. However, at eleven, Bill Morrison made his usual inspection of the cowsheds only to discover that one of the animals was clearly going into labour. The local vet was quickly summoned and at five minutes to midnight Bill's herd was increased by one to fifty-seven.

3

Birthday Party

Bill Morrison was normally an unemotional and carefree character, at one with nature and all her foibles, but that equanimity had been sorely disturbed by something that seemed to him to be more than a little unnatural. For a man barely out of his thirties, his prematurely greying hair always seemed to be at odds with his ruddy and healthy complexion and it had turned a touch whiter by the following morning. He had had an unusually restless night after he had eventually got to bed at one-thirty. He just couldn't get 'young Ed's' words out of his mind: '*You have fifty-seven cows, today, Mr Morrison*'. It wasn't the accuracy of Ed's estimate that bothered him so much as the use of the word '*today*'. If his new calf had been born even just five minutes later, he would still have had just fifty-six cows '*today*'.

His wife, however, didn't seem to be suffering from the same apprehension but knew her husband well enough to recognise something was troubling him. After the early morning milking, Bill returned to the farmhouse for his breakfast just after seven-thirty. Light was just breaking over Fenton-on-Sea but the dark and brooding presence of Peewit Hill did nothing to raise his troubled spirit as he made his way inside. He'd hardly had time to wash his hands before Evelyn remarked,

"What's up, love? You were tossing and turning all night."

Evelyn placed Bill's usual platter of bacon and eggs in front of him and placed both hands on his shoulders. He looked up into the warmth of her equally ruddy face surmounted by her jet-black tresses that dangled to her shoulders. Only her weathered complexion gave a hint of her daily routine. The rest of her demeanour said beauty model or raven-haired film star. Bill Morrison was helpless, as usual, and he couldn't do anything else but unburden himself to the person he loved more than anyone or anything else in the world.

"It's nothing really, I suppose, but I just can't get that friend of Edward's out of my mind. I mean – how could he be so accurate with his guess? It's almost as if …."

Bill paused, unsure of what to say next.

"As if?" queried Evelyn.

"As if he wasn't guessing – he just knew. Did you see the look in his eyes? It was spooky; like he was remembering what he'd seen and was doing the counting there and then or even …."

Again, Bill went silent, struggling for the right words. His wife tried to help him out.

"Or even that he was communicating with a spirit?"

"Ye-es. Did you notice it too, then? said Bill excitedly, as if his suspicions were about to be confirmed. His hopes were soon dashed.

"Oh, come on, love, lighten up – I was joking! He just made a lucky guess – he didn't actually get it right, did he?"

Then Evelyn regretted what she'd said as her husband retorted,

"He did by the end of the day. By midnight we had fifty-seven cows, just like he said: '*You have fifty-seven cows, TODAY, Mr Morrison*'. Remember?"

Either his wife didn't remember or she didn't *want* to remember – she didn't like the way the conversation was going.

"I wasn't really listening, Bill. It did strike me a bit odd at the time that he should be so close with his guess, but I just put it down as precisely that – a guess. Now forget about it and eat your breakfast before it gets cold."

"Alright, love, you're probably right – but I'm going to ask Minor about his friend when he gets up. The boy just seemed strange to me – it was those eyes; they just stared at me. I didn't like it."

Evelyn Morrison was getting cross with her usually unflappable husband.

"Oh, give it a rest, will you – you're letting your imagination run away with you. Ed Compton-Jones is not strange – he's just a very observant little boy. He's only five for goodness sake and his mum appears a very nice girl. She was telling me how hard it has been for her, raising Ed on her own. He probably isn't used to talking to men, especially one so 'strange' as you, to quote you."

Bill Morrison actually then managed to raise a laugh and put out a long arm to hug his wife.

"Sorry, dear – I'm just being silly," he said, and the debate was finally at an end. Evelyn Morrison looked satisfied that she had placated her husband, but as far as he was concerned, memories of his first meeting with the little 'magpie' would remain with him for some time.

In all the excitement of his friend's visit to the farm the day before, Minor had forgotten to ask his mother if he could go to Ed's 'birthday party' on the coming Monday and he was therefore somewhat surprised when his mother pre-empted him when he came down to breakfast at eight-fifteen, just as his dad was finishing reading that week's Fenton Times.

"Mrs Compton-Jones says you are going to Ed's for tea on Monday – you haven't asked me yet, have you? Ed's mum told me yesterday."

"Forgot, Mum. Can I go? Will you take me?"

Bill Morrison looked up from his newspaper. A frown had returned to his face. He started his investigations.

"Where does the little magpie live, son?"

Minor seemed offended by his dad's nick-name for his friend and he replied somewhat indignantly,

"His name is Ed, Dad – not 'agpie."

"Sorry, son – I mean Ed. Well, where does he live?"

"I don't know, Dad, but I think his grandad works at the station."

"Ah," said Minor's dad as if things had suddenly become clearer, which to some extent they had. Bill Morrison knew Fred Compton and he had vague recollections of his daughter Jennifer who once worked in Arleson's the bakers in the High Street. Sam Arleson bought his cheese and butter for his rolls and sandwiches from Peewit Hill Farm. Little Ed's double-barrelled surname also brought back memories of Jennifer Compton's marriage to Gary Jones. It had taken Bill Morrison only a couple of seconds to put all the facts together. He repeated his acknowledgement.

"Ah, I see. Well, let's hope this Edward doesn't disappear, then."

With that and without explaining his apparently cryptic statement, Minor's dad got up from the table, kissed his wife on the cheek and left for the duties of the day. Farmers didn't really distinguish weekends from weekdays. Mother and son were both left slightly bemused by the farmer's concluding remark, though it jogged something in Evelyn Morrison's memory about a past tragedy in the Compton family. Minor put no such connotation on his dad's words and said innocently,

"Ed only disappears when he goes back to his house, Mum. He comes back every morning at school."

"Yes, dear," said his mum sympathetically. "We all disappear sometimes. Your dad didn't mean anything else."

Minor's mum paused and then continued.

"How are you going to get to Ed's house on Monday, then?"

"Can you take me in the Lan' Rover?"

"Of course I will – there's just one problem, dear."

"What, Mum?"

"You said you don't know where Ed lives."

"Oh, figglesticks," replied Minor with a childish mock grimace.

"Fiddlesticks, Edward. Please talk properly – you're not a baby anymore. It's just as well that Ed's mum gave me all the instructions yesterday, then, isn't it, young man?"

The weather turned for the worse that Saturday lunchtime and by mid-afternoon, Fenton-on-Sea was clothed in a blanket of snow. Bill Morrison's pure-bred Holstein-Friesians were confined early to the cowsheds to graze on the stored hay, and by three-thirty, the farmer was back in the parlour with his feet up. Ben Filsom had joined him for a quick afternoon drink. Ben was a couple of years older than his boss and lived in a farm cottage on the other side of Peewit Hill close to the banks of the River Wentham. He and his wife, Mary, had rented the small dwelling from Bill for the past five years, ever since Ben had come to work for him after a spell serving in the army in Northern Ireland. Though he was a local man by birth, he'd left Fenton-on-Sea when he had joined up to do his National Service and had stayed on as a regular soldier until he left the army when he turned forty. Finishing as a corporal, he had an unfortunate habit of treating Bill's other worker, Aaron, with some disdain, ordering him about as though he was an army private under his charge. Aaron seemed to put up with Ben's overbearing nature, whether by choice or by fear. Bill did his best to keep them on separate jobs around the farm; Ben tending to the cows on the western pastures below Peewit Hill and Aaron the farmyard, the milking and the meadow down to the pond which marked the eastern boundary of the farm facing the outskirts of Fenton. The two men had just finished their second glasses of

Bill's home-made beer when Ben got up to make his way back to River Cottage in his own rusty Land Rover.

"Better be going, Bill – before the snow gets any worse. Mary'll only worry."

"Alright, Ben …."

Bill Morrison stood up beside his farmhand and, after a pause, said,

"How many cows have we got, Ben?"

Ben looked oddly at his boss.

"You know how many we've got, Bill. You keep an accurate record – it's in your book and you've never shown me that. You seem to like to keep it secret from me. You told me we had enough grazing pasture for up to a hundred at full capacity and I know you said we had about eighty when I first came here, but that's all I know."

"Yes, *I* know how many we've got, but do you? Have you ever counted them for yourself?"

"No, boss – I didn't think I was supposed to. I always lead them down for milking so I don't really see them altogether like, and when they're in the upper pastures they're so scattered it's impossible to count them. I bet even Aaron doesn't know and he helps with the milking when they're in their stalls."

"No, I know it's not part of your job. Don't get me wrong, I'm not getting at you, mate. I just wondered if you could estimate how many."

Ben Filsom stroked the two-day stubble on his chin.

"I should say there are less than a hundred – maybe seventy or eighty. I know there's one more since last night, boss. Am I close?"

"Not bad, Ben – there are fifty-seven to be exact."

"Oh," said Ben with some disinterest. "Not as many as I thought."

Bill Morrison smiled and with that Ben made his way out of the farmhouse, shouting his cheery farewell to Evelyn who was in the kitchen making some bread. Bill sat down in his fireside chair and scratched his head in thought. His little test had confirmed what he had suspected – it wasn't easy to count a herd of cows when they were wandering aimlessly in a field. Even his own cowhand hadn't ever bothered to do it, yet a five-year-old boy who had never seen them before had come up with the exact number. It couldn't be a coincidence; it just couldn't.

Jenny Compton-Jones only just got back from her part-time job at 'Curls and Twirls', the hairdressing salon in Hamsden, before the snow started in earnest early that Saturday afternoon. The drive from the nearest large town to Fenton-on-Sea took her ten minutes longer than the half an hour that the twelve-mile journey normally took. It was fortunate that she only worked every other Saturday morning from nine till one; otherwise she might never have made it. By the time she reached her parents' house in Fir Tree Close where her son had spent the time while she'd been at work, driving conditions were becoming difficult and she wasted no time in bundling him in to the car for the short trip home to Acacia Avenue. Though it was a journey of only a few hundred yards, it proved to be almost as tiring as the drive down the A132 from Hamsden, particularly with Ed offering up his opinion on the wintry scene at every minute of the way.

"Can we build a snowman, Mum, when we get home? Can we?"

"Let's just get home first, Ed."

"I wish Minor could come and play – we could make snowballs."

"You'll see Minor on Monday – it looks like the snow will still be here then, love."

"Granny said that Uncle Eddie fell over in the snow, Mum. Did he? She says a nice man carried him home from the big road. You have to be extra careful when it snows, Mum – Granny says, or you may break your legs."

Jenny smiled at the distant memory when her brother had been about twelve; more than ten years ago now, she thought as she manoeuvred the Austin 1300 onto the drive of her semi detached house – the house that she was now trying to buy courtesy of the Eastern Shires Building Society and with the help of a substantial deposit from her parents. Her part-time job at 'Curls and Twirls' – on three and half days plus alternate Saturday mornings – enabled her to just about make ends meet with her mother acting as baby-sitter for the time when Ed was not in school.

Unfortunately for Ed, the snow continued to fall heavily until well after dark and the snowman had to wait until the following morning. The front garden at number 26 Acacia Avenue looked like a battlefield by the time Ed and his mum had erected a Grandad look-a-like as Ed called their masterpiece. The snow was deep – over eight inches had fallen and the drifts in places nearly dwarfed Little Ed. No cars moved down the Avenue that day and very few on the morning of his sixth birthday too, causing Ed to continually look through the front room window, anxious as he was in case his friend might not be able to come that afternoon. Ed's mum was calm about the matter, reassuring Ed that farmers got around in all weathers and if a Land Rover could cross fields deep in muddy ruts, getting to Acacia Avenue would pose absolutely no problems whatsoever. And when, at two o'clock, Mrs Morrison telephoned to confirm that Minor was still coming – she had already been into town in the Land Rover – Ed finally forsook his position at the window. Jenny was more concerned about her parents getting there by their intended time of three o'clock, let alone them being able to get home after dark. Fortunately, it was only a short trudge through the alley from Fir Tree

Close and they arrived on time, as punctual as one of Fred's trains at the railway station. Ed was more excited than usual to see his grandparents because his mum had only allowed him to open a few of his presents – she wanted Granny and Grandad to witness the occasion and see the excitement on their grandson's face when he opened her present, their present(s) and, of course, that other present. She felt she needed their support when Ed opened *that* present. It was bound to raise comment whatever it was. She just hoped that Minor would not arrive till his directed time of four-thirty, giving them time for all the remaining presents to be opened and for the inevitable recriminations that *that* present would ferment.

Ed led his Granny Ann by the hand into the lounge to show her his remaining three unopened presents; two from his mum and one from his dad. Fred Compton followed and could not restrain himself from passing comment even though his grandson had obvious pride in his voice when he pointed out the brown paper-wrapped package on the sofa.

"And about time too. If I ever …."

Ann Compton tugged at her husband's sleeve and whispered,

"Shh – be quiet, Grandad. Let Little Ed open his presents. Here you are – this is from Grandad and me."

Ed took the large rectangular present from his grandma and replied with some indignation,

"I'm not little anymore, Granny – I'm six now."

Ann Compton smiled and said,

"Of course you are, dear – I'm sorry, Ed. Which one are you going to open first?"

Grandma and grandson sat down beside each other on the sofa while Jenny ushered her dad into the kitchen – she didn't want him spoiling Ed's surprise when *that* present was opened. She might have to sacrifice her own joy when her son opened her presents.

Four presents now lay on the sofa and Ed seemed to be uncertain which to open first.

"Well, come on, Ed – open your presents," said his grandma.

Ed paused, and grabbing his grandparents' present, said,

"I'll open mummy's when she comes back."

He tore at the wrapping paper to reveal the cardboard box inside.

"Ooh – it's a farm just like Minor's. Are there cows inside, Granny?"

"I think so, dear – and pigs and sheep. We'll set it up later when your friend comes. He'll know where everything goes, won't he?"

"Yes – he can have three cows and I'll have four. Thank you, Granny."

Ann Compton didn't bother to check whether the number of cows was marked on the outside of the box. If she had, she wouldn't have found reference to the quantity of any of the animals. She was more curious about the brown-paper package.

"You're very welcome, dear – now let's open your dad's present. I wonder what he's sent you."

This time, Ed held back on telling his grandma precisely what he thought (knew) it was.

"I bet it's not a Jaguar car, like I wanted," he said.

"Well, you're not going to find out unless you open it."

The parcel was so well taped that it took his grandma's help to reveal the box inside the several layers of paper.

"Oh – it's my mum's car," said Ed with almost mock disappointment. Opening the box revealed that Gary Jones had done his homework as Ed pulled out the sizeable 1:12 scale pale yellow Austin

1300 with friction wheels to power it. Within seconds, Ed had it racing across the lounge carpet, colliding with chair legs and walls. On its fourth journey it met with a human buffer – his grandad's feet – as Fred Compton entered the lounge after hearing the mechanical noises and squeals emanating from within.

"Now then – what's all this? What have you got, young Ed?"

"It's a car just like mum's, Grandad."

His daughter had obviously reasoned with Fred in the kitchen for his response was quite out of character.

"Well, you are a lucky boy, Ed. Let's hope you're able to see him one day and thank him."

"I will, Grandad – and thank you for my farm. It's brilliant!"

Jenny had followed her father into the lounge and smiled warmly, even though she had no idea how her son would accomplish his promise – she didn't know where Gary lived. Another thought came to her as she looked at her son and his grandad: '*Was this going to be the start of something she couldn't or didn't want to handle?*' She shuddered slightly at the thought and then shook herself together as she said,

"Come on – you haven't opened my presents yet."

Ed turned back to the sofa and picked up the smaller of the two remaining presents. His grandparents moved silently out to the kitchen.

"This one first, Mum," he said excitedly. His special talent didn't seem to have revealed to him what was inside as he continued, "Feels soft."

A few seconds later and his mum's first present lay in front of him on the sofa.

"Ooh – it's a Jaguar jumper!" he exclaimed as he picked up the British Racing Green pullover with the familiar Jaguar emblem emblazoned on the front.

"It'll keep you warm when you go out to Minor's farm, if you get invited again", said his mother. "It may be a bit big for you at the moment but it was the smallest size Osborne's in Hamsden do."

"Thanks, Mum," replied Ed as he looked at his last present. There were no histrionics as he opened it. Even at his tender age, he was learning to exercise care with his special foreknowledge. His response would have done an experienced actor proud.

"Ooh, ooh – it's an E Type! Wow, Mum – thanks!"

He placed the similarly coloured S4.2 Jaguar down on the sofa and reached over to hug his mother.

"I love you, Mum – how did you know I wanted one?"

"It wasn't hard, dear – you've mentioned it enough times over the last few weeks. I wasn't sure whether Father Christmas would remember you wanted one so I got it for your birthday."

What Ed said next barely registered in Jenny's mind and she wasn't sure she'd heard him correctly anyway. She made no response and kept her thoughts silent, fearing that part of the magic of Christmas had been lost forever from the special mother-son relationship. It would only be some time later that she would admit to herself the full significance of his words. In a low voice and to no one in particular, her son whispered,

"There isn't a Father Christmas."

Minor Morrison arrived amid another snowstorm and, at first, there was a concern that it might get so bad that his mum wouldn't be able to drive back, let alone come out again to collect her son at six-thirty. Fortunately, however, by the time Evelyn Morrison had deposited her charge, the snow had stopped and the temperature seemed to be rising a degree or two as well. The birthday tea passed off without any problems, and though no party games were forthcoming from any of the adults, the two friends played happily for an hour or so afterwards, alternating between Ed's new farm and races between Graham Hill and James Hunt. Surprisingly – no matter who handled it – the Austin 1300 seemed to come out on top every time, prompting Ed to say finally,

"I knew my dad's car would be the best," as if, by so saying, he was attempting to elevate his unknown father's status in his friend's eyes. Ed bore no grudges against his father, unlike those contained in the odd remark he had occasionally overheard from his mother or grandparents. Whatever he had done in the past, Gary Jones was still, and would ever be, Ed's father and the little magpie was beginning to warm to the idea of actually having one for real.

Mrs Morrison arrived to collect her son slightly earlier than arranged – at twenty past six – but, in any case, the two boys seemed to be ready to finish their playing as one or two squabbles had inevitably surfaced, particularly over who could send their car the furthest. While Ed's grandparents acted as referees and provided some much needed child control, Evelyn accepted Jenny's offer of a quick cup of coffee and chat about their two sons. Seated at the kitchen table, and well out of earshot of their offspring, the two women began to relax in each other's company.

"It must be hard bringing up Ed on your own, Jenny," said Evelyn.

"Yes – sometimes. He does need a father now he's growing up."

"Does he see him often?"

"No, he doesn't," replied Jenny quietly. "In fact, he ...."

And then Jenny found herself unburdening her life story, trying to be as honest and unbiased as she could with Evelyn Morrison who, after all, was still a relative stranger. It seemed easier, however, to talk to this woman about Ed and his non-existent father than if she had been talking to her own mother. A friendship was beginning to form. The conversation expanded to the problems of bringing up only children and the need for both their sons to form associations outside of their immediate families. Evelyn Morrison was clearly grateful that Minor had struck up, what seemed to be, a long-lasting and trusting friendship with Ed. A trust was also beginning to form between the two mothers as Evelyn then began to talk about her desire for more children, which obviously seemed to be a bone of contention with husband Bill. It appeared that, having produced a son and heir, with all the additional responsibilities that that entailed, he was reluctant to increase his overall flock. By the time her mum poked her head round the kitchen door, Jenny was even beginning to sense that her own son might be used by Bill Morrison as an excuse for not having more children. She could almost hear his argument: '*Well, he's always got young Ed to play with, Evelyn*'.

As soon as Jenny became aware of her mother's presence in the kitchen, the conversation changed to the more immediate need to get Minor home. It wasn't the right time – Jenny felt – to bring her mother into a discussion of the delicate issues associated with bringing up children, with or without two parents. Within five minutes, Minor and his mum were on their way back to Peewit Hill Farm, followed soon afterwards by Fred and Ann Compton making the short trudge back to Fir Tree Close. It had been a good afternoon for Jenny and Ed; both had cemented necessary friendships with Jenny being particularly pleased that she now had someone, other than family, to talk to about the one thing that was currently bothering her – the lack of a relationship between her son and his father, Gary Jones.

4

Reconciliations

Later that evening, with her son safely tucked up in bed, Jenny looked again at the model car that her ex-husband had sent Ed for his birthday. In addition, and out of curiosity, she went to the dustbin outside the back door and retrieved the brown wrapping paper it had come in. She knew deep inside it couldn't have been just a lucky coincidence that Gary should send an exact model of her own Austin 1300 – he had to have done it for a reason. Sitting there on her sofa staring at its now scratched paintwork, she realised that it must have taken quite a deal of research and no little effort to find such a toy. The question was: Why? She hadn't seen Gary, let alone spoken to him, for over three years and Ed had been only three when he had last sent his son even a card. Jenny wasn't even sure that Ed's father was still living in the area or that he was still a fireman with the Hamsden fire service. Though she too worked in Hamsden, she hadn't seen him around town since before Christmas four years previously and any of his colleagues she bumped into never mentioned his name in her presence, whether out of sympathy for her situation or simply because, as she suspected, he *had* left the fire service and probably the area as well. It was therefore with mild surprise that when she inspected the brown paper wrapping more carefully, she could just make out a Hamsden postmark in one corner. She knew it was Gary's writing on the brown paper but she also knew that his dad still had his second-hand car showroom in Hamsden and Richard Jones could easily have posted the parcel for his son. And then a thought struck her – she had bought her own pale yellow Austin 1300 from Richard Jones' Cars three years previously, while she had still been talking to Gary's father, so at least he might remember what type of car she owned. If not, Gary himself would probably have access to the garage records. It was so obvious, she almost laughed out loud – Gary hadn't needed much investigation; he had only to ask his dad – but at least it showed to Jenny that he had taken an interest in what she was doing. A strange warm feeling suddenly came over her – a feeling she hadn't experienced since before she ….

After a few more minutes of silent reflection, Jenny put the model Austin 1300 back in its box to be taken up to her son's bedroom later that evening. The wrapping paper would eventually end up in one of her bedroom drawers.

Gary Jones *had* left Hamsden and the fire service, where he had worked since he was nineteen. If he hadn't resigned from the service four years previously, he would, no doubt, have faced disciplinary proceedings leading to his dismissal in any case. Twice he had been sent off duty, having appeared at work under the influence of alcohol, which state had probably gone unnoticed on numerous other occasions as well. The drinking had started soon after he and Jenny had been married and was one cause for her leaving him; the other being his apparently less-than-platonic and continuing relationship with an old girlfriend. Humiliated and jobless, Gary had tried his luck in London, working as a garage mechanic in several seedy establishments in and around Tottenham, staying at each garage just long enough before his sloppy work was discovered. The drinking had continued and with most of his free time spent in the local bookies, Gary reached a position of degradation where even the long-suffering Richard Jones eventually refused to have anymore to do with his son.

It had taken a tragic piece of news to jolt him to his senses earlier that December. He had been walking in Oxford Street on a Saturday morning with no particular purpose in mind when he had chanced upon a former colleague from the fire service who was on a Christmas shopping trip to the capital with his wife. Dave Brooks stopped right in front of Gary, barring his path, before the ex-fireman showed any recognition whatsoever.

"Gary? Gary Jones? It is you, isn't it?"

Gary raised his head and was about to make some angry comment when recognition finally dawned.

"Ye-es – who the …."

"Dave – Dave Brooks – from Hamsden. Remember me?"

And Gary Jones suddenly remembered, but the next few words he would hear would be the catalyst for the change of life he desperately needed.

"I'm sorry to hear your dad's news. We all hope he's going to beat it – he's always been well-liked in Hamsden, you know, Gary."

"What news? What are you …?"

The cough had started that summer and two courses of antibiotics hadn't shifted it. A chest X-ray and follow-up bronchoscopy had confirmed the worse in late November – Gary's dad had cancer. Dr Reid at Hamsden County Hospital broke the news to Richard Jones and his wife, Mary – the tumour was inoperable and the course of drugs might only stave off the inevitable rather than provide a lasting remission. The prognosis had been kept under wraps within the town and only a very select band of people knew of Richard Jones' illness. Dave Brooks' wife, Shelagh, was one of that select group, working, as she did, in the office at the car showroom.

Gary Jones made his way home as quickly as he could that day, Saturday, December the 6th 1975, driving his battered MG at breakneck speed back to Hamsden and his parents' home. Within a week he had moved back in with them on a temporary basis at least. His mother was more welcoming than his father who continually made comments to his son like: '*It takes me to be seriously ill for you to put in an appearance*'. Gary took them all on his chin and eventually even gained a modicum of respect from Richard Jones as he took over the running of the car showroom with his father keeping a watching brief on the days when he felt well enough to join him. The transformation in Gary's character quickly included thoughts of his own son and the futility of his own situation when faced with the probability of the impending loss of his father. A chance meeting in London had prevented him finding out about his father before it was finally too late and the relationship had been more or less repaired. He made up his mind. He had much more to accomplish with his own son, with whom he had never even *had* a relationship, with no one to blame but himself. That journey began for him on Monday, December the 15th, exactly one week before his son's birthday. At least Gary hadn't forgotten that day six years previously. He hit upon the idea of sending his son the present which would have a special significance for his former wife, in the hope Jenny would recognise his attempt to start the relationship as both honest and rightly beneficial for Ed. As Jenny suspected, Gary had been idly checking the garage's sales record over the previous years and had discovered Jenny's purchase of the yellow 1300. Contacts in the motor trade enabled him to quickly obtain the scale model which was quickly dispatched to the Jenny's address, easily gleaned from the local telephone directory.

Gary had no idea how the present would be received or even if Jenny would know it was from him, as in his haste that week, he forgot to put any card inside to identify him as the sender. What he did know was that his son and, indeed, former wife still bore his name. It had been quite a nice surprise to see the double-barrelled surname both in the garage records and the public directory. It gave him hope that any kind of contact, no matter how tenuous, might not be rejected out of hand. After Jenny's quiet contemplation on the evening of her son's sixth birthday, it would have been clear that – to any independent observer – his contact had not fallen on deaf ears. In both Gary's and Jenny's minds it was a start.

Richard Jones passed away on April the 10th, 1976 – much more quickly than the doctors and consultants had thought he might. It had been a short illness and his will to live had probably been affected by his reconciliation with his son. He knew that the car showroom would continue in Gary's reasonably safe hands. In the months between December and April, father and son had formed a bond stronger than even that which had existed before Gary had moved away from Hamsden. Thoughts of pursuing any kind of bond between Gary and his own son were put to one side as Ed's dad took control both of the showroom and all the other matters that needed dealing with – from support for Mary, his mother, to funeral arrangements at the end of the family's ordeal.

The first sign that Gary's original olive branch had not been ignored by Jenny was the bouquet of spring flowers which arrived on the day of the funeral. The card attached to them read simply,

'Suffering with you all at this time – sincere condolences,
Jennifer and Ed'.

Jenny, too, had made reconciliation with Gary's father through one short visit to him in hospital when she knew his son would be at work.

Meeting them both together in such sad circumstances would have been too much for her and, indeed, a mistake – given that it would have taken some of the focus of attention away from the person who needed it most. Though brief, the visit had enabled Jenny and her ex-father-in-law to say some things to each other that they hadn't been able to when she had been married to Gary. One short sentence would remain with her as a guide for what had to happen next with regard to Ed and his father.

'*Please forgive Gary, Jenny – I know he wants to see Ed. He just doesn't know how to do it*'.

So when Jenny and her father turned up at the funeral at Hamsden crematorium on the afternoon of Thursday, April the 15th, the opportunity was there for the process of reconciliation to begin, albeit in the most tragic of circumstances. Jenny's mum did not attend as she had offered to collect Ed from school. As was etiquette, the mourners filed past Gary and his mother outside the tiny crematorium chapel after the cremation and service, shaking their hands as they did so and giving their individual words of sympathy. Gary had spotted Jenny and Fred Compton earlier at the service and was therefore at least partially prepared for the face-to-face encounter. Jenny's dad offered his hand first to Gary. Mary Jones was weeping too much to acknowledge many mourners and was stood to one side in the arms of an elderly lady who bore all the hallmarks of her mother. Fred Compton was simple and reasonably eloquent for a man of few words and who still harboured animosity towards Gary.

"Sorry, Gary – he was a nice man; an honest businessman."

"Thanks, Fred."

Jenny moved forward and, for one moment, Gary thought she was going to kiss him, but the movement had only been to enable her to whisper something in private.

"Ed says thank you for his birthday present. Give me a ring sometime."

Gary made to shake Jenny's hand or make even more intimate contact but she had already moved away, taking her dad's arm for support. Consequently, she didn't see the tears begin to roll down Gary's cheeks for the first time that day and, indeed, for almost the first time since Dave Brooks had given him the news about his father on a cold Saturday the previous December in Oxford Street.

In the wake of his dad's funeral, it took a couple of weeks before Gary found time and, indeed, the courage to phone Jenny. It was just before six on the evening of Friday, April the 30th and Jenny had only minutes before returned from collecting Ed from her parents' house where he had been taken after school. The ensuing conversation was to be both brief and semi-formal. Ed himself had taken to picking up the phone whenever it rang, despite Jenny's pleadings for him not to.

"Hello – who is it, please?"

There was a short pause while Gary gathered himself having guessed who had answered his call.

"Oh – er, is Jenny there, please?"

Silence – then in the background Gary heard,

"*Mum! It's a man for you.*"

A few more seconds passed and then Jenny picked up the telephone, seemingly just dropped by her son.

"Hello? Fenton 43891. Jenny speaking."

There was another pause before Gary answered.

"Jenny – it's me – Gary."

A few weeks previously and Jenny's answer would probably have been: '*Gary? Gary who?*' but her actual response was polite, short and apparently unemotional.

"Oh, hello, Gary. Just hold on a minute, please."

In the background Gary thought he could hear Jenny telling his son to go to his bedroom for a few minutes. There seemed to be a muffled debate about this unusual instruction that Ed had received, with him obviously insisting that he hadn't been naughty. Then there was silence until Jenny came back on the line.

"Sorry – just making sure that Ed couldn't listen in."

"Jenny – you asked me to phone you, so I ...."

Jenny cut in and her tone was not as welcoming as her whispered comment at the funeral had suggested.

"Well, you took your time."

"Sorry, Jenny – I've had a lot to do helping Mum sort out Dad's affairs and there's the garage ...."

Jenny then seemed more conciliatory.

"Of course – sorry. I just thought we ought to meet – for your son's sake."

"I'd been thinking the same thing, Jen. When?"

Jenny seemed prepared with the arrangements. She was obviously determined to see her ex-husband on her own before allowing him to see Ed. Things had to be taken a step at a time. There were so many implications for the future.

"Tomorrow – Saturday, in Pritchard's Coffee House at one-fifteen. Right?"

"O.K."

"And Gary?"

"Yes?"

"Be prepared to discuss your son's future from a financial point of view as well."

Another pause – longer than before.

"Gary?"

"I'll be there."

The line went dead. Jenny tried to continue.

"Gary? Gary? Oh, …!"

Unlike most other occasions when someone phoned Jenny, Ed didn't immediately inquire as to the caller's identity, but whether he had guessed or just simply 'knew', the phone call that his mum made to his grandma five minutes later confirmed what had crossed his mind, special talent or not. He had been allowed downstairs again and was listening from the lounge doorway.

"Mum – I need you to extend your normal help tomorrow. Can you keep Ed till three or maybe four? I've arranged to meet you know who after work in Hamsden."

The response seemed to be positive as Jenny then said,

"Oh, thanks, Mum. You know why I'm doing it."

Ed was 'shooed' back into the lounge while mother and daughter discussed the 'why'. When Jenny appeared in the lounge a few minutes later, Ed pre-empted her.

"You're going to see my daddy, aren't you? Why can't I come?"

"Because Mummy wants to talk to him about lots of things, Ed – you know – grown-up talk."

"Oh," replied Ed thoughtfully. "Can you ask him if I can have a go in one of his sports cars, Mum? Can you?"

Jenny had already begun to tell her son a little bit about her former husband, trying to prepare him for an eventual meeting. Gary's role as the new manager of Richard Jones' Cars had been useful in establishing some sort of common ground between son and estranged father. Keeping things simple in the early days seemed the best way forward to Ed's mum.

"Maybe – I'll have to ask him tomorrow, dear. You will have to be good, though, and not pester me to see him until he's able to see you. He has a very important job in Hamsden, you know."

The slight over-exaggeration in Gary Jones' status seemed to satisfy Ed's immediate questions. Jenny just hoped that she wasn't building her ex-husband up too much. Though he had seemed more reserved and mature at his dad's cremation, she knew of old – and to her utmost cost – the dangers of putting too much faith in the reliability of his character.

Ed Compton-Jones nodded thoughtfully and said,

"Hope he can take me in a Jaguar – like the one you bought me, Mummy."

And with that, he wandered off into the lounge to watch the television. Jenny was relieved – her son was keeping things simple too. Fortunately for her, he had never seemed too interested in why his daddy didn't live with them. Jenny was torn between hoping that father and son would get on well together and fearing that, if they did, Ed would eventually ask her the question that she had always dreaded: *'Why doesn't Daddy live with us?'* or worse: *'Can Daddy come and …?'*

Though Jenny knew she had to be confident and assured when she met Gary the following day, she had a few butterflies in her stomach as she made the short walk from 'Curls and Twirls to Hamsden's premier coffee parlour. She had also made one or two elementary errors at the hairdressing salon that morning – including mixing up Mrs Philpott's hair dye incorrectly and nearly turning her into a redhead instead of a platinum blond!

Gary was punctual and was waiting for her at Pritchard's when she got there. He had already reserved a table near the front in one of the more private alcoves. One or two of the customers nodded pleasantly at Gary and some even spoke a few words to him – his father's death had been a shock in the town where he had been such a well-known and respected businessman. There was clearly a lot of sympathy about for Gary, despite his wayward past. This gave him an air of confidence that she hadn't seen in him before and instead of hoping to be in control of the meeting, Jenny found herself on the back foot. She tried to reassume control when Gary returned with two coffees.

"So, when did you come back to Hamsden?"

"As soon as I found about my father, back in December."

Jenny was determined to get some stored-up feelings off her chest and retorted,

"More fool you for doing what you did and becoming a drunk and a gambler in London – no wonder your dad disowned you, like …."

Gary finished Jenny's sentence for her.

"Like you did, Jenny."

When Jenny said nothing, Gary continued,

"Anyway, you seem to know more about what happened to me over the last four years than I do about you."

"I spoke to your dad when he was in hospital. He was one of the reasons for me eventually agreeing to see you."

Gary looked down.

"I didn't know."

"He didn't tell you?"

"No, Jenny, he didn't."

"I expect he wanted you to come to your senses without any help from me."

"Why did you go and see him, Jenny?"

"Oh, come on, Gary – he was dying and we'd fallen out over you. I needed to make reconciliation before it was too late."

"Same as I did, I suppose."

"Yes."

Gary took a sip of coffee and raised his head to look directly at Jenny.

"Jenny, I have to …."

Jenny was silent. She averted her eyes from his stare and picked up her cup.

"Jenny, I have to say things to you and I don't know how to start."

"What things?"

"Jenny – I'm sorry."

"Is that all? You think it's as easy as that? Just say you're sorry and we can move on."

"Jenny – please listen. I know I was bad to you. I didn't realise it at the time but I wasn't really ready for marriage, let alone having kids. I was too immature. I may have had the body of a man but I had the mind of a kid. I knew you wanted to get married and I thought it would be alright. I did love you – I still …."

Jenny was quick to interrupt.

"Don't say it, Gary – just don't say it. And don't try to blame me for getting married. I haven't forgotten the drinking and the womanising and the total disregard for married life and all the responsibilities that go with it. Why do you think I've prevented you from seeing Ed? Do you think I wanted him growing up knowing his father was a drunkard and a gambler – a father that never raised a finger to help me in the first few months of his life; a father that was only interested in the status of being married and a father that still wanted his pleasures and who shamed me in front of my friends and family? Don't talk to me about wanting to please me by getting married, Gary."

Jenny was finished – five years of frustration and she had finally got most of what she'd wanted to say off her chest. She felt better. She was also crying; emotion had got the better of her. Gary offered his handkerchief. Jenny took it and wiped her eyes and looked at Gary.

"Thanks."

"No," said Gary. "Thank *you*. I deserved that and worse. I just want to put the past behind me, Jenny. Since moving back to Hamsden, I haven't had one drink or been in one betting shop. It's taken until I'm thirty-two for me to realise that I've been a fool for most, if not all, of my adult life. I've got a job now that secretly I always enjoyed. It was just hard, working for my father, even though I know now that he wanted the best for me and he probably deliberately made it hard for me when I worked at the showroom. I think he knew before he died that he could safely pass the business over to me and that made him happy, I hope."

"What about the fire service? Why didn't that work? You couldn't even stay sober for that, I hear."

"I think it was other people who thought I'd be good at it and I just went along with the flow. I wasn't getting any status and credit by working at dad's showroom and joining the service gave me some kudos of my own. It was the complete opposite of the kind of thing that Dad was interested in and it made Mum proud, so …."

"So you put lives at risk by turning up worse for drink, Gary."

"O.K., Jenny. What do you want me to say? I can't say anything more. I don't want forgiveness – I know I did wrong and I've got to prove to myself that I've changed. It will be up to other people to judge in a few years whether I make it. I hope, in time, you will recognise that I can do it and be a good father to Ed and help him in whatever way I can and, yes, Jen, that does mean financially, too. All I ask – though you may say I have forfeited the right to ask – is to be able to see Ed occasionally and have the chance to form a relationship with him before it's too late. You may not think I'm a very good role model but at least I can help him avoid certain vices – from bitter experience."

The last phrase almost raised a smile on Jenny's tear-smudged face. Both of them had had their say and despite her original intention to discuss financial assistance and paternal arrangements, it was clear that Jenny wanted to leave the discussion there. The emotion had drained her and she wasn't in the mood to talk about practicalities.

"O.K., Gary – I think I want to go now."

"Oh, but …."

Gary could see Jenny's strained face, but he had to ask one question.

"When can I see Ed?"

"Can we leave that decision today, Gary? Now that we've cleared the air a bit, I'd like to make it another time when we can discuss that and other things. Now that I've seen you, I'd like to talk a bit more to Ed before we get there."

"Alright, Jen – when?"

"How about next Saturday – same place, same time?"

"O.K. I'll be here and, Jenny …."

"What?"

"Just tell Ed I love him – that's all."

"I have – many times."

5

Trouble at School

Jenny couldn't believe the time after she had eventually left a slightly bemused Gary and wandered back to her Austin 1300 parked in the municipal car park behind the main shopping thoroughfare in Hamsden. She breathed a sigh of relief when she discovered that she hadn't received a parking ticket, as she had only paid enough till two-thirty and the town hall clock was already reading a quarter to three. She had been with Gary for well over an hour.

Her mind was in a whirl as she drove back to Fenton. Gary had seemed a bit too good to be true, but – as he had indicated – time would tell. Some progress had been made, Jenny thought, but she was soon to discover that one particular little boy had been hoping for her to report considerably more.

Ed was waiting for her at the front gate of his grandparents' house – the weather was warm for the first day of May and he was dressed only in shorts and T-shirt. He ran across the lawn to greet his mum as she pulled the car onto the drive. In his strange six-year-old mind he seemed to have been expecting an extra passenger in the car.

"Where's Daddy, Mummy? Didn't he want to come?"

Jenny emerged from her car and smiled at her son as she led him by the hand to the front door of number 38.

"Now slow down, Ed – Daddy has to work in the car showroom on a Saturday afternoon."

"Oh," said her son with obvious disappointment. "When's he going to take me for a ride in a Jaguar?"

"Soon, love; I promise – very soon. He sends you his love."

This seemed to satisfy Ed and as his granny opened the front door, he said simply,

"Good."

Jenny's dad arrived home from the station soon afterwards at four o'clock – his days were getting shorter as young Gordon was given more responsibility. His arrival gave the two women an opportunity to discuss Jenny's meeting with Gary while Fred Compton entertained Ed with an old Hornby train set that had once belonged to his own son, Eddie. Jenny and her mum repaired to the kitchen. With coffees poured, Jenny's mum said,

"Well – how did it go? Ed says he isn't going to see his father yet. Did you ask Gary about maintenance?"

"One thing at a time, Mum. It wasn't easy, you know. I had to find out one or two things first."

"And?"

"And I think it's going to be alright. Gary seems to have changed. I think losing his dad has had an effect on him. He was more …."

"More what, love?"

Jenny seemed to be searching for an accurate description of how she thought Gary had changed.

"More thoughtful, I suppose, or … at least, I hope."

"Well, that's a start, Jen. What's going to happen next? Are you going to arrange for Gary to see Ed now?"

"I'm going to see Gary on my own just once more – next Saturday at the same time, if you can help me out again, Mum."

"Of course, dear. Did you not ask about money?"

"I kind of didn't need to – Gary said he would help without me having to ask him. That's what I want to sort out next Saturday."

"I hope you remind him that he owes you, and me and your dad, for that matter, a lot of money already over the last few years."

"I think we must put the past behind us, Mum – I'll just be happy for some support from now on. What's done is done and I want to forget it and not have to squabble over what he should or should not have contributed in the past. After all, he might turn round and argue that he didn't get to see Ed in all that time so why should he …?"

Jenny paused and then added,

"Anyway, I'll pay you and Dad back for what you've given me and Ed – I promise."

"Now you know there's no need for that. We don't want anything back. Just seeing you happy and get on with life has been payment enough, love."

Ann Compton reached across the kitchen table and gently squeezed her daughter's hand. Jenny responded by saying,

"Thanks, Mum – I'll sort everything out with Gary next week, including making arrangements for him to have Ed for a day, on his own. I just hope Gary is prepared for the little fellow and has some ideas of what he would like to do. I think it will involve Gary getting hold of a Jaguar for a day."

"Do you think it's a good idea for Ed to be on his own with Gary the first time? After all, he's almost a complete stranger to the little boy. Ed was less than a year old when he last saw his dad."

"Got to start somewhere, Mum – he's not really a stranger. And anyway, Ed is desperate to see him – he is his dad, for goodness sake!"

Jenny's mum still looked uncertain until Jenny reassured her.

"Well, we'll all go for lunch or something first and then they can go off on their own. O.K?"

"That sounds good, Jen – sorry if you thinking I'm poking my nose in."

"You're not, Mum – I suppose I hadn't really thought about it carefully enough. It has been an exhausting and emotional day, but I think it has been worth it."

Ed's over-enthusiasm to answer questions in class eventually got him into trouble at school by the Tuesday, prompting a phone call from Miss Sandbuck that afternoon. The previous day had been exceptionally sunny and warm for early summer, and class 1Sb had been taken on an exploratory trek down to the south end of Fenton, collecting shells from the beach and learning a bit about their seaside town. Miss Sandbuck had pointed out one of the older buildings – the old Beach Railway Station, which was now a row of holiday flats. The beach and town trail provided the material for Tuesday afternoon's lesson. Ed had remained unusually quiet for the first part of the lesson which had been concerned with a discussion of what the children had found on the beach. Miss Sandbuck then turned to the walk back.

"Now, can anyone remember seeing any unusual buildings?"

Susan Long was first with her raised arm.

"Yes, Miss – the old station near the beach."

"Very good, Susan. Now I wonder if anyone can guess how old it is?"

Several hands shot up.

Miss Sandbuck ignored Ed's insistent arm and turned to Jack Collison.

"Yes, Jack."

"Older than my house, Miss?"

Miss Sandbuck smiled calmly – the Collison family had only just moved into a brand new house on Jenny's development.

"Yes, Jack, it certainly is. Anyone else?"

After a few more guesses had narrowed the old station's age from *'hundreds of years ago'* to *'sometime last century'* – the second concept being difficult except for only one or two children to comprehend – Miss Sandbuck inevitably had to tell them the exact date it had first opened as a railway station, even though, again, the actual number would mean very little to them.

"Well, children, Peter was closest when he said *'last century'*. It was actually opened nearly a hundred years ago in 1879."

Ed's hand shot up and he almost jumped out of his seat in excitement.

"Miss – you're wrong! It opened in 1889."

"Edward – please *do not* shout out and certainly do not contradict me. Do you understand?"

"Yes, Miss – sorry Miss Sandbuck, but it *was* 1889."

Although Gabriella Sandbuck was furious that one of her charges should dare to answer her back, she was also extremely curious as to how a six-and-a-half-year-old could possibly have an opinion on such an unusual matter. Even hearing a child of that age pronounce the date correctly was a rarity in her long teaching experience.

"So, Ed – just how do you know that?"

The rest of the class had fallen silent. The children waited for their classmate to answer. Not one of them was smiling – Ed Compton-Jones was a strange boy in their opinion.

"I just know, Miss – because I was …."

Minor Morrison attempted to lift atmosphere.

"Because he was there, Miss!"

Class 1Sb descended into laughter. The tension had been released. Ed himself added to that release.

"I know, Miss, because my granddad told me. He works at the station."

"Oh, does he, Ed? I'm afraid that doesn't matter – you must never contradict me in future. Understand?"

"Yes, Miss."

The confrontation was over. Miss Sandbuck made her phone call to Jenny after school, it being a day when she worked only in the morning. Ed was severely reprimanded by his mother and threatened with all kinds of punishments if he made an exhibition of himself at school again, including ringing his father to inform him of his son's behaviour. That seemed to upset Ed the most and Jenny had found an extra weapon in her disciplinary arsenal. It would not be the last time that the warning, *'I'll tell your father'*, would be used. From Ed's point of view, he hadn't regarded his friend Minor's jovial interruption in the same spirit as his classmates because that was precisely what he had been about to say himself, and not as a joke, either. Additionally, Ed hoped that his grandad would never have occasion to talk with his teacher, because even Fred Compton was not aware of the precise date the Beach Station opened, despite being the fount of all knowledge when it came to railways.

Later that evening, Gabriella Sandbuck did eventually go to her small book on local history and check the details of Fenton Beach Railway Station. Opening it at the right page, the entry raised a wry smile on her face when she read:

'The Beach Station finally opened on June 14th 1889 nearly ten years after the plans had been first been mooted by the District Council in 1879'.

It had been her mistake – she had remembered the wrong date; a simple error that could have happened to anyone. Nevertheless, she decided she would have to keep a careful eye on Master Edward Compton-Jones from then on. His unusually powerful memory bothered her at times and, if nothing else, it meant she would check her facts more carefully in the future.

Saturday, May the 8th arrived without Ed getting into further trouble at school, whether the restraint was of his own doing or not. Indeed, when Jenny picked him up from school on the Friday afternoon, Miss Sandbuck even made a point of coming out with him to tell his mum how impressed she had been with his local knowledge and that, despite his earlier behaviour, he was doing really well in his first year. Fortunately, both earlier in her phone call and on that Friday, Miss Sandbuck made no mention of the particular piece of local knowledge she had been referring to. Jenny was so overwhelmed with Miss Sandbuck's compliment that she didn't ask Ed for the full details of the issue.

6

Fast Cars and One That Nearly Got Away

Gary was five minutes late the following day and was profusely apologetic as he escorted Jenny to their table.

"I'm sorry, Jenny – had a customer arrive just as I was leaving."

"No problem, Gary – I'd only just arrived myself."

"I'll get the coffees," said Gary.

As Gary made his way to the counter, Jenny observed that her ex-husband seemed unusually nervous. While she waited, she hoped it was to do with his rush to get to the coffee parlour and not with any second thoughts he might be having over maintenance for Ed. Everything seemed alright when he returned as he got straight to the point.

"Right, Jen – about the money. Would fifteen pounds a week be O.K?"

This wasn't the dithering Gary she had known and his forthrightness threw Jenny for a moment. The weekly amount had hardly registered with her. When she didn't say anything, Gary said,

"It's as much as I can afford, Jen."

When Jenny suddenly realised that the amount Gary was offering was nearly half what she was getting weekly at 'Curls and Twirls', she nearly dropped her cup. She stammered her response.

"Are you sure? It sounds an awful lot, Gary."

"I know, but it's what I want to do. After all, Ed is my son and he should enjoy the fruits of my labours. The showroom is doing very well at the moment."

Jenny's heart rate had shot up and she could feel the pounding in her chest. A huge increase in her income was coming her way. She didn't take long to respond.

"Well, it would certainly come in handy. I could treat Mum for picking him up from school and keeping him till I get in from work."

"Maybe I could help sometimes, too – pick him up and entertain him till you come home. I could treat him every so often."

"Maybe," replied Jenny thoughtfully. "Let's take things one at a time. You haven't even seen him yet."

"So when can I?"

"Well, I'm not working next Saturday. Why don't I bring Ed to Hamsden – we could go for lunch somewhere and then you could take him for the afternoon."

"Sounds good," said Gary. "Is there anything special he would like to do?"

Jenny smiled and said,

"Oh yes, Gary – there's something special alright. He wants a ride in a Jaguar like the model one I bought him last Christmas."

Gary smiled coyly.

"I'll see what I can do. I thought we might do a spot of fishing on the Wentham – I know a good spot. Would he like that, do you think?"

"I think as long as he gets his ride in the Jaguar, you'll have him eating out of the palm of your hand and he'll do anything. Do I need to buy a rod?"

"Of course not – it's my treat."

Jenny then discussed with Gary the details of how he would send the maintenance, with him promising to bring thirty pounds in cash on a fortnightly basis when he picked Ed up for a couple of hours after school or at the weekend. Jenny wanted to try the arrangement for a couple of months and if everything was alright, the frequency of the visits could be increased to once a week. Finally, Jenny agreed to bring Ed to the showroom at noon the following Saturday – May the 15th. From there they would go for something to eat with Gary's special surprise to follow. Gary also agreed to bring Ed back to Acacia Avenue by seven that evening.

A few minutes later, Jenny and Gary parted amicably and Ed's mum was back in Fenton by three o'clock, where, understandably, her son was anxious to find out what was going to happen. He rushed to the car when she arrived and hugged Jenny.

"When's Daddy coming, Mum? When can I see him?"

Ed's mum soon realised that Ed had been hoping that the meeting was going to be that very day as he seemed slightly disappointed when she replied,

"Next Saturday, love. We're going for lunch and then Daddy has a couple of surprises for you."

"Oh – can't we go now?"

By this time they were inside Jenny's mum's house and Jenny didn't need to reply as Ed had already run to his grandma in the kitchen, shouting,

"I'm gonna' see Daddy next Saturday, Granny!"

Jenny didn't hear what her son said next and her mother would assume that she already knew the information anyway, thus eliminating the need to mention it. If she had done so, it would have left Jenny speechless and somewhat bemused, let alone frightened by her son's apparent foreknowledge, if that's what it turned out to be.

"And we're going to the Old Market Restaurant for dinner."

The fine warm weather continued and the following Saturday was no exception. Jenny seemed as nervous as her son was excited and, in the end, she bundled him into the car before eleven. By twenty to twelve they were parked and strolling in Hamsden, giving Jenny enough time to take

Ed to 'Curls and Twirls' to show him where she worked. From there it was less than a hundred yards to Richard Jones' Cars where they arrived at one minute to twelve. Gary was waiting for them at the front of the showroom. Ed seemed to have no inhibitions and ran forward to meet his dad while Jenny hung back nervously.

"Hello, young fellow," said Gary as Ed hugged his father for the first time. There were tears in Jenny's eyes which she struggled to hold back. Gary lifted his son up into his arms, saying,

"What a big lad you are," even though Ed was still small for his age.

"Put me down, Daddy," were the first words Gary would hear from his son, followed by

"I want to see my Jaguar?"

Jenny laughed – the reunion she had been dreading for years was complete. Gary put his son gently down and, taking his hand, led him through to the rear of the showroom and through the office. Jenny followed but she already felt she was intruding on something special. She nodded to Shelagh Brooks who was doing some paperwork and just managed to catch her son up as he squealed,

"It's the same as mine!"

There, parked in one of the two private spaces at the back of the showroom, stood a shiny British Racing Green S4.2 E-Type open-top Jaguar. Jenny was suitably impressed.

"Gary – how on earth did you manage to get it? And how did you know the one I bought him at Christmas was green? I didn't tell you the colour."

"Lucky guess, I suppose. A friend of mine in the trade got it for me for the weekend. He owed me a favour after I sold him a car cheaply."

By this time, and almost unnoticed, Ed had managed to open the driver's door and was sitting behind the steering wheel with his short arms stretched to their limit, clutching the bottom rim.

"Now then, young man – out you get. We're having lunch first. Will the Old Market Restaurant be alright, Jenny? They do nice kids meals there on a Saturday," said Gary. "It's just behind the town hall."

"Yes, I know – we sometimes go there from work."

Neither Jenny nor Gary noticed the knowing smile that appeared on Ed's face as he climbed out of the Jaguar.

Lunch was a reasonably pleasant affair for Jenny, and to some extent for Gary, as both parents let Ed monopolise the conversation – Jenny had hardly ever known him to be as voluble especially with someone as unfamiliar as Gary. Gary found it a little awkward at times, as he struggled to cope with the six-year-old's chat, unused, as he was, to dealing with someone so young. By one-fifteen, he clearly wanted to curtail their stay at the Old Market Restaurant, particularly as one or two of both his and Jenny's friends had acknowledged the apparently happy family, thus causing them some embarrassment, with explanations hurriedly and only partly offered to explain their gathering. After one such encounter, Gary said,

"Come on, Ed, it's time that we gave you that ride in the Jaguar."

Ed needed no second invitation and after his dad insisted on settling the bill, he led them to the back of the showroom. It was a beautiful sunny afternoon and while Gary lowered the Jaguar's roof, Jenny went through all the usual warnings that Ed would eventually get used to. From, *'now do everything that daddy tells you to do'* to *'he won't take you out again if you not good'*. Finally, she leant down and lightly kissed her son's head and with a quick goodbye to Gary, she walked away without turning back, in case either of them should see the tears rolling down her cheeks.

Once his mother had left, Ed became a little more reserved and, at first, Gary thought that the afternoon was going to be a bit of an ordeal. However, as soon as he pulled the Jag onto the A132 dual-carriageway outside of Hamsden and pushed the accelerator most of the way to the floor, Ed started to scream with delight as the powerful motorcar scythed its way through the warm May air. No doubt Jenny would also have been screaming – screaming for Gary to slow down – but it was a boy's afternoon out and little Ed's eyes were wide with delight. They covered the six miles to Linham Junction – the recognised half-way point between Hamsden and Fenton – in less than five minutes, prompting Ed to call out above the guttural sound of the engine,

"Am I going home already, Dad?"

"No, son, just be patient – we're not going to Fenton," shouted Gary above the engine and the wind's rush. "We turn left, now!"

Gary slowed the sleek green sports car in a matter of seconds and pulled the steering wheel over to his left as the Jaguar slewed onto the narrow B1123. The country lane prohibited speeds much above forty and the E-Type's legendary handling came to the fore. Though sitting low in his harnessed seat, Ed was able to take in much more of the scenery than he had been able to in the ninety-mile-an-hour dash down the A132. After about five miles, he seemed to have some recognition of his surroundings.

"I think my friend lives over there – behind that big hill. His dad's a farmer and they've got lots of cows."

Gary managed a glance to his right at Peewit Hill, dotted with said black and white animals.

"Well, we're going to the other side of that hill. Do you know what's there, Ed?"

Ed said nothing at first. His dad still hadn't told him what they were going to do that afternoon. Then he said,

"Mr Morrison's farm? Are we going to see Minor?"

"No, son – we're not going to a farm. Anyway, who's Minor?"

"He's my friend – he's real name is Edward – like mine."

Suddenly, the car came to a T-junction; to the right lay Peewit Hill Farm, but Gary pulled the big car in the opposite direction onto an even narrower lane.

"We go this way, Ed."

The road began a gentle descent and wound past high-hedged banks, thus suddenly obscuring the view of the surrounding countryside. They continued to wind left and right for ten minutes or more until eventually, the narrow lane levelled out and the hedges receded on each side. The River Wentham was at its most peaceful here, edged on either side by wide lush meadows. Joining the two banks, and directly in front of them, was a fairly modern one-lane bridge, which seemed solely for the purpose and use of the local framers to get their sheep or cows from one side of the river to the other. It definitely didn't appear wide enough to take even the smallest of farm vehicles. The next proper road crossing was five miles upstream in Hamsden, although a small foot-passenger ferry ran in the summer months between Fenton Ferry and the village of Canford on the north bank of the Wentham.

"Ooh, are we going swimming, Dad?" asked Ed as the Jag began to ascend the slight incline onto the bridge.

"No, Ed, just be quiet for a minute – the next bit's tricky."

Gary manoeuvred the E-Type onto the concrete bridge and shouted,

"Keep your arms inside the car, Ed."

Gary edged the car along the top of the bridge with only an inch or two to spare each side. Crawling at less than walking pace, with both wing mirrors nearly scraping the low balustrades on either side, it took nearly a minute to complete the fifty-yard crossing to the far bank. It soon became apparent why Gary had chosen the north bank, as right next to the bridge, and extending under it, was a grass-covered apron where several cars could be parked. The apron's fairly level surface, which gently sloped into the river, was perfect for what Gary had in mind for that afternoon's entertainment. Having pulled the car round so that it faced the river, Gary turned to Ed and said,

"Now, what do you think swims in this river?"

And then it dawned on Ed.

"Fish! Can we catch some fish?

Then his face dropped a little.

"But we haven't brought any rods, Dad."

"Haven't we?"

Ed's dad climbed out of the car and went to the boot. Ed jumped out and followed. Though the Jaguar's boot was compact, it still had enough room for two folding rods, net and assorted boxes containing flies and worms. Gary reached in and pulled out a three-section rod with simple line and reel attached which he opened up and fixed into its rigid form.

"This is yours, Ed. Hold it carefully while I get mine and all our tackle out."

Ed took the rod in his hand and, in so doing, nearly stuck the end in his dad's eye until Gary shouted,

"Hold it upright!"

A light breeze suddenly got up as Ed and his dad set themselves up at the edge of the river. It was soon clear that Gary was not a very experienced angler, even though the river at that point was still tidal and the niceties of fly fishing weren't really needed. Threading a worm on the end of each line and casting the line roughly into the water was the order of the day. After about half an hour when nothing fruitful happened, except for Ed getting his line tangled round his dad's collapsible canvas chair, they decided to try further upstream on the far side of the bridge. As they moved their gear, the breeze had become a moderate wind and the skies were suddenly darkened by some heavy clouds overhead. In the short space of time that it took for them to walk through under the bridge along the grassy bank, the weather had completely changed. One or two heavy drops of rain started to fall causing them to take shelter back under the bridge.

"We'll just wait till it passes – it'll just be a shower," said Ed's dad as they put all the tackle down under the bridge. Gary made Ed put his little yellow anorak on in case they had to make a dash for the car. It suddenly seemed to have got quite dark – darker even than to be expected under the low bridge. Ed was getting frightened.

"I don't like it, Dad – it's going to thunder."

They could hear the rain getting harder and Gary made a dash for the car to put the roof back up, shouting back as he ran,

"Stay there, Ed – I'll only be a minute."

Ed did not reply; a smile had formed upon his face, quite out of keeping with his apparent nervousness. It took Gary a good deal longer than a minute to wrestle with the Jaguar's roof, and with the intensity of the sudden rainstorm, he was hardly able to see more than a few feet in front of his face until he reached the shelter of the bridge again. Rubbing his eyes, he said,

"It's worse than I thought – I could hardly see a thing, Ed."

Gary's son made no reply. His dad opened his eyes fully and looked around him. Ed was nowhere to be seen. Gary began to panic and shouted,

"Where are you, Ed? Stop messing about and come out wherever you are!"

As Gary's eyes adjusted fully to the light under the bridge, he soon realised that there was absolutely nowhere for his son to hide under the smooth-faced concrete bridge if, indeed, he had started a game of hide-and-seek with his father. The rain seemed to be easing and Gary ran out from cover and up the bank to the topside of the bridge. The rain had stopped and the sun was peeping out from behind the clouds. He was in the middle of his worse nightmare. His son had completely disappeared. Gary ran to the centre of the bridge and from this high point he could see for several hundred yards in all directions across wide open green meadows on both sides of the river. He steeled himself to look downstream in the direction of the current. At first he could see nothing and then something caught his eye, glinting on the surface about a hundred yards downstream. He ran – past the Jaguar, skidding on the wet grass. It couldn't have happened – it couldn't be ....

"Oh no – oh God, no!" he screamed as he got level with the floating object. It was yellow. Gary waded into the fast-flowing river and made a grab for his son but his hand only brought out the yellow anorak. It wasn't attached to his son. He floundered around in the water, smacking it in his frustration and panic. This just could not be happening; after all he'd gone through to make amends with Jenny, this was unreal. He tried to stay calm and waded out of the water. He ran back to his car – he had to get help. Then he looked up and he stopped dead in his tracks. There, not twenty yards in front of him, and trying to open the Jaguar's door, was Ed. Gary ran forward and pulled his son towards him, as if checking he was real.

"Oh, thank God! Where on earth were you?"

With a puzzled frown, Ed looked at his father. He began to get upset at the panic etched on his dad's face.

"Nowhere, Dad. I wanted to get in the car."

"But how did you get here without me seeing you?"

And then, between apparently genuine sobs, Ed tried to explain that once his dad hadn't come back immediately from putting the Jaguar's roof up, he had rushed forward to find him. It soon became clear to Gary that they must have run blindly past each other in opposite directions in the murk, and it was also to transpire that there was a simple (?) explanation for the floating anorak.

"How did your anorak end up in the river?" asked Gary in as calm a voice as he could muster.

"I took it off and put it over my head when I ran to find you at the car. I couldn't hold on to it, Dad, and the wind blew it out of my hands."

Ed sobbed some more as Gary tried to reassure him he wasn't in any trouble. After a few more minutes, the picture suddenly became clear. While Gary had gone to the top of the bridge, Ed had stayed by the Jaguar trying to get in, but on the far side and thus hidden from Gary when he had looked downstream from the bridge. Gary didn't look back when he ran past the Jaguar and it wasn't until he came back from the river clutching the yellow anorak that he'd seen his son for the first time.

It made some sort of sense to Gary, but only because, in his joy at finding his son, he hadn't noticed that Ed's clothes were bone dry, despite him having crouched in the torrential rainstorm for several minutes. Though Ed's complicated explanation of a series of chance events seemed to satisfy his father, Ed himself knew that it wasn't really what had happened. He was discovering that he had more special talents other than foreknowledge of events or unusual facts about old buildings.

Gary was able to change out of his sodden trousers, shoes and socks into a pair of shorts and trainers he'd brought with him in the car in case the sun had got too hot. The warm afternoon sun completed the drying process. It was nearly four o'clock by then and the appeal of any more fishing seemed to have worn a little thin for both father and son. Both of them, for their own reasons, remained quiet while they packed the fishing tackle away and headed for the car. As Gary pulled back the Jaguar's roof, flipping away any remaining water, Ed seemed to have regained his enthusiasm for the outing. As he opened the passenger door, he remarked,

"What are we going to do next, Dad?"

Gary checked his watch and replied with his plan B – already prepared in case the weather had been bad from the start.

"How about we try the pier at Fenton-on-Sea? There's lots to do there and we may be able to catch some crabs – I've got a crab line somewhere in one of the tackle boxes."

"Ooh, yes, Dad! I can take Mummy one home."

Gary turned the Jaguar round and approached the bridge with less caution than when they had arrived. Unfortunately, in his haste, he didn't quite line up the sports car properly and there was a faint scraping sound of metal on concrete as the rear nearside wing caught the balustrade. Quickly putting the car into reverse, Gary managed to correct the angle of approach and slowly edged the Jag across the bridge. He stopped the car at the side of the narrow road and got out to inspect the damage. He muttered to himself as he climbed back into the car.

"Just my luck – I'll have to get our paint shop to touch that up on Monday morning."

Ed leaned across to his dad and said with surprising maturity,

"Don't worry, Dad. I won't tell anyone – including Mum."

The ride back to Fenton was uneventful, although, at his son's insistence, Gary did take them past Peewit Hill Farm. They didn't stop as there seemed to be no activity going on and there was no sign of Ed's friend, Minor.

Gary faced a bit of embarrassment when they reached the seafront at Fenton. He had just parked the car by the promenade at the foot of Steep Hill and was getting the crab line and small plastic bucket from the boot when he heard a woman's voice call to Ed from across the road.

"Hello, Ed! Are you alright?"

Ed glanced to his right and waved to an elderly lady dressed somewhat inappropriately for the warmth of the day in a brown tweed suit. Rather than just acknowledging Ed's wave, the lady crossed over The Undercliff and made a beeline for Gary who seemed to want to avoid a meeting with someone he obviously knew of old.

"Hi, Mrs Thompson," said Ed as she came towards them. Mrs Brenda Thompson seemed concerned for Ed's welfare and replied,

"And who is this, Ed? You'd better introduce me, young man."

Ed looked proud when he said,

"My dad, Mrs Thompson."

"Oh – I didn't recognise you, Gary. We haven't seen you around for ages."

"Yes, Mrs Thompson, I've been living in London till quite recently. I'm staying with my mother and I now run Dad's car dealership now that he's no longer with us."

Ed clung to Gary's arm as if offering his own sympathy. Mrs Thompson smiled and said,

"Yes, I know, Gary – it was so sad to hear of your dad's ...."

Being its resident busybody, Brenda Thompson knew most things that went on in and around Fenton-on-Sea. She and Ed's grandmother were active members of St Andrew's Church, which stood above the seafront a short distance away from where they were standing. Though Ed had acknowledged her politely, he had never really taken to her on the odd occasion he had accompanied his grandma to church. He was clearly anxious for his dad to cut the meeting short and he began to tug at Gary's arm. Gary responded to his son's urging and said quickly,

"Well, it's nice to see you again, Mrs Thompson. We have to be going – I'm taking this one onto the pier for some crab fishing. Goodbye now."

Brenda Thompson looked a little put out and replied brusquely,

"Goodbye, Gary."

As Gary and Ed walked away, she called out,

"And give my love to Jenny."

With her final remark, Mrs Thompson had been doing some 'fishing' of her own. She had much gossip to circulate and that gossip would include the possibility that Jenny was 'seeing' her ex-husband again. Though nothing could be further from the truth, Brenda Thompson was prone to see such things in a different light and the rumour would still be all over Fenton-on-Sea in a matter of days.

The one-armed bandits and other entertainments in the covered section of the pier were being fully used when Gary and Ed eventually slid away from the town gossip. In any case, Ed had already set his mind on some crab fishing. Gary led his son the two hundred yards to the very end of the pier where a mixture of worms and bread was quickly fixed to the hook on the end of the line. With Ed insisting that he held the line, Gary fed the hook, with weight attached, through the iron railings and dropped the simple tackle to the sea, calling out,

"Hold the reel tightly, Ed – here we go!"

The reel spun round in Ed's little hands as the line hit the waves.

Gary looked down.

"She's in – now all we do is wait."

And they didn't have to wait long for their first bite – to Ed's great excitement.

"Got one, Dad!"

"Wind her in, son."

Gary helped his son wind the reel until a small brown crab was quickly landed and dropped into the bucket, suitably filled with seawater collected from underneath the pier on their arrival. In all, they caught seven crabs of varying shapes and sizes, throwing all but the largest back and only stopping when Gary's supply of bait ran out.

When St Andrew's Church clock struck the hour and Gary had counted the six strikes, he turned to his son and asked,

"Chips and an ice-cream, young man?"

Gary's timing was perfect as, minutes before, Ed had struggled to cope with the news about the lack of bait and had been about to vent his disappointment and frustration. All such thoughts were quickly erased from his mind.

"Ooh, yes please, Dad!"

After chips with tomato ketchup, followed by a chocolate ice-cream consumed on the way back to the car, they finally left the seafront at twenty to seven and were back outside 26 Acacia Avenue ten minutes before their allotted deadline. When Gary got back home to Hamsden that evening, he found himself to be physically and emotionally drained. He hadn't told Jenny fully about his brief nightmare when he thought he had lost Ed permanently in the River Canham, describing it rather as an impromptu game of hide-and-seek brought about by the sudden downpour. His report on the afternoon's events concentrated more on the wind blowing Ed's anorak into the water and his son's natural talent for catching crabs off the pier. Jenny seemed grateful that Gary's first outing had passed off with nothing worse than a slightly damp anorak. For his part, Gary went away that evening with the distinct impression that she had actually feared he wouldn't have been able to cope with his son on his own for such a long time. Though he had allayed her fears, Gary knew deep down that it had been a close run thing.

Later that evening, Ed expanded on his dad's description of the afternoon, leaving out the full truth about his 'disappearing act'. Like his father, Ed was also physically exhausted and, after falling asleep on the sofa, he was safely tucked up in bed by nine. In her mind, Jenny had rated Gary's first performance as a father at seven out of ten. She had been able to tell from her son's obvious volubility that evening that a real bond had formed between father and son.

7

Knowledge is Power

Minor and Ed's friendship had grown slowly over the first half of 1976 and though the farmer's son had played with the little magpie several times at Acacia Avenue on Saturdays, Ed had only paid one more visit to Peewit Hill Farm, and that for a reciprocal birthday party in late March for Minor's sixth birthday. There had been no cow-counting issues to disturb Bill Morrison's otherwise peaceful existence and he seemed to have put the event behind him as he warmed to his son's bonding with Ed. March the 26th had been a Friday, and the few hours after school that Ed had spent at the farm had all been passed inside the farmhouse owing to some seasonal wet weather. The May Saturday of Ed's first outing with his dad was the first time since then that he had been anywhere near Peewit Hill Farm.

Minor's part in the unfortunate trouble that Ed had got into at school with Miss Sandbuck earlier in the month didn't seem to have been taken by Ed entirely in the way that it had been intended. Consequently, Ed hadn't really spoken much to his friend at school for the rest of the month and with half-term intervening, it wasn't until Friday, June the 11th that the two boys struck up any kind of meaningful conversation again at morning break. They had wandered separately over to their special corner of the playground and Minor started the conversation.

"Fancy coming to the farm tomorrow? Mum says you can come if you're not doing anything."

"Maybe – what do you want to do?"

"Mum's got a horse."

"What's it like?"

"It's a black mare. Dad says it's the same colour as her hair. Mum puts me on it sometimes and leads her round the lower field near the duck pond. I can't really ride properly yet and Ben or Aaron has to hold me on. I could ask Mum if you can have a go."

Ed didn't seem too keen at first and said,

"I don't think my mum would let me ride a horse. I might fall off and hurt myself."

"I've got a helmet you can borrow or you can just watch me if you like. We can feed the ducks and look for sticklebacks in the pond."

Ed was curious and he did his best with the pronunciation.

"What are stipplebacks?"

"Little fish – you catch them with nets and put then in a jam jar. Mum's got loads of jam jars in the kitchen. And I saw a newt once."

The mention of the word 'fish' suddenly cured Ed's diffidence and he said,

"O.K., but I don't think my mum can bring me – she's working tomorrow."

"Mum says she can always bring you," said Minor, who had obviously received instructions from his mother about inviting Ed to the farm again. That seemed to settle it for Ed.

"I'll ask my mum after school."

The bell sounded for lessons and the arrangements for the following day would be finalised when the two mothers exchanged phone calls later that day. Mrs Morrison would pick Ed up at ten-thirty from his grandma's house in Fir Tree Close.

The weather on the Saturday morning behaved itself and though breezy, it was sunny with only some light high cloud. After an exchange of introductions between Evelyn Morrison and Ann Compton, the boys were soon on their way to Peewit Hill Farm where they arrived shortly after eleven. The breeze had eased considerably and it began to feel quite hot; both boys having suncream rubbed into faces and arms by Minor's mum before they set out for the duck pond with strange looking floppy white sun hats covering their tender heads. With a jam jar each and Minor in charge of the net, they looked like something out of a Mark Twain novel – Tom Sawyer and Huckleberry Finn look-a-likes to a tee.

Before they reached the pond, Minor was able to show Ed the new black mare, called simply, Shadow. Black Beauty had seemed too obvious to Minor's mum and her son had been allowed to pick the name from one of the characters in his comics. Shadow wandered over as the two boys leant against the wooden fence that enclosed a sizeable paddock in the lower field. Minor's mum had had it put in so that she could ride and exercise Shadow in the bigger meadow and over the ditch into the woods beyond, using the maze of paths contained therein. A five-barred gate at the far corner of the paddock gave access to the main meadow. It was always kept shut and secured since the meadow was unfenced, edged only by ditches and the farm track that led to the roundabout at the start of the A132. While Minor stroked Shadow's mane, Ed seemed to be looking at the distant gate. Minor noticed his friend seemed to be daydreaming.

"What have you seen?"

Ed didn't answer immediately until Minor asked,

"Have you seen some rabbits?"

"What? Oh, no – there's nothing to see."

But Ed had seen something or, at least, knew something, since nobody's eyes would have been powerful enough to see what his special mind had registered. The gate, though apparently shut, was *not* secured with the large metal ring that was normally hooked and padlocked to one of the gateposts. Even a gentle breeze might blow the gate open. And then Ed realised what he ought to do but something prevented him from doing it. After all, it wasn't his problem and who would believe him anyway. No one would comprehend how he could possibly know such a fact from a distance of over a hundred yards. He couldn't be to blame if Shadow got out, could he? As far as Ed was concerned, at that moment in time, and on the first occasion in his life, the old maxim was true – *knowledge is power*; power to do good or evil. But silence wasn't evil, was it?

With shoes and socks off, the two friends paddled carefully in the shallow pond, with one or two friendly ducks in attendance seeking offerings of food. Each boy caught a stickleback within a few minutes of each other and Minor even tried in vain to net a particularly elusive newt which eventually swam away to a deeper part of the pond. Even at the centre of the pond, the water was no more than a couple of feet deep and, in any case, Minor's mum had given them strict instructions that they should stay right at the pond's margin where the water was only inches deep. Aaron had been told to keep an eye on the boys from his position in the field on the opposite side of the farm track, where he was scything some tall grass. With Shadow an equal distance away, the Mark Twain analogy was perfected. What could possibly disturb such a tranquil scene?

It only took a slight increase in the strength of the breeze. Ripples began to form on the pond's surface. Some half-remembered thought stirred in Ed's mind. Minor's hat blew off into the pond. He made a lunge for it before it hit the water – then he tripped, and fell face first into the pond. Ed grabbed his arm and with much splashing in the shallow water, accompanied by squeals of laughter, the two friends extricated themselves from the pond ending up in a heap on the grass by the pond's edge. Aaron looked up from his work, and smiled – Ed and Minor were up on their feet, jumping up and down in an effort to shake themselves dry.

Meanwhile the gentle breeze had become stronger, ruffling Shadow's mane in the paddock behind the pond. She raised her head and, spooked by the sudden increase in the wind, lurched away into the middle of the paddock, kicking her hind legs out behind her. The boys glanced across at the mare's sudden antics. The thought that had been lingering at the back of Ed's mind was about to become reality. Whether she knew what was going to happen or not, Shadow bucked and hurdled her way to the far end of the paddock. As if on cue, the wooden gate swung inwards allowing Shadow to continue her jittery progress into the open meadow beyond. Minor shouted to Aaron across the track, jumping and pointing at the same time,

"Shadow's got out!"

Aaron dropped his scythe and ran towards the opposite meadow, calling back to Minor,

"Fetch you mum, Minor!"

Shadow had several hundred yards start and after initially charging for the familiarity of the woods, she veered right and headed back towards the farm track – the farm track that led, after about a mile, to the roundabout on the busy A132.

Aaron tried to head her off and force her back into the meadow but his frantic urgings only caused her to head straight down the track and away from the farm. Aaron soon realised his pursuit was pointless, as the horse, now truly frightened, was galloping blindly at full speed and much faster than Aaron could run. He doubled back towards the farm to be met half-way by Mrs Morrison in the Land Rover, driving furiously towards him. She slowed just enough for Aaron to jump in the still-moving vehicle and they roared away down the track, scattering dust and stones in all directions as they were thrown from side to side by the Land Rover's inadequate suspension.

Back at the farm, Ed and Minor, together with an animated Nelson – who was wondering what all the fuss was about – stayed with Bill Morrison who had just phoned Fenton police station of the possible danger to traffic on the A132. The aging, but calm Sergeant Owen Hughes had despatched two patrol cars to the area of likely chaos and alerted the fire service in Hamsden.

Bob Ingham had driven taxis for nearly twenty years, plying his trade in and around Fenton-on-Sea as Coastal Cars' senior and most experienced driver. But, no matter how much experience he had had in his long career, nothing could have prepared him for what was to happen that lunchtime as he returned from dropping off one of his regular customers in Hamsden. With the heat of the morning, Bob had both front windows wound down as far as possible, and was enjoying the relaxing cruise back to Fenton in his silver Ford Cortina. He was hoping there would be no more calls when he got back and he could get out and enjoy the sunshine.

As Bob approached the roundabout at the end of the A132 on the outskirts of Fenton, he thought he could hear the wailing siren of a police car. Bob had long been able to differentiate between the sounds made by vehicles of the various emergency services. '*Sounds like there's been an accident*', he thought as he slowed for the roundabout. In the distance he could see blue flashing lights approaching from the Fenton direction. Little did he know, in those last few seconds, that no accident had yet taken place and that he ....

As the silver Cortina reached a spot about fifty yards from the roundabout, Shadow was an equal distance back up the track, still being pursued by Evelyn and Aaron in the Land Rover which, owing to the narrowness of the farm track, had clearly been unable to get in front of the crazed horse or alter its path. Bob Ingham was too busy looking for traffic coming from his right to notice the black horse heading straight for the centre of the roundabout. As the big silver car entered the roundabout, Bob glanced left and was suddenly presented with the sight of the horse bearing down on him at a full gallop. At first, he thought that the animal would swerve or even try to hurdle his car, but he had no such luck as Shadow ploughed its front hooves into the passenger door. The Cortina shuddered and lurched right with the sound of breaking glass and mangled metal. Fortunately for Bob, the taxi stayed upright in its slide into the embankment on the roundabout. Shadow was not as lucky as the impact catapulted her over the car. There was an excruciating thud of shattering bone as she landed on this earth for the very last time, in the middle of the roundabout. The first of two police cars pulled onto the roundabout and screeched to a halt beside the scene of devastation and carnage as the chasing Land Rover did likewise. Constable Mike Sutton was first out of the police car, making straight for the Cortina, now perched at a slight angle on the grassy roundabout. The driver's door was already open and as Mike peered in, he could see quickly that the driver was more or less alright.

"Stay still, sir," he shouted as Bob Ingham had been about to get out of his taxi.

"I'm O.K., officer. Just shaken – I think."

Mike Sutton helped the dazed taxi driver out and to his feet. Though unsteady, he was able to walk to the first police car where he was carefully put in the back seat. By this time, officers from the second car had put up road blocks and diversions would soon be in place. Vehicles approaching from either Fenton or Hamsden were sent back in their respective directions. In the meantime, Evelyn Morrison and Aaron Coppick had jumped out of the Land Rover and gone to Shadow's aid. The farmer's wife knew, even before she saw her dead horse, that there was nothing that anyone could do. She flopped down in the centre of the roundabout in floods of tears. Aaron stood beside her, at a loss to know what to say or do, until another policeman came over to take details for his report.

Apart from a few cuts and bruises, Bob Ingham had survived the ordeal without serious injury. Though his taxi was a write-off, he was back driving within a fortnight in a brand new car, provided by Coastal Cars' insurance company, after negotiations with the Morrisons' company. Loss of their no claims bonus on their policy was the least of their concerns after the tragic loss of Evelyn's horse. No criminal charges were brought against the Morrisons for leaving the paddock gate open, since the only real damage had been sustained by something that belonged to them anyway. Bob Ingham pressed no charges – he was thankful to be alive and in possession of a brand new car. He thought that the Morrisons had suffered enough over the accident. He would tell his story countless times in the Red Lion in Fenton – about how his superior driving skill saved his life. Of course, in truth, he had been incredibly lucky to survive the strange encounter over which he had actually had no control.

Arguments raged for several days between Evelyn and Bill Morrison over who had left the gate open and, whether out of guilt or sympathy, Bill bought his wife a brand new white pony which she aptly named Sunshine, thus providing some kind of ironic memory of her first horse.

At home in his bedroom later that day, Ed reflected on what he had 'seen' at Peewit Hill Farm. He continued to dismiss any real feelings of guilt over the affair. He kept reminding himself that no one would have believed him if he'd said anything and, indeed, no one would have had the time to check and secure the gate anyway before Shadow freaked out. No one had been hurt and though Shadow had been killed, she was only an animal, wasn't she? The use – or, in this case – non-use of one of his special talents had started to show him what power he might have at his disposal – the power over life and death.

8

Surprises

Gary continued to see Ed on a fortnightly basis throughout that summer, which proved to be one of the hottest and driest on record. Apart from a full day's visit to a small wildlife park just north of Hamsden during half-term at the end of May, the outings were confined mainly to a few hours, either directly after school or at the weekends. In all, by the beginning of August, there had been eight such jaunts. Father and son had not visited the River Wentham again and fishing was confined to Fenton-on-Sea pier which, together with the amusements housed there, was the mainstay of their times together. Their relationship had developed well with Ed able to confide in his dad over some issues that he hadn't even mentioned to his mother. Gary was able to use his son as a channel for information on Jenny's welfare, for which he seemed more concerned than might have been expected, given their history.

Jenny did her best to quash any rumours, which she heard circulating Fenton, about the possibility that she and her former husband were getting back together again. Gary was largely oblivious to such stories, living and working, as he did, twelve miles away in Hamsden. Had he been aware of them, they might have raised a warm smile to his face.

Ed and Minor spent a good deal more time together at Peewit Hill Farm and, sometimes, a delicate balance had to be struck between loyalty to his dad, playing with his friend and being at home in his mum's care. Given this three-way pull on his time, Jenny often had more time to herself, particularly at weekends. At first, she seemed to be at a loss to know how to fill such occasions until she reminded herself that she needed to develop her own life again – a life which, for nearly seven years, had been devoted single-handedly and single-mindedly to her only son. Latterly, that development had extended to the occasional night out with her friends from 'Curls and Twirls', while Ed was looked after by a combination of goodwill provided by grandparents and father.

Once such night was to occur on Saturday, August the 14th and it required some special arrangements to be made. Three fellow workers from Jenny's hairdressing salon had obtained four tickets to see the West End musical '*A Chorus Line*' for the early evening performance starting at six p.m. at London's Theatre Royal in Drury Lane. With her parents entertaining some old friends for the weekend and Gary tied up with a two-day garage promotion, Jenny appeared to have no one to look after Ed for what would need to be most of Saturday – from lunchtime till after midnight. At first, Jenny had declined the invitation, but with her friends anxious for her to come and enjoy herself, she racked her brains in the week before to find somewhere her son could go to for the second half of Saturday and the first part of Sunday morning. In the end, it was a chance remark from Ed as late as Friday teatime that solved her problem.

"Can I go to the farm tomorrow? Minor says it's alright and Dad's busy, Mum."

Jenny smiled to herself and offered up a silent prayer of thanks.

"Absolutely, Ed. And would you like to sleep there tomorrow night if Mrs Morrison says it's alright? I will have to phone to check."

At first, Ed wasn't quite sure of the arrangement that his mum was suggesting. He had never slept apart from his mother before – not even at his granny's house.

"Are you coming as well, then?"

"No, dear – I have to go to London for the evening with some friends."

"Oh."

Ed didn't seem too sure until Jenny added,

"And I'll bring you back a surprise."

Ed cheered up and said,

"I want a car like Dad's."

Whether she got it in Hamsden or London, Jenny knew that she would have to find a model version of Gary's MG. The deal was sealed when she said,

"You shall have a car like Daddy's."

Jenny paused and then said,

"As long as you're good at Mrs Morrison's."

"I will be, Mum."

Jenny went to make three necessary phone calls, praying to herself that Evelyn Morrison could indeed have Ed overnight and also that her three friends hadn't given the spare ticket to anyone else. She was soon relieved to hear that the ticket was still available and also that the farmer's wife had been going to suggest that Ed stayed overnight anyway, but had been a little too shy to ask. It was haymaking time and with everyone fully involved at one of the busiest times of the year, Minor would be left to his own devices for most of the time. Ed would provide company for him for the weekend and she would only be too happy to take him from Saturday morning till after lunch on Sunday, if Jenny wished. Jenny did indeed wish – and the arrangements were made, with Evelyn picking Ed up at ten the following morning. She gave Evelyn her parent's telephone in case of any emergency. The third phone call was to her parents – whose friends had just arrived to stay for the weekend – to tell them of her last minute plans and arrangements. Ann Compton was pleased that her daughter had been able to join her friends on the trip to London.

It was a scorching hot day when Evelyn Morrison called for Ed the following morning. Shorts, T-shirt and sun hats were to be the order of the day. This time, Minor had joined his mum for the short journey to Acacia Avenue. Within ten minutes, the rusty old Land Rover was negotiating the rutted and bone dry track to Peewit Hill Farm and two things struck Ed immediately – the change in the colour of the surrounding meadows and the total lack of cows.

"Where have all the cows gone, Aunty Evelyn?" he asked.

"Oh, we had to move them to the other side of Peewit Hill. There's still some decent grazing pasture there next to the river. Everywhere else is tinder dry."

The Land Rover slowed almost to a stop as Mrs Morrison tried to avoid a particularly deep rut and Ed noticed her new white pony in the paddock to the right. Sunshine had wandered over to the fence to inspect the Land Rover as it passed.

"That's Mum's new pony, Ed," said Minor. "He's called Sunshine."

"Oh," said Ed, without much emotion in his voice, even though memories of that tragic day in June had suddenly come flooding back. "He won't get out this time," he continued cryptically.

Evelyn Morrison glanced briefly in her rear-view mirror – the comment hadn't gone unnoticed by her, but she said nothing as all her concentration was suddenly needed to avoid further ruts in the track.

As they neared the farmhouse, Ed glanced to his left to see Mr Morrison driving a tractor with a small hay cutter attached. Ben and Aaron were walking behind using large rakes to form numerous small haycocks. All three men were shirtless and their backs gleamed with sweat.

"You boys can help me take some drinks out to the lads in a minute," said Mrs Morrison. "It's about time for their mid-morning break – they've been at it since eight."

Evelyn Morrison pulled the Land Rover into the shade of one of the hay barns and the boys quickly made their way across the farmyard to the house. It was getting unbearably hot – dust and particles of hay choked the atmosphere, causing Ed to cough. As they reached the wide-open front door of the farmhouse, Mrs Morrison patted him lightly on the back, saying,

"We better get you a drink, Ed, before we take the men theirs and then I suggest that you two play round the back of the house where there's some shade. It'll be a bit cooler and there's less dust. I think Minor's got something to show you, as well, Ed."

Minor Morrison had a coy smile on his face almost all the time while he and Ed helped his mum take two large jugs of iced squash, together with some fruit and some towels, out to the men in the hay field. His dad gave the game away about his son's surprise just as he had finished his first glass of squash.

"I suppose you two are going to play with Minor's new toy, while we sweat and toil out here, eh?"

"Oh, Dad – it was supposed to be a surprise," exclaimed Minor.

"Whoops! Sorry, son – I thought you'd have told him by now. You can't usually keep a secret for very long. Anyway, he doesn't know what it is yet, does he?"

"No, Dad, he doesn't," said Minor. "I'm gonna' show him in a minute."

Ed turned and looked back reflectively at the farmhouse. '*Of course, I know*', he thought. '*I knew the moment Mrs Morrison patted me on the back.*' Ed Compton-Jones had had another 'vision' and he'd never been wrong before.

A few minutes late and Ed feigned his surprise when he saw his friend's new 'toy'.

"Ooh! It's a tractor like your dad's."

"Yes, and you can sit on it, and it goes too," gabbled Minor breathlessly as the two boys stared at the shiny red model tractor with bucket seat and pedals. "You have to pedal, but it can go over the grass and we can push each other down the slope by the back door."

"Ooh, can I go first?" asked Ed, apparently with real excitement. A split second earlier, another vision had entered his head. He knew they'd have to be very careful.

For the next forty minutes, the two friends alternated as pusher and driver, trying to see who could freewheel furthest down the slope and into the rear meadow. With lunch fast approaching – indicated by Minor's mum issuing a ten minute warning from the back door – Minor took his last turn as driver. What was to happen next was played out in Ed's mind and he knew he had to do something. He knew there was going to be an accident.

"Push me!" shouted Minor, when Ed had seemed reluctant to do so. When there was no response from his friend, Minor put his feet on the pedals and pedalled for all he was worth. The slope started just beyond the opening for the back door and Minor knew he only had to pedal until the gentle incline took over. Ed made up his mind and ran forward, shouting,

"Look out, Aunty Evelyn!"

The back door to the farmhouse seemed to open slightly as the tractor approached at speed. At the last moment, Ed managed to grab the back of the bucket seat and, with almost superhuman strength, hauled the tractor to a halt, inches from the door. Minor pitched forward in the seat but remained in contact with the tractor, shouting some unintelligible words of surprise. When he sat back in the seat, he turned round and said,

"What did you do that for? I was going really fast – I was going to break the record."

"Your mum was just coming out of the door and she wouldn't have seen you."

Minor looked to his right at the half-open door. There was no one there.

"My mum's in the kitchen making lunch, you clown."

Ed trotted to the door and pushed it open wide. The back hallway was empty. He frowned and turned back to his irate friend.

"Sorry, Minor – I thought I heard her coming."

A minute later and Mrs Morrison did come – to tell the boys that lunch was ready. Ed was confused. He had either misinterpreted his vision or someone, or something, had deliberately played a trick on him. Whatever the reason for the erroneous foreknowledge, Ed began to doubt, for the first time in his short life, whether he could always rely on one of his special talents. He had been absolutely convinced that the 'accident' would happen – just as convinced as he had been on one or two other occasions when he had seen into the future.

Ed's appetite was poor for the home-cooked lunch provided by Mrs Morrison. Though it consisted of many of his favourite items – ham and cheese sandwiches on fresh bread, followed by peaches and ice-cream, he ate very little and seemed ill at ease, with Minor's mum making comment on his lethargy.

"You two had better play inside this afternoon. Ed here is looking a little pale. Have you been working him too hard, Minor? Did you make him do all the pushing? Whenever I came out, you were always on the tractor."

"No, Mum – we took it in turns, but I think the sun may have gone to his head. He started seeing things outside!"

Minor winked at his slightly embarrassed friend who sat in silence while Minor related the story of his panic over the non-existent accident. Ed's inability to attempt to explain away his antics convinced Evelyn Morrison even more that the weather had taken its toll on him. After lunch, the boys were confined to the relative coolness of the dairy parlour with its cold stone floor where they played for a couple of hours, alternating between Happy Families and Minor's superior model farm, until they went to help Minor's mum in the kitchen where she was baking some cakes for tea.

After some more refreshments, with Ed's appetite returning, the two friends went back outside and wandered off to do some stickleback fishing in the duck pond. It was four-thirty and a light breeze off the sea began to provide some much needed relief from the strong August sunshine. With trainers and socks removed, that relief was made all the more complete when they paddled in the cool water searching for the somewhat elusive fish.

At about the time that Ed was having his mind apparently play tricks on him, Jenny and her friends, Sue, Carol and the manager of 'Curls and Twirls', Jean, were boarding the coach to London from Hamsden Bus Station. The journey to Victoria Coach Station was scheduled to take three hours with a couple of other pick-up points before they reached the capital. With the performance due to start at six, they had at least a couple of hours to shop or take in the sights.

It was equally as hot in London as it was back in Fenton-on-Sea that afternoon; the atmosphere made all the more oppressive by the lack of any sea breeze. Though the four women took a taxi up to Oxford Street, they were still wilting by the time they arrived outside the Theatre Royal in Drury Lane. Judging by the many happy faces that were just emerging from the afternoon performance, the show was going to be a good one, and the evening was about to get even better for the four friends. Jenny had managed to buy Ed his model MG, though not in the same colour as his dad's, and with several other souvenirs of their short shopping excursion, the theatre party looked slightly bedraggled, being weighed down with several bags as they were. It was just after five-thirty as they stood outside the theatre, all of them hoping that the ladies toilets would not be too busy and they could obtain a quick wash and a recovery of their ladylike composure.

"Come on, ladies," said Jean. "Let's go in before the last minute rush. I'm dying for a …."

Three voices chimed in unison.

"Me, too!"

The surprise awaited them at the ticket kiosk. As soon as the lady in the booth looked at their tickets, she said,

"Ah – you're the party from Fenton-on-Sea. I'm afraid there's been a change to your seats."

Carol Johnson moved forward and said,

"Oh? They've been booked for ages. I sent the cheque in over a month ago."

"I know you did, dear," said the ticket lady warmly. "But you've been upgraded since."

"Upgraded?" queried Carol.

"Yes – we had a telephone call late this afternoon from our ticket agent in Hamsden to say that a gentleman had just been in to request a private box for you all. We had two left and he paid the agent in cash for the upgrade. He was most insistent that you should have the box for the evening."

"How did he know *we* were coming?" asked Carol. "And what gentleman?"

"Easy, dear. When I checked your tickets just now, they matched those recorded by our Hamsden agent. As for the identity of the gentleman – apparently he didn't leave his name. Though the agent only had *your* name on the booking, the gentleman seemed to be certain there were going to be four of you. If you don't want the box, I can sell it to another party. I think you'll like it."

"No! No!" exclaimed Sue and Jean almost simultaneously. "Tell her we'll take it, Carol."

And they took it. And it was magnificent – with a lavishly appointed ladies room across the corridor. With places to store their shopping bags and a superb vantage point from which to watch the show, the girls were in seventh heaven. After a quick improvement to their appearances and with suitable physical relief, the four friends settled back in their luxurious seats. Before the curtain went up, the main topic of conversation was the identity of their anonymous benefactor.

"I bet it's your hubby, Jean," said Sue Malham. "You know mine is still serving overseas with the army."

"Well it wasn't mine," added Carol Johnson. "We haven't been talking to each other all week."

"No way it's Derek," said Jean Cooper.

"Well, it must have been one of your husbands – I'm not married anymore and I certainly don't have any admirers at the moment," said Jenny.

"There is another possibility. Something similar happened when I worked in London," said Carol, after some thought.

"And that is?" asked Jean.

"That it has come via one of our clients."

"They're all women, Carol, dear," said Sue.

"Maybe – but there's hardly been a day over the last month when we haven't discussed today in the salon. I bet one of the women was so pleased with us over the years that she got her husband to pay for a treat for us."

In the end, the women decided that Carol was probably right. Failing that, the only other possibility seemed to be that the theatre had made a mistake, but, as the curtain went up, they were determined to enjoy their good fortune, however the upgrade had been provided.

Though Jenny had denied the existence of any admirers, she would find out later that she would not be able to sustain that denial for very much longer. Somewhere in the back of her mind she suspected who the mysterious gentleman had been. The question she asked herself that evening was: '*How did he know that she was coming when she had only made her mind up the previous teatime?*' It just didn't make sense. It wouldn't be until the next time she spoke to her parents and the stand-in manager back at the salon in Fenton-on-Sea that the penny would finally drop.

Earlier that Saturday, Gary had decided that, because of the hot weather which was inducing many possible customers out of Hamsden to make for the beaches on the coast, he would close the showroom three hours earlier than the intended time of six o'clock. With the extra time available, he decided to see if he could take his son out for a couple of hours. When he phoned just after two, he got no answer from Jenny's house and so he tried her parent's number. Ann Compton answered.

"Hello – Fenton 3566."

"Oh, hello, Ann – it's Gary. Are Jenny and Ed there with you?"

"Oh no, Gary – didn't she tell you? She's gone to London with some friends from work. They're off to the theatre for a show."

"Last time I saw her, she told me she couldn't go since she didn't have anyone to look after Ed," said Gary.

"Oh – she managed, at the last minute, to get Mrs Morrison out at Peewit Hill farm to look after him. Fred and I only found out yesterday evening. It was a last minute decision."

"O.K. – thanks, Ann. What have they gone to see?"

"I think she said it was *A Chorus Line* at the Theatre Royal in Drury Lane. Why? Do you need to contact her?"

"Oh no, Ann. I just wondered, that's all."

After the phone call, Gary sat back in his office chair and pondered how nice it was that Jenny was out enjoying herself again. He was reminded of their honeymoon, spent in London nearly eight years previously and how he used to like to treat his wife with surprise trips to restaurants and cinemas. He'd never realised that she liked the theatre. Soon, he made up his mind – he wanted to treat Jenny again. He owed her so much. Five minutes later he was at 'Curls and Twirls', where the stand-in manager gave him all the information he needed. '*Yes,*' she said, '*the trip had been booked through the East Shires Travel Agency located on the way to the station*'.

After not getting back home till well after two o'clock on Sunday morning, Jenny didn't phone the farm until early on Sunday afternoon to arrange to pick Ed up. Evelyn Robinson said she would bring Ed back in the Land Rover by three o'clock as the farm track was so badly rutted. Jenny had just returned from lunch with her parents and their friends where she had soon learned of Gary's inquiries into her whereabouts on the previous evening. Her suspicions as to the identity of the anonymous gentleman were finally confirmed when, later the next week, the stand-in manager would casually mention to her in passing about Gary's visit to the salon the previous Saturday afternoon.

The rest of Ed's time at Peewit Hill Farm seemed to have passed off without any further problems, Evelyn Robinson reporting that, apart from Ed having a bit too much sun on Saturday, the two boys had had a great time and had been well behaved. Ed described to his mum most of what had happened over the weekend, leaving out any reference to the 'phantom' accident. He did seem a bit upset at something else though. When his mum gently asked him what the matter was, he replied quietly,

"People keep calling me names, Mum."

"What people?"

"Minor's dad and Aaron."

"Who's Aaron?"

"He works at the farm for Mr Morrison."

"What do they call you?"

"Little magpie and ...."

"And?"

"Shorty."

Jenny smiled. She had feared that her son's size could become a topic of fun, but the first nickname baffled her for a moment."

"Why magpie, Ed?"

"Don't know, Mum. What is a magpie?"

Even before she replied, Jenny had guessed the connotation, given her son's jet black hair and pale skin, though the latter now had a distinctly red tinge.

"It's a large black and white bird."

"I'm not a bird, Mum."

"Of course you're not, love. I'm sure Mr Morrison meant nothing by it and, as for this Aaron – just stay away from him next time you go."

Ed mumbled something about not wanting to go again if Mr Morrison was there and Jenny made a mental note to have a word with Evelyn about it if the opportunity arose naturally. She didn't want to make a fuss over something that Ed would have to learn to cope with on his own. It might give him a complex.

As Ed lay in bed that night, and prompted by the name-calling, he began to reflect on how different he must be from other boys. For some time, he had realised he had talents that other people didn't possess, but the weekend stay at Peewit Hill Farm had made him start to think that those people didn't like him as well.

9

A History Lesson

Jenny kept the realisation that Gary had been the mysterious benefactor for the theatre trip to London from her three friends. She also didn't take it as a romantic gesture; perhaps as Gary had intended. For his part, Gary was a little disappointed when she didn't mention it the next time he saw her as he picked Ed up for the afternoon on the last Saturday before the school term started on Monday, September the 6th. When he tried to probe his son that afternoon, Ed seemed to know little about the trip, other than the white model MGB GT his mum had bought him in London.

Ed didn't quite seem himself during their visit to Fenton pier for some crab fishing and it wasn't until the drive back home that the reason became clear to Gary. His son was not looking forward to going back to school on the Monday. Mentioning it to Jenny on their return gave her a chance to talk about the name-calling, particularly with regard to his size. Though Gary appeared relieved when she told him that she didn't think it was happening much at school, and certainly not from his friend, Minor Morrison, he did ask Jenny to let him know if it happened again. Neither of them had realised that the name-calling wasn't the real problem, but rather that Ed had got it into his head that people were jealous of him in some way.

September in Fenton-on-Sea, like most of the country, remained hot – uncomfortably so for sitting in stuffy classrooms at Fenton Central Junior School. Miss Sandbuck made a basic teaching error on the afternoon of Friday, September the 24th – she tried to teach class 2Sb some local history. It would not have been such a bad idea if her pupils had been two or three years older, but they were only six or seven and possessing of little knowledge or interest of anything other than their immediate home surroundings. With temperatures outside in the high seventies, it would take an exciting delivery to keep her pupils' attention – even keeping some of them from nodding off would prove to be a challenge. The topic was on Victorian England and what life would have been like in Fenton-on-Sea all those years ago. Miss Sandbuck managed to keep the attention of some of her charges while she was asking for their thoughts on what it must have been like before there were cars and decent roads. What would the seafront have looked like with no promenade? Which of the present buildings in Fenton would have been there nearly a hundred years ago? By this time she had lost all but a few pupils and any answers only seemed to come from those children who had grandparents who had been born in the town. Eventually, one of the brightest pupils, Susan Long, recalled the town trail they had taken earlier in the summer.

"Miss – the Beach Station was here, wasn't it?"

Ed's head ceased its downward journey as he struggled to keep his eyes open.

"Why yes, Susan – it was. How clever of you to remember. I believe it was built in 1889. Isn't that right, Edward?"

Minor Morrison was jolted awake at the mention of his name but returned to his slumbers as soon as he realised that Miss Sandbuck was looking at his friend and not him. Ed, himself, nearly said something like: *'How clever of you to remember, Miss Sandbuck'*, but what actually came out was,

"Yes, Miss."

"And what do you think the trains would have been like all those years ago? Did the trains go on the roads? How did …?"

Ed Compton-Jones didn't hear the completion of his teacher's next question. The combination of stuffy classroom and her soft tones had had its effect. He was already in another world.

Gabriel Thomas was sixteen. His father, Joshua Thomas, was thirty-nine and a member of the recently formed Old Fenton Parish Council. It was May. Joshua was a fisherman and owned the Rosalind Ann, a small fishing smack that operated out of the newly-built harbour. The only other building of any significance in Fenton was the imposing St Andrew's Church which stood near the edge of the cliffs at the bottom of Sea Lane.

"No, Jack – there wasn't a pier or as many buildings as now along the seafront. Just fishing cottages and private ...."
"And the big church, Miss Sandbuck."
"Yes, Susan, St Andrew's would have been there."

Gabriel worked on the Rosalind Ann with his father and old Amos. Nobody knew Amos' second name, if, indeed, he knew himself. It was late afternoon and they were approaching their mooring with a moderate catch of mackerel to be sold in the fish market on the South Quay. They could see the small crowd of regulars awaiting the Rosalind Ann. Joshua and his two-man crew were in luck – they were the first boat back that day. With soused mackerel an ever popular supper dish, Joshua Thomas was hopeful of a decent price for his fish. His rough mental calculations had given him an estimate of over seven pounds for the entire catch. With local average wages running at about six pounds per week, it had been another good day.

As the sun went down on the South Quay on that Friday in late May, Gabriel helped his father organise the various coins into the stacks of their individual denominations. With the final tally on his chalk slate, he prepared to make his announcement of the day's takings to Joshua Thomas. Old Amos had long since repaired to the Coach and Horses; a two mile trudge across the fields to the Hamsden road. Amos didn't need his day's wages as free beer was always obtained from his many fishing tales, most of which were exaggerated beyond the belief of all but the most naïve of any passing strangers. It was Saturday and there would be a few of them still left on their way home from the seaside. Their horse and carts or simple carriages would wander from side to side on their way back to Hamsden, all of them hoping they could make it before the darkness of night set in – the time for robbers to be abroad for any tardy and unsuspecting day trippers.

Gabriel folded his arms proudly and announced,

"Eight pounds, sixteen shillin's and fourpence ha'penny."

"Not bad, Gabriel – and we have three mackerel left for our suppers. Ma will be pleased."

"Ooh – I trust she has some bread and ale to go with it."

"She will, my boy. Now let's get the baskets back onto the Rosalind Ann and secure her for the night. It'll be dark in an hour and I want my supper."

With the sun still just above the horizon, Joshua and his son walked the half mile to their modest white clapboard dwelling at the south end of the small seaside town. The walk took nearly fifteen minutes with a steep climb up the cliff path to negotiate before it levelled out opposite St Andrew's Church, whose stained glass windows glinted bright red in the dying rays of the sun.

'Ma' was waiting for Gabriel and Joshua in the low-ceilinged kitchen that seemed to smell permanently of a combination of fresh bread and coal smoke from the big cast iron range that dominated one wall. The temperature in the kitchen never varied more than a few degrees all year and, without the single window, it would have been difficult to determine whether it was summer or winter without peering through its smoke-stained glass. Ma – or to give her her birth name, Annie – had pans ready and waiting for their fish tea. In the centre of the solid oak kitchen table stood a tall jug of ale with two large round loaves for companions. With hardly a word of acknowledgement, Joshua poured himself a glass of the frothy home-made beer and plonked himself in the chair at one end of the table. He was immediately reprimanded.

"Get yourself up Joshua and go and wash that awful smell from you!"

Gabriel had already made his way to the small brick-built outhouse which doubled as laundry room and washroom. When father and son returned to the kitchen a few minutes later, the smell of frying fish dominated the atmosphere.

"I'm starving, Ma," said Joshua.

"Good – now what have you to give me?"

It seemed that despite Ma being cook, cleaner and laundry maid, she was also keeper of the purse strings as Joshua then proceeded to give her the leather bag that contained the day's takings. She would find less than eight pounds there when she counted it later that evening. The shortfall would never be accounted for, but Joshua was never without a few coins for beer and cribbage.

Joshua picked up his mug of ale and took a long swig. His work was done for the day and he leant back in his tall-backed chair and closed his eyes. Gabriel cut the first loaf into man-sized chunks. The air was stuffy – the heat of the day still trapped inside. Stomachs churned at the rich smell of the fish cooking in butter. Ma turned to look at her husband.

"Wake up! Are you asleep, Joshua?"

"Wake up! Are you asleep, Edward?"

"Huh? No, I'm just hungry, Ma."

"No, Miss, I'm just tired."

Ed had been jolted awake by his 'Ma' – Miss Sandbuck and it took him a few seconds to readjust to the reality of 1976. It had been so warm and comfortable in the kitchen. He had felt at home and safe. Within a few more minutes, however, he would have forgotten all about his interlude in a bygone age. The school bell sounded for the end of school. It was time to go home. All memories of another home wiped, at least temporarily from his mind. Miss Sandbuck was still talking.

"Well, some of us have found it hard to concentrate this afternoon. I suspect that some of you need to go to bed earlier at night – Edward, Jack, Davy; to name just a few."

One or two voices gave their somewhat sleepy response of '*Yes, Miss*' against the livelier background chorus of '*Bye, Miss! See you Monday!*'

Jenny was waiting for Ed when he emerged from school that warm September afternoon. She thought he seemed happier than usual. She didn't know it, but that happiness wasn't only due to the fact that nobody had poked fun at him that day. As she took his hand for the walk back home, he had just one question on his mind.

"Can we have fish for tea, Mum?"

10

'Family' Outing

By half-term at the end of October, Gary was beginning to see Ed on more or less a weekly basis, thus enabling Jenny to socialise more. As was to be expected with such an arrangement, there were often occasions when each parent needed Ed to be with them at the same time. One such occasion happened on the last Saturday of October, before Ed was due back at school on the Monday. Jenny had put off buying him any new clothes, in case he should have a sudden growth spurt. However, it had been clear for some time that his school uniform had worn so much that the entire outfit needed replacing anyway. She had thus decided that she would take him shopping in Hamsden for the requisite items, it being a Saturday when she wasn't at work. Unfortunately, she had forgotten that Gary had promised Ed that he would take him to see Hamsden Town play at Freeman Street with kick-off at three o'clock the same afternoon. It was to be his first visit to see the local first division side. Though both events were not mutually exclusive, they quickly became so. Unbeknown to Jenny – because Ed had neglected to mention it until Friday teatime – his dad had also promised to take him shopping in the morning, followed by lunch at the Old Market Restaurant before the match. When Jenny went to phone Gary just after tea on the Friday to see if he could take his son the following weekend, Ed followed her into the hall sobbing and pleading with his mum not to change the arrangements.

"Dad promised me, Mum. Why can't I go for my silly uniform next weekend?"

"Because I'm working," retorted Jenny somewhat angrily with phone in hand.

Suddenly, Ed stopped crying and said quietly,

"Why can't we all go together?"

Jenny appeared to ignore her son's obvious, if naïve solution, and dialled Gary's number. Ed sulked away into the lounge, as though resigned to the inevitable disappointment. As he did so, a familiar knowing smile formed on his face. He 'knew' what was going to happen.

Gary's mother answered Jenny's call.

"Hello – Mary Jones speaking."

"Oh hello, Mary – it's Jenny. Is Gary there?"

"No, dear – he hasn't got in from work yet."

"Oh – will you tell him I called, Mary, and ask him to call me this evening? It's quite important."

"Of course, Jenny. There's nothing wrong, is there?"

"No. I just need to check his arrangements for Ed with him."

"I'll let him know you called as soon as he gets in."

The two women exchanged their goodbyes and Jenny went to check on her son. She had to talk to him about one or two things. However, when she looked at him happily watching one of his favourite television programmes, she decided it was the wrong place and the wrong time. He was far too young to understand the problems caused by split families. After all, it wasn't his problem. Gary would just have to change his plans and she wouldn't tell Ed until the morning, hoping that Gary wouldn't phone until after his son had gone to bed.

The phone rang ten minutes later and Jenny reluctantly picked it up.

"Gary?"

"Yep. What's up?"

And then Jenny explained the situation, but, like his son, Gary couldn't see that there was a problem and, in any case, as he remarked, he had had to go to great lengths to organise cover for the showroom for the day. He didn't know when he would have a Saturday free gain. Jenny was cornered. He even used some of Ed's words: '*Why can't we all go together. You don't have to come to the match afterwards if you don't want to*'. She began to relent. Where was the harm? It wouldn't mean anything – if they were seen out together as a 'family'. Suddenly, Jenny realised that that was really her only objection. As long as Gary didn't read anything into the joint day out, why should she be bothered about what anyone else might think? If she could cope with Mrs Thompson's snide remarks and rumour-mongering, she could cope with anything. After all, the most important thing was her son's happiness.

There was a touch of autumn mist in the air as Jenny and Ed set off for Hamsden after a light breakfast in advance of lunch at the Old Market Restaurant. Though his mother was understandably apprehensive about the day's prospects, Ed was full of excitement for his first football match. After a brief spell in the top division in the early sixties, Hamsden Town had only just regained their place, having finished a creditable thirteenth in their first season back earlier that year. In this, their second season, they had not fared so well and were currently languishing second from bottom of Division One. Of course, statistics like that meant nothing to Ed – he wasn't even sure who Town's opponents were that afternoon.

Jenny had just reached the A132 and had pulled out of the last of the sea mist that was shrouding Fenton-on-Sea. With blue sky suddenly appearing all around them, she said,

"It's going to be nice day for the match, Ed. You are so lucky to be going and you know who the Town are playing, don't you?"

"No, Mum. We'll beat them, though."

"You'll be lucky! They're up against Liverpool who just happen to be top of the league at the moment."

"So? I know we will win," replied Ed with unusual but assured authority. Jenny smiled at her son's innocence.

"Well, let's hope so. Grandad will be pleased if they do."

During that week, Fred Compton had been predicting a four or five nil thrashing to his colleagues at Fenton railway station and local bookmakers were offering the lowest odds against similarly high victories for the talented opposition.

Hamsden was busy when they arrived just after ten o'clock and Jenny had some difficulty in finding a parking space behind the Town Hall. She had arranged to meet Gary outside Osborne's department store at ten-fifteen and, as the Town Hall clock had already struck the quarter when she eventually found a vacant space, they were clearly going to be late. Fortunately, it transpired that Gary had had similar parking problems and he arrived almost at the same time as Jenny and Ed. His son immediately ran to his dad and gave him a hug. Jenny made a mental note, as she observed this demonstration of affection to be at least equal to that which she usually received from her son. Taking Ed's hand, Gary asked,

"Where to first, Jenny?"

"Shirts and trousers on the top floor."

"Right, let's get the boring bit out of the way, eh, son?"

Ed groaned his agreement. He wasn't looking forward to the inevitable humiliation when the shop assistant was bound to say something like, '*I'm not sure we've got anything in your son's size*' or, even worse, '*Maybe the 4 to 5-year-old size will still fit him*'.

Fortunately, the shop assistant knew Jenny and managed to smuggle the trousers to her without Ed realising their size. Gary looked on proudly as his son behaved immaculately while shirts and trousers were carefully tested for fit. With a new navy blazer purchased from Cornfoot's, the school outfitters, the necessary shopping was completed by eleven-thirty. Jenny then managed to persuade Gary and Ed to return to Osborne's where she wanted to look for a new winter coat for herself. Ed protested a little at the suggestion but his dad seemed quite happy to concede half an hour or so for the exercise. It had been a few years since he had accompanied Jenny for such an event and, secretly, he was quite looking forward to offering his advice as to style and colour. Whether or not she would take it remained to be seen.

After his mother had tried on four coats of varying styles and sizes, Ed was getting impatient and, indeed, hungry for something to eat. He was also finding it hard to contain his excitement for his visit to Freeman Street. Though nearly seven, Ed still had no real sense of time. When Jenny was about to try on the first coat for the second time, Ed remarked,

"Can't we go and watch the football now? And I'm hungry, Mum."

When Gary assured Ed that lunch was booked at twelve-thirty and that it was still three hours to kick-off, it did little to relieve his impatience.

"But this is boring, Dad."

Then he added something that, if his mum had been listening, would, no doubt, have registered with her.

"Besides, she wasn't supposed to be coming with us, Dad."

"Shh, Ed, and let your mum finish her shopping. We have to go in ten minutes anyway if we're to get to the restaurant on time," replied Gary, just loud enough so that Jenny couldn't fail to hear. Jenny *had* heard.

"Oh what, Gary? When's lunch?"

"Twelve-thirty."

"O.K. – but I can't make up my mind. What do you think, Gary? This one or this one?"

Jenny held the two coats up for him to see; one black and one cream-coloured. Gary's heart nearly missed a beat – she was asking *him* for his opinion. He studied each coat carefully and gave his advice.

"The cream one."

He regretted immediately what he said next.

"Cream always suited you, Jenny."

Jenny scowled and put the cream coat back on its hanger. She bought the black one.

Lunch was a slow affair with the Old Market Restaurant packed with shoppers and several football fans who – as Ed remarked when one spoke to him – *'That man talks funny, Mum'*. Liverpool F.C. were in town and, judging by the many red scarves and banners, there were a lot of them, too. Jenny was a little quiet, having been thrown a little by what she saw as Gary's over-attentiveness. By a quarter to two, Gary was anxious to relieve the somewhat tense atmosphere and make for the ground to get a reasonable seat. Ed needed no second asking as he jumped up and said,

"Come on, Mum – we've gotta' go."

Gary had already suspected what her reaction would be. He had guessed right when she replied,

"You go with your dad, love. I'm a bit tired and I want to do a bit more shopping as well." Then she added, "If that's alright, Gary. You can bring Ed back, can't you?"

"Yes – no problem."

Ed didn't seem to be as disappointed as Jenny thought he would be. He gave his mum a quick hug and took his dad's hand with a cheery,

"See ya later, Mum."

Gary said goodbye and told Jenny that they would be back in Fenton about six, depending on the post-match traffic. Jenny mumbled her thanks for lunch and for helping with Ed's uniform and called after Ed,

"Have a good game and I hope they win."

Gary smiled inwardly. '*No chance,*' he thought, as he went to pay their bill. Having paid, and with more change than he had expected, he was suddenly reminded of his former vice. He led Ed back to where Jenny was still finishing her coffee.

"Sorry, Jen – can I leave Ed with you for a just a few minutes?"

"Ye-es – what's up?"

He leant down and whispered in Jenny's ear.

"I just want to put a small bet on over the road."

Jenny gave Gary a knowing look as if to say: '*You still can't leave it alone, can you?*'

Unfortunately, Ed had heard his dad, and though he didn't really understand the ins and outs of gambling, he'd gathered what his dad meant. He gave his own prediction for the result.

"Town are going to win 2–1 and I'll bet you a million pounds they do so, Dad."

With that, he pulled a 50 pence piece out of his pocket and gave it to his dad. Gary looked guilty and immediately handed back the coin that had been his pocket money to Ed that week.

"No, son – you're not gambling."

Jenny was cross.

"You see what you've started, Gary. Now go – and if you're not back in five minutes, I'll take Ed to the game myself."

Gary was quick – making two wagers; one for five pounds on Liverpool to win 4–1 at 9/2 and one for 50 pence on Town to win 2–1 at 66/1. The betting assistant laughed when she saw the second slip and, to preserve face, Gary had to explain that it was for his son. He laughed with her. He was back with Jenny and Ed in under four and half minutes.

Jenny didn't do anymore shopping – it had been an excuse to foreshorten her time with Gary. As she made her way back to the car park behind the Town Hall, she tried to understand why she had found Gary's remark over her choice of coat so difficult to take. She knew she shouldn't let it bother her, but she hadn't been sure of his intentions when he had tried to flatter her, even though she had sought his advice. In the time they had been a couple, he had hardly ever made mention of what did or what did not suit her, even in the heightened romance of their courtship. Was this an attempt to strike up romance again? What would she do if it was? What if she found that she began to like further remarks?

Jenny was back in Fenton-on-Sea by half past two and decided to visit her parents' house in Fir Tree Close. She knew her dad would be at work at the station until at least four. Her mother was surprised to see her Jenny walked in.

"What's happened, love? Where's Ed? I thought you were going to the match."

"Gary's taken him on his own. I was feeling a bit tired. He'll bring him back afterwards. I never really wanted to go," she lied.

"Oh?"

Jenny could tell from her mother's tone that she hadn't really convinced her of the reason for her early return, and over the next hour, mother and daughter discussed Jenny's main concern of the moment. It was clear to Jenny that her mother had spotted some signs of romantic intentions in Gary's conversation when he had picked Ed up from Fir Tree Close on the odd occasion. As Jenny was about to leave, hoping to miss her dad, who might still have strident views on his former son-in-law, Ann Compton said quietly to her daughter,

"I think he still loves you, Jenny, love."

Jenny said nothing. All the signs were leading her to the same conclusion. As she drove home she asked herself two simple questions: '*Did she mind? Did she feel the same about Gary?*

Gary had to take great care with his son on the way to Freeman Street. Though it was normally only a ten minute walk, the streets on the way to the ground were packed with supporters, thus hindering their progress and jostling them from side to side. The crowd seemed to be more red than blue as the visiting fans outweighed the home ones by about two to one. Fortunately, as they arrived outside the ground, the crowd split into two as the Liverpool fans headed for their allotted positions in the South Stand. It was soon clear that Gary and Ed would have no problem finding seats in the North Stand, as Town's notoriously fickle supporters had stayed away in droves despite the visit of their illustrious opponents. Even with only a third of the season gone, they had decided what awaited the Town in a few months time and had gone to do other things on what might be one of the last fine days that autumn.

Ed had never before seen so many people together in one place and he sat in awe of his surroundings for several minutes, hardly saying a word. Freeman Street's compact ground and stands were larger and more imposing than any structure he had ever seen too. Looking around, Gary could see that their stand was about three parts full, while the South Stand opposite was a mass of red scarves and flags. It was five to three and Gary felt the hairs stand up on the back of his neck as Gerry Marsden's voice sang out the Liverpool anthem over the loudspeakers. The Liverpool captain led his team onto the pitch from the tunnel adjacent to the South Stand. Five thousand Scouse voices erupted in unison with their rendition of '*You'll Never Walk Alone*', while a small section of the East Stand offered their unsubtle alternative, changing the last word of the title to '*Again*'. Fortunately, this cruel and nasty response was drowned out by the North Stand's usual anthem, '*Keep Right on to the End of the Road*', which avoided any awkward questions from Ed as to the meaning of the alternative chorus.

The home team quickly followed with the loudspeakers blaring out a crackly pre-war version of Town's anthem. Centre half Mick Crawford took his blue and white team to the north end for the prematch warm up. The noise was incessant and Ed had to shout to make himself heard.

"Which way are we kicking, Dad?"

"They have to toss a coin first. Look – the captains have just been called to the centre-circle."

"Hope we're kicking this way."

Ed got his wish, though for most of the first half, he was to see little of the ball from close quarters as the Reds camped almost permanently in Town's half at the opposite end. The Blues survived until the thirty-seventh minute when the opposition's diminutive number seven scored with a mazy dribble and shot into the top corner.

Ed sat back in his seat with an eerie silence all around him. Both his father's betting slips remained live. The far stand was a mass of waving red scarves and flags. Ed didn't seem to be too upset that Town were behind.

"Who scored, Dad?"

"That's the great Peter Hughes, son. He plays for England."

"I like him," said Ed, contrary to his expected allegiance.

"Why?"

"Because he smaller than the other players."

120

Gary smiled at his son's affinity for the Liverpool striker. He was beginning to see for himself how self-conscious Ed was of his size.

The half-time whistle blew and Gary and Ed made for the toilets and refreshment bar. As they climbed the last few steps to the top of the stand, a voice called out from behind,

"Hey, Shorty! What're *you* doing here?"

Ed turned round to see Greg Patterson standing behind him with a broad and slightly sarcastic smile on his face. Ed clung tighter to his dad's hand. At first, Gary didn't seem to realise that his son was the intended butt of the remark and he continued forward until his son's tight grip forced him to look behind him. Greg Patterson had disappeared into the crowd congregated behind the goal.

"Who was that, son? Were they talking to you?" asked Ed's dad with a concerned look on his face.

"Oh – that's Greg. He's in my class at school. I hate him."

"I can see why, Ed. If I catch him, he won't be calling you names again."

"He's not the only one that calls me names. Jack Collison does as well."

Gary didn't reply and Ed then said,

"But I'm not bothered, Dad, because I'm cleverer than them and I know things they don't."

Gary smiled somewhat proudly at his son's self-confidence, even though he had misinterpreted Ed's intended meaning. He hadn't been referring to simple facts learned and remembered at school or in his everyday life. Little did Gary realise that his son knew things he wasn't supposed to, and sometimes, couldn't even possibly know. He might get an indication within the hour.

With soft drink and packet of crisps in hand, Ed returned to his seat with his father. The players had emerged for the second-half. Unusually, a couple of opposing players seemed to be holding a conversation with each other and it didn't look to Gary as if it was a particularly friendly exchange. He checked the numbers in the programme and discovered that centre forward Danny Hogan of Town and defender Sammy Wilson of Liverpool had been the participants in the 'debate'.

The second-half started in the same fashion as the first with the Reds constantly attacking the North End goal. Ed now got a much better view of the action and, unlike his dad or the referee, spotted that the argument between Hogan and Wilson was continuing. The tall Liverpool defender, shadowed by Hogan, had come up for a corner and appeared to be sent flying in the penalty area by a sly, but deliberate, elbow in the side. The ball was cleared by Town and Wilson took his revenge as they ran back upfield. Unfortunately for the Liverpool player, the return elbow to Danny Hogan's face occurred right under the referee's nose with the Town player's identical facial protrusion spurting blood for all to see. The referee blew his whistle. Players of both sides gathered round in sympathy or in anger. The medical staff was summoned from the touchline. The referee had no choice and he reached for his pocket and Sammy Wilson quickly became one of the first players in England to get red-carded. Liverpool suddenly only had ten men. Arguments continued as Danny Hogan was taken off the field for repairs – eighteen-year-old Steve Lillis replaced him for his debut for the first team.

The tenor of the game changed drastically. What had been a one-sided and reasonably friendly affair suddenly became more even and bad-tempered. Tackles flew in from both sides. Four yellow cards were shown in the space of ten minutes. One such card had been for a late challenge by a Liverpool defender on the edge of their box. Town's Mick Crawford placed the ball carefully and, with only one thing in mind, strode back to take the free-kick. He ran forward and blasted the ball through the wall and into the top left-hand corner of the net. The score was 1-1. Both Gary's betting slips still remained 'live'.

Most of the remainder of the match remained a stalemate with Town giving as good as they got. With time running out, it looked like both teams had settled for a draw. Seconds remained as Town's goalkeeper, Roy Marshal, booted the ball into the opposition's penalty area where it bounced once between two Liverpool players who had left it for the other to deal with. Steve Lillis darted between the static defence and rose stylishly into the air to nod the ball past the advancing keeper. Only one of Gary's betting slips still remained live. Ed leapt out of his seat with the rest of the North Stand and shouted to his dad,

"Told you we'd win 2-1. I just knew it!"

Gary's emotions were torn three ways – between cheering the winning goal; coping with the disappointment at the loss of his five pounds and realising that his other bet might return him £33.50 in winnings. No sooner had the referee restarted the game than he blew his final whistle. Gary's winnings were confirmed. He congratulated his son on his 'lucky' guess, but he appeared less excited than might have been expected at such an unlikely prediction coming true – it reminded him too much of his bet.

"Well done, Ed," was all he could bring himself to say.

Gary knew that he wouldn't be able to collect his winnings from the bookies as he and Ed made their way slowly back to the car. He would have to leave it till Monday when he could return on his own. He desperately wanted to tell his son of his good fortune and confirm to him at the same time that he had actually taken him up on his forecast, but he knew also that the serious responsibilities of a father did not include such obvious condonation of gambling.

In fact, Ed didn't need his dad to remind him of his prediction, and it hadn't caused him personally as much astonishment as it had to the thousands of other fans present at Freeman Street that day, or, indeed, anywhere else for that matter. He would probably have been more surprised if the score *hadn't* finished 2–1 in favour of the home side. That was a testament to his growing confidence in his special powers. Consequently, Ed made strangely modest reference to the result on the way home after his initial '*told you so*' remark. It suited his father, as the chances of him letting slip the details of the secret bet diminished considerably.

11

Dreams

Ed was understandably tired when Gary brought him home that evening. It had been a long and exhausting day, both physically and emotionally for him and his dad. Surprisingly, Jenny invited Gary in for a cup of tea before his drive back to Hamsden. After her chat with her mother, she had decided not to act nervously in her dealings with him, but rather face up to any attempts at flattery in a calm and collected manner. Time alone would tell whether she could absorb any further such comments without emotion or whether she would warm to them instead.

Ed retired to the lounge to watch television while his parents sat in the kitchen. Jenny would find her son fast asleep half an hour later. In the absence of his son, Gary began to relax a little, relating much of what had gone on at the game, including Ed's prediction for the match score. Though suitably impressed, Jenny was reminded of one or two other occasions when her son had made similarly good predictions.

"He's a good guesser, our son. Mrs Morrison out at Peewit Hill Farm told me recently that he had more or less correctly guessed the number of cows they had out to pasture one day."

Gary didn't seem to think the two events were comparable.

"He might have counted them without anyone knowing."

"Evelyn Morrison says not. He didn't have the opportunity. Besides, do you really think he could have counted accurately up to fifty-seven at his age? It was nearly a year ago, Gary."

"Maybe – he seems a clever lad, or so you said his teacher told you. Anyway, today's guess wasn't about counting things that were already there. No one knew how the game would turn out and I know this, Jenny ...."

"What?"

"That I bet very few people anywhere in the country would have gone for a win for Town, let alone give the exact score as well."

"Just luck," said Jenny finally. "Like your gambling, it's just luck! Oh, and by the way, I suppose you lost money at the bookies, didn't you?"

Gary hesitated before he replied,

"Yes, but only a couple of pounds."

Jenny smiled knowingly at his hesitation.

"You should have followed your son's advice, then, shouldn't you?"

Gabriel Thomas had always been a dreamer, from his short time at the local church school run by the Fenton School Board to his times on the Rosalind Ann, gazing wistfully out to sea. Unlike his father who had no formal schooling whatsoever, other than that gleaned from St Andrew's Sunday school, Gabriel had attended until he was twelve after the Education Act of 1870 established compulsory education for all but the very poor. His teacher at St Andrew's Elementary School, the Reverend Hezekiah Morton, often had to correct, and sometimes punish him for daydreaming. His simple essays were full of rich ideas of what the future would be like. In another life, and with a better brain, he might well have become an inventor of note, rather than a humble fisherman.

It was Tuesday, May the 28th and Gabriel was dreaming of faraway places. He and Amos were alone on the Rosalind Ann, moored at the South Quay. Amos was busy repairing nets while Gabriel was supposed to be scrubbing the deck, under strict instructions from his father who that afternoon was attending a meeting of Fenton and Canford Parish Council.

Meanwhile, his son had assumed a comfortable prostrate position in the warm sunshine, disturbed only by occasional snippets of sea shanties from Amos. Gabriel had a new addition to his normal daydreams – the railway was coming to the beach at Fenton. In just over a fortnight, Fenton would have its second station and his father, Joshua Thomas, was in charge of the opening ceremony. The meeting of the parish council that afternoon was finalising the arrangements, with the main item on the agenda being, no doubt, the hospitality needed for the local dignitaries, of which the Duke of Suffolk was the most eminent.

In his daydream, Gabriel was imagining how much easier it would be to go to Hamsden. No more the two-mile walk into Fenton to catch the train at the main station. He would only have to saunter out of his front door and across Beach Road to the new one. He would have more time to explore further afield – maybe even to London. No more lugging a cart laden with fish up the town. He and his dad could load the early morning catch directly onto the train for the market in Hamsden the same day. It could be on the stalls, freshly caught, within not much more than an hour of landing. There had been talk for years about a Beach Station and now it was at last going to happen – for the benefit of fisherman and tourists alike. Several boarding houses had sprung up all along Beach Road in the last couple of years and some fishermen had had their own humble dwellings converted as well.

"Wake up, Master Gabriel – you ain't even started a-scrubbin' yet. Just wait till your father catches you asleepin'."

Gabriel lazily raised one eyelid.

"I wasn't asleep, old fellow – just resting my eyes from the sun. Them nets fixed yet?"

"Yes, Gabriel, and I'm off for me tea."

"Be quick then – the governor's due back at six to inspect our work. He'll expect to see you here, Amos."

"And I shall be, young sir. My work is done – just a bit of tidyin' to do. More 'an can be said for thee, Gabriel."

When Joshua was not with them, Amos assumed a fatherly role which, as far as Gabriel was concerned, did not extend to ordering him about or commenting on his work or the use of his time. Gabriel pulled a face at the old fisherman who climbed down onto the quay with surprising agility, belying his advancing years.

Gabriel 'rested' his eyes for another few minutes before he suddenly realised from the position of the sun that the afternoon was advancing quickly. He jumped up, threw back his shock of black hair and set to work with bucket and brush. The job, which normally took nearly two hours to do properly, was completed in less than one, with fish baskets and other gear carefully placed in positions where his cleaning had been less than perfect. By the time Amos returned from his 'tea' at the Mariner's Inn on the cliff top behind his three-roomed shack that he called home, Gabriel had his feet up on deck once again, awaiting the arrival of his father.

"All done, Master Gabriel?"

"Yes, Amos – take a look round, if you will."

"No need – the governor will do that awhile."

Amos climbed aboard with pipe in hand and headed for his seat at the stern.

"I'm for a smoke, Gabriel. I'll keep an eye out for tha' father from there."

Gabriel did not reply as he had already closed his eyes against the bright sun. With no sea shanties to disturb him and seagulls hovering over the north quay a quarter of a mile distant, he drifted off to real sleep and further dreaming – he hoped.

"Come on, shake a leg, son."

Gabriel stirred.

"Come on, time for bed, son."

Ed stirred. It had been another pleasant dream. He opened his eyes. His mother was standing over him. He was back in his lounge at 26 Acacia Avenue and he mumbled,

"Is my dad here yet?"

Jenny smiled.

"No, dear – daddy's not coming. He's just gone back to his house."

"But he has …."

The dream faded from his mind and Ed didn't finish the sentence. He had been about to say: '*But he has to check the deck and the nets*'. Whatever he had dreamt that last Saturday evening in October had gone, but an image of another time was building slowly somewhere inside him – a time where he felt happy, no one called him names and he was respected. Within five minutes he was in his bed and within another five he was fast asleep again.

It was never easy to fool Joshua Thomas – it took him less than a minute to discover Gabriel's sloppy work but, as usual, he seemed to hold back on his criticism. Whether it was the fact that the parish council meeting had gone well, or just that his relationship with Gabriel had always been like that of best friends – rather than the traditional one between father and son – his reaction was mild and forgiving.

"Not bad, Gabriel, lad. You've missed a plank or two, but never mind – it'll suffice. Now let's take a look at the nets."

Amos had done his work to his usual fine standard and, after the three of them had stowed everything away and made the Rosalind Ann ready for the morning, they made their way home.

Annie had a platter of best sausages, potatoes and bread waiting for Joshua and Gabriel. It was no surprise as they had smelt the aroma wafting down the cliff path.

"Ah – my favourite," exclaimed Gabriel as he went to sit down at the table while his father changed out of the Sunday best he always wore to council meetings.

"Get up and get yourself washed, Gabriel."

"Yes, Ma."

Joshua returned and put his arms round his amply proportioned wife.

"Now, Annie, love. Where would a man be without a wife like you?"

"Dead, more like, Joshua. Get thyself sat down – supper's ready and hot."

"I'll wait for my favourite son, Ma."

Annie smiled at her husband's adjective for his *only* son. She turned away to hide the tear that was about to fall as she thought of her daughter – the daughter that they'd taken away and put in ….

"Oh Ma, I *am* hungry," said Gabriel as he returned to the kitchen. "I could eat a pound of sausages. It's hard work scrubbin' the boat."

Annie presented her tear-free face and said,

"Good – they'll make you more handsome than you already are. The girls'll take a fancy to you if you're not careful."

Gabriel's dad laughed and said,

"Not too many then – maybe give him just four, Ma. My stomach is rumbling as well. I could smell them sausages from a mile away," he exaggerated with a broad grin.

"Me, too," echoed his son.

"*Me, too*," murmured another boy in a different century. "*Me, too*," Ed called out in his sleep. He woke with a start, the smell of cooking sausages fresh in his mind. But the smell wasn't only in his mind. It was real and all around him. It was dark and he called out loudly again,

"Ma! Ma! I'm hungry!"

Jenny came running upstairs from her kitchen and into his bedroom.

"Whatever is the matter, Ed?"

"Ma – er, I mean, Mum – I'm hungry. I haven't had my supper."

"Supper? You didn't have any tea, never mind supper. You were so tired, Ed, and less of the Ma, by the way – it makes me sound old. Do you want one of my hot dogs?"

"Mm, yes please, my tummy's rumbling."

12

Romantic Liaisons

The following weekend, Gary arrived after lunch to pick up Ed for the Saturday afternoon. He had a surprise for Jenny, after he had announced to that he was going to take Ed to Freeman Street for the reserve game with Borchester United, a neighbouring team from about thirty miles north of Hamsden. While Ed was still upstairs tidying up his bedroom before he went out with his dad, Gary gave Jenny an envelope containing the fortnightly maintenance for his son. Jenny took it and was about to place the envelope, unopened, in a kitchen drawer when she noticed it seemed to be slightly thicker than that she had become accustomed to.

"What's this, Gary? There seems to be more here this time."

"Open it then, Jenny," replied Gary with a smile.

Jenny slit open the brown envelope with a kitchen knife and took out its contents. She carefully counted the stack of crisp new five-pound notes. She took a deep breath and counted again.

"Gary – there's seventy pounds here. Why …?"

Gary was prepared with his explanation.

"Well, it's not long till Christmas and I thought you might need some extra for presents and so on."

"But, Gary, it's too much. I can't possibly …."

"Yes, you can, Jenny. Can't a father treat his own son? And besides, some of it is for you. Go and buy yourself something nice."

Jenny tried not to blush or show any emotion, but she failed, and another side of her personality took over – a side that she had kept under strict control for a long time. Her unusual warmth would not go unnoticed by her former husband.

"Oh, that is so nice of you, Gary. Thank you. I do need a new pair of shoes for work. They wear out so quickly when I'm on my feet all day."

"Good – no thanks necessary. It's just nice to see you happy, Jen …."

Gary just managed to stop himself from adding the word '*love*' to his sentence and Jenny nearly overstepped her mark with an even more intimate display of affection. But she, like Gary, just managed to restrain herself and her former spouse did not receive the kiss that a small part of her thought he deserved. The emotional tension was suddenly broken by Ed's cheery greeting for his dad.

"Hi, Dad. I'm ready to go."

As Jenny waved goodbye to Ed and Gary from her front garden gate, she thought about the extra money Gary had just given her. A worrying question nagged her. Had it come directly from his normal income or was he back to one of his old habits again? She had known Gary give her treats before when they had been married, courtesy of local bookmakers. Though unaware that she had quite correctly guessed the source of the extra money, she had, however, failed to realise that it had been entirely due to her son.

Despite Jenny's concerns, Gary had not had another bet since the previous Saturday. He was well known in the bookies in Hamsden and word could easily get back to her via the salon. He had something to prove to his ex-wife if she was to accept him as more than just her son's father – and that was proving to be a much stronger motivation than his own will power.

Nevertheless, in the car journey up the A132, Gary was interested in his son's opinion of that afternoon's game. Surely he wouldn't have a prediction for such a lowly encounter with little or nothing known in the media about either reserve team. He was surprised with Ed's response.

"Borchester Reserves will win 4–3, Dad."

Gary didn't notice the look in his son's eyes as he gave his prediction – he was too busy concentrating on the road ahead. If he had, he might have seen a touch of slyness there, suggesting to a casual observer that he hadn't quite been telling the truth. By this time in his short life, Ed knew he had power and, more importantly, he was beginning to know how to use it. Even though it was very unlikely that Ed was aware that his dad or, indeed, his mum had profited from his previous prediction, he was not about to aid and abet a habit that his father now had under firm control.

The game that afternoon was attended by less than a couple of hundred spectators and Hamsden Town Reserves lost a miserable game 4–2 with a November mist swirling around the ground from half-time. As they walked back to his car, Gary teased Ed on how close his match prediction had been.

"Not bad, son – at least you got the result right."

"Yep," replied Ed with a smile. "I just knew we'd win."

Of course, Ed had 'known' that the score would in reality be 4–2, but he had had his bit of fun and said nothing more.

The journey home was a little slow, Gary's vision being hampered by the fog that became denser as they approached Fenton-on-Sea. As on the previous Saturday, Jenny invited Gary in for a cup of tea, but this time together with the offer of some home-made apple pie and cream which he and Ed accepted gratefully. After two helpings of his favourite pie, Ed quickly did his disappearing act and, though it took a little longer this time, he was soon asleep on the sofa.

Gary and Jenny chatted for a good hour this time as they both seemed to relax more in each other's company, with Jenny even managing to laugh when they exchanged a few memories of the times when they had been together. She was warming to her ex-husband in a way that she never had before, when the attraction had been mainly physical and tempered with their individual and, alas, separate ambitions for the future. Now both of them seemed settled in what they wanted out of life, with their concern for Ed's upbringing being of paramount and shared importance. She began to see Gary in a new light that evening. Many of the features and traits that had attracted her to him in the first place were still in evidence, but now they were coupled with the maturity that his need to be a good father had given him.

Friday, June the 14th 1889 was due to be one of Fenton's biggest and most prestigious days ever. After nearly ten years of wrangling and much hard work, the Beach Railway Station was finally to be opened by the Duke of Suffolk at 3 p.m. With his father a mainstay on the parish council committee charged with the organisation of the ceremony, Gabriel had been invited to attend as Joshua's guest – a rare privilege for him, as many of the councillor's wives, including Joshua's own, had not been awarded such an honour.

Gabriel was excited that morning by the added prospect of trying to sneak a ride on the inaugural train that was scheduled to leave the new station at three-thirty for Hamsden via Fenton Town. A specially chartered Great Eastern Iron Duke class steam locomotive was to haul four carriages for the fourteen mile journey. Even with a ten minute stop at Fenton Town, the trip would take less than forty-five minutes at speeds up to a rumoured maximum of fifty miles per hour. Gabriel had only read about such speeds in books, given that the vastly inferior steam engine that plied between Fenton Town and Hamsden only ever got to about thirty. He had no idea how he would make the return journey as the special train was to be the last one out of Fenton that afternoon. In any event, it would be an adventure for the handsome sixteen-year-old fisherman and parish councillor's son.

Gabriel's black-haired and tanned good looks had not gone unnoticed by the local girls of Fenton and one, in particular, was to be present at the opening ceremony, her father holding no less a position than that of Mayor of Fenton. Naomi Eliott was as attractive as a young lady as Gabriel was as handsome as a young man and, whether engineered by both, one or neither of their respective fathers, the two sixteen-year-olds found themselves standing next to each other in the welcoming party for the Duke and his entourage.

"Good afternoon, Gabriel," said Naomi politely.

"It is, Naomi – and an exciting one, too. How is your father?"

"He is well and yours?"

"Well."

Their conversation was too formal and stilted for either of their likings and Naomi tried to lighten the mood.

"Oh look, Gabriel – Mrs Weatherspoon has lost her hat. She'll lose her wig if she's not careful and I hope her petticoats are securely fastened in this breeze."

Gabriel laughed at Naomi's mischievous remark. He began to relax as he glanced at Beach Road where the Duke of Suffolk was arriving in a black and brass three-wheeled 'horseless carriage', the like of which Gabriel had never seen before and his jaw dropped in wonder. His mouth remained open as, coughing and spluttering, the Daimler-Benz shuddered to a halt, causing the lead horse pulling the first of the ducal party's non-mechanical carriages to rear into the air.

"Close your mouth, Gabriel," chimed in Naomi. "You'll catch a fly."

Gabriel did as he was told and Naomi poked him playfully in the side. For the first time in his life, Gabriel found himself warming to a member of the opposite sex. In the distance, a steam whistle blew to announce the imminent arrival of the inaugural train from Fenton Town. By this time, the Duke of Suffolk and his entourage had been formally greeted by the mayor, members of the parish council and the railway and other local dignitaries. The silk tape had been drawn taut across the station entrance between two suitable posts. Mayor Richard Eliott checked his pocket watch and consulted with a couple of councillors. It was three o'clock and His Grace the Duke of Suffolk stepped forward and took the shiny brass scissors from Mr Joshua Thomas, head of the ceremony organising committee. Gabriel looked on proudly and playfully tapped his new friend on the arm.

"At least my father didn't drop them, Naomi!"

The Duke gave a brief and standard speech, thanking the town for giving him the honour of performing the opening ceremony and for their welcome and hospitality. Finally, with the equally standard, '*I now declare Fenton Beach Station open*', he stepped forward and cut the tape.

It wasn't going to be easy to accomplish their daring escapade. Firstly, neither of them had a pass for the inaugural trip out of the Beach Station and secondly, all seats on the brown wooden carriages were reserved. By this time, it was nearly twenty past the hour and with the Windsor Castle suitably fuelled and ready for its journey to Hamsden, Naomi explained her plan. The two youngsters had watched as the majority of dignitaries had boarded the carriages and only the mayoral party remained. They had already stationed themselves in the middle of the 'Up' platform and loitered a few feet from the remaining passengers.

"All we do, Gabriel, is follow my father and yours onto the train and hope that the guard assumes we're with them. As long as they don't look back, we can immediately duck down behind one of those wooden partitions near where we climb aboard, while they find their seats. We wait until the train has started and then try and find somewhere more comfortable. They can't throw us off at least until we get to Fenton Town."

"And if the guard wants to see our passes?" asked Gabriel.

"He won't – I'll use my persuasive powers."

"And if your father or mine looks back?"

"I'll use my persuasive powers on them."

Gabriel wasn't sure what 'persuasive powers' meant but Naomi seemed confident and, after all, what could anyone do? The worst that could happen, as Naomi had said, was that they would be asked to leave the train, and would anyone want the embarrassment that such an ejection might cause? Gabriel thought not.

Richard Eliott and Joshua Thomas moved forward to board, followed by two other councillors. Naomi nudged Gabriel forward. His father turned and nodded to his son as he assumed Gabriel was just moving forward to wish him bon voyage. Richard Eliott took Joshua's arm and guided him into the carriage. The two remaining bona-fide passengers followed. The mayor was last to board and, seeing his daughter directly behind him, he gave her a mock mayoral bow. Naomi looked nonchalant. The guard smiled as he interpreted Richard Eliott's gesture as an invitation for his daughter to follow him into the carriage. Immediately, Naomi's father turned, and ducked into the train. Just as quickly, his daughter linked arms with Gabriel, as if to confirm that it was a dual invitation, and the two young people boarded the train with the guard's blessing. He shut the door behind them and moved away to give his signal to the driver. Fortunately, both fathers had already found their seats at the opposite end of the carriage. Naomi tugged Gabriel's jacket sleeve and the two of them just managed to squeeze themselves into the space behind the wooden screen near the door. The carriage lurched forward. Scent of lavender permeated the enclosed space and began to set Gabriel's pulse racing. He'd never been this close to a girl before and Naomi smiled warmly as, in order to retain his balance against the motion of the train, Gabriel had to wrap his arms round her in a tight embrace; his legs entangled in a cascade of skirts and petticoats.

When the Windsor Castle reached Fenton Town, the majority of the local parish council members and other prominent residents of the seaside town alighted from the train. Naomi poked her flaxen-haired head around the screen and just managed to spot both her father and Gabriel's among those leaving the train. She immediately whispered to her new friend,

"They've gone – I had assumed that father was going all the way to Hamsden."

"Oh? Mine didn't tell me what was going to happen afterwards, but I suppose there would have to be some sort of gathering of the parish council in the church hall. Now I come to think of it, father did mention something about refreshments after the opening."

The two 'stowaways' crept out of their hiding place and found a pair of vacated seats nearby. The remaining guests in the carriage seemed to be either Hamsden businessmen or rail company officials, easily identifiable by their constant need to consult their pocket watches. A quick glance round confirmed to Naomi and Gabriel that they were not acquainted with any of the other passengers. They sat back in their upholstered wooden benches and began to relax. Naomi put her arm through Gabriel's and leant over to whisper in his ear,

"There you are, Gabriel – I told you it would work. We're off to Hamsden."

It was clear that Gabriel wasn't as enthusiastic for their dubious achievement as his beautiful new companion.

"We have a problem, though, dear Naomi."

"What problem is that, my dear Gabriel?"

"We have no way of getting back to Fenton today. There isn't a train coming back. I think this one returns to Norwich."

Naomi cuddled closer to her fellow adventurer and said audaciously,

"Well then – we'll just have to lodge the night somewhere."

"But I …," Gabriel protested.

"But?"

"But I'll be in trouble with my father. We are out on the Rosalind Ann at six sharp in the morning. I have to be back in my own bed tonight, Naomi. I want to go to my bed."

"*What – now?*"

"*I want to go to my bed now.*"

Ed stirred from his exciting dream as the adventure began to make him feel uneasy. His mother was standing over him. He heard two voices in his head.

"*You've worn him out, Gary.*"

"*Poor little fellow. He looks dead beat.*"

His power of speech returned.

"I want to go to bed now, Nao…, Mum."

"And so you shall, Ed, my little love. Would you like Daddy to carry you?"

"Mm, yes ple…."

Ed's eyes closed once more as Gary carefully lifted his son up. He was asleep before his father reached his bedroom. His dreams of another and more peaceful age were over for the time being.

Gary went home soon afterwards. On the drive back to Hamsden, he actually shed a tear or two, not only for the privilege of tucking his son up in bed, but also for Jenny's reaction to his more than usually intimate farewell. She had not recoiled when he had kissed her lightly on the cheek as they said goodbye on the doorstep of 26 Acacia Avenue.

As for Jenny, she spent most of the remainder of Saturday evening with her emotions in turmoil. What was happening to her? She had thoroughly enjoyed her extended chat with Gary – in fact, she had been positively warmed by it. Sharing common problems, and being open about what had led to their separation and divorce, had put her ex-husband in a whole new light, and she was warming to him once again for a whole new set of reasons. She had long ago promised herself that she would never allow displays of affection from another man to unsettle her; yet here it was happening with Gary, the one man she had come to despise. Perhaps, Gary had just behaved as a friend who shared common interests. After all, it was only a kiss on the cheek. On the other hand, a little part of her had *wanted* him to kiss her and that part could still be swayed by the thought of a new romance, even with an old and rejected partner. Jenny was caught between two emotions – tossed from wanting her ego to be boosted to a fear of being dreadfully hurt again. It wasn't to be long until she would find that she would have to make a decision as to which side she wanted her coin to fall.

The phone call came the Wednesday following and Jenny was inadequately prepared for it. It was just after Ed had gone to bed at eight o'clock and she had settled down to watch a favourite soap on television. She hoped she wouldn't be disturbed till it was finished, particularly by her son, who seemed to be having 'dreams' on a regular basis. She had taken to giving him his tea soon after he got in from school, suspecting eating too late to be the cause. None of the dreams, so far, had developed into outright nightmares, but Jenny had found herself starting to listen for the telltale noises from his bedroom. Ed, himself, didn't seem to be too upset at his 'dreams', invariably just mumbling and then shouting some unintelligible words in his sleep. He would then return to the land of the living; often to greet his concerned mother with a warm smile on his face.

On hearing Gary's voice after picking up the phone, she was more than a little awkward and nervous in her response to Gary's opening, 'Hello, Jenny'.

"Oh – er, hello, Gary. What's the matter?"

"Nothing, Jen. I just thought I'd give you a call to see how you were."

Jenny regained her composure.

"Oh, fine, Gary – just watching some television."

"Oh, I'm sorry. I didn't mean to disturb you."

"You're not, Gary."

The line went silent for a moment.

"Are you still there, Gary?"

"Yes. The reason I phoned, Jen, was to ask you a question and I hope you're not going to be offended by it."

Jenny's heart began to pound. He wasn't going to, was he?

"Fire away, Gary," said Jenny after a pause. "Just don't ask me for money."

"No, I won't. I just wondered if I could buy you dinner sometime – just the two of us like."

"Oh, er, I don't know, Gary. There's Ed to think of and I …."

"Could your mum babysit him for a few hours one evening?"

"When?"

"Saturday?"

"This Saturday?"

"Yes."

"I don't know. I'd have to ask. Aren't you taking Ed this Saturday?

"No – I did tell you last weekend that I had to work all day this Saturday, and Sunday is Mum's birthday."

"Oh, I forgot."

Jenny had almost but exhausted her prevarication. Gary interrupted her thoughts.

"It's only dinner, Jen, and I so much enjoyed our chat last Saturday."

"Me, too," said Jenny.

"Well – what do you say?

"Well, yes, provisionally. I'll have to check that Mum can come and look after Ed, though."

"Of course – let me know sometime tomorrow. I'll pick you up about seven if everything is O.K."

Jenny and Gary then exchanged a few less controversial pleasantries and after hanging up, Gary mumbled to himself: *'How hard can it be to say yes?'*

When Gary picked Jenny up on the Saturday, his refusal to tell her where he was planning to take her for dinner was causing her some concern. It was ten past seven and Gary had done his best to keep its location a surprise. They had just pulled onto the A132 and were heading for Hamsden in his MG. The night was clear and starlit. The moon illuminated the flat landscape.

"Look, Gary, if you don't tell me where we're going you can take me back home right now."

"Why do you want to know? It's supposed to be a surprise."

"Because, if you must know, I'd rather not go anywhere that people know me. You know how tongues wag in Hamsden."

"Just as well that we're not going to Hamsden, then," said Gary with a smile and gently patted his passenger's knee. As he did so, Jenny looked down at her modestly stylish combination of loose white blouse and black trousers covered with her new black coat.

"O.K., but it would also have been nice to know what kind of place it was so that I could have dressed accordingly. Are you sure I'm alright as I am? I'd have felt more comfortable in jeans and a jumper."

"Perfect, Jen."

Jenny glanced at her dinner date's smart blazer and open-necked pale blue shirt. '*No*', she thought, '*jeans and sloppy jumper would not have been right*'.

By Linham Junction, Gary swung the car left down a B road and headed south.

"Where *are* we going, Gary? There's nothing down this way," said Jenny.

"Just a short cut."

The road wound for several miles down high-hedged lanes and even in daylight it would have been difficult to see much of the neighbouring countryside. Jenny peered at her watch in the weak yellow light from the car's dashboard. It was twenty to eight.

"What time have you booked dinner for, Gary?"

"Eight – and we'll just make it."

The road appeared to widen and Jenny could see the headlights of cars as they merged onto another dual carriageway. It seemed familiar.

"We're on the London road, aren't we, Gary."

"Got it in one. Not far now."

Gary had avoided Hamsden and they were now five or six miles south of it with Colchester the next town about twenty miles ahead. Five minutes after joining the A12, Gary again turned left with Jenny just able to read the sign: '*Clayton Ferrers* 4'. After another ten minutes of even windier roads, they reached the small village the sign had indicated, where Gary slowed to a stop.

"Here we are," he said, and Jenny looked to her left at their brightly illuminated destination. "The Angel Inn is supposed to be good, Jen, and it's well out of the way, isn't it? I think we're safe here."

Jenny patted Gary's knee and said,

"Yes – and thank you. It looks just perfect."

The dinner date went as well as Gary could have wished. Jenny appeared more relaxed than her diffident reaction to his phone call suggested she would be and they continued to exchange memories of old times as she dug deeper into Gary's life over the previous five or six years. Though he didn't come right out and say it, it was clear to her that his womanising had stopped soon after she had upped and left him. Jenny absorbed most of his compliments with just a smile and without much of a visible response, but towards the end of the evening she found herself reciprocating with some of her own. Unlike the Gary of old, he appeared genuinely appreciative of Jenny's compliments and acceptance of his intentions to right the wrongs of the past. At last she seemed to be recognising the vast improvement in his moral fibre.

During dinner, both of them had listened intently to each other's conversation and had occasionally offered reassurance with semi-intimate pats on the hand. When Gary eventually drove them back to Fenton-on-Sea, Jenny found herself tapping his knee in the car as a further sign of that reassurance, and also that she now accepted him as rather more than only a friend and her son's father. When Gary finally drew the MG to a halt outside Jenny's house, there was a tense silence between them for a few seconds. That silence was suddenly broken when Jenny kissed him impulsively on the lips, immediately jumping out of the car before he had time to react. Romance had returned – in Gary's eyes at least. It had returned in Ann Compton's eyes as well, when she met her daughter in the hall before she went back home that night after babysitting her grandson.

"You look as if you've enjoyed yourself, Jenny."

"Yes, Mum – Gary was a perfect gentleman."

"And?"

"And what, Mum?"

"I don't know – you tell me, but I know one thing, love."

"What?"

"There's a look in your eyes that I haven't seen since you first started dating Gary when you were sixteen."

Jenny blushed, and then her mother knew what she had guessed was true. Her daughter was in love for the second time and with the same man. Feeling her face redden, Jenny attempted to steer her mother away from delving further and said,

"How was Ed?"

"Oh, O.K. – mostly."

"Mostly? Wasn't he good?"

"Oh yes, he was good – went to bed without any fuss at half past eight, like you said you wanted him to. He must have had some dreams later. I heard him talking in his sleep when I went to the toilet, that's all. Not nightmares, as when I went in he was sleeping fast and appeared to be smiling contentedly."

Jenny looked curious.

"What did he say?"

"I didn't hear much, but I think he must have a girlfriend at school."

"Why?"

"He called out a girl's name – it sounded like Naomi."

"Naomi? I don't think he knows anyone called Naomi, Mum."

"Might have been Nanny, I suppose," said Jenny's mum finally.

"He calls you Granny."

13

Out of School

In his short life so far, Ed had never been able to remember his dreams, other than some transitory impressions of another world – a world where he felt happy and contented; where he was respected for who he was and where he didn't have to suffer taunts about his size or anything else. In this respect, his mother never had problems in persuading him to go to bed each evening; indeed, he seemed to positively look forward to the daily occurrence. He even found himself daydreaming at school, desperately trying to capture fleeting visions of his other, temporary world. Sometimes, it annoyed him when he would be just on the verge of recalling what that world was like when, in a flash, the memory would be wiped from his subconscious. A casual question from his mother on the penultimate day of the autumn term somewhat jogged that memory. Ed was having his breakfast before school on Thursday, December the 16th, and his impending seventh birthday was the topic of conversation. Jenny had suddenly recalled her mother's words after the first of several 'dates' she had had with Gary back in mid-November.

"Are you going to invite any of your friends to your birthday party, Ed?"

"Don't know, Mum – just Minor, I suppose. No one else at school likes me really."

"Oh, that's a shame. You could have two or three you know, if you would like."

Then Jenny was bolder as she tried to probe deeper.

"What about Naomi?"

Though Jenny didn't spot any obvious facial signs that her son was acquainted with a person of that name, Ed himself had been reminded of

148

several transitory feelings of his other world. After a little hesitation, he replied,

"Naomi? Naomi who?"

"I don't know, dear, but your granny told me that she heard you say the name in your sleep one night when she babysat while I and Daddy went out for dinner."

"Did I? I don't remember, Mum. I don't know anyone called Naomi."

Ed paused as if he needed to convince his mother further.

"There is a Nadine Johnson in my class, but I don't know her, Mum."

"Oh, O.K., then – we'll just invite Minor next Wednesday for a birthday tea. It'll hardly be a party, though."

"I don't mind, Mum – honestly. He's my best friend."

Jenny nearly added, '*and your only friend, by the sound of it*'.

All morning at school that day, the illusory visions, prompted by his mum's question, began to haunt Ed; so much so that by lunchtime he was feeling anxious and almost as if he should be somewhere else. At one p.m. precisely, and with no one noticing him, Ed Compton-Jones walked out of Fenton Central Junior School and into the town.

With no particular destination or purpose in mind, Ed wandered coolly down the High Street, his mind still anxious as to what was going to happen. In no time at all, he had reached the promenade on the seafront. The day was crisp and cold but sunny. He continued down onto the beach and wandered to the water's edge. There was no wind and the sea was a flat calm. He was simultaneously apprehensive and excited. He looked out to sea, shading his eyes against the low sun. He closed his eyes and felt the feeble warmth of the sun's rays on his eyelids. It was peaceful and quiet, apart from the gentle lapping of the waves at his feet. If only he could go to that place in his dreams – if only. Reluctantly, he opened his eyes. A mass of yellow greeted them. He felt happy again. He wasn't dreaming this time, surely. This had to be real.

"Are you tired once more, my beloved Gabriel? We haven't come all this way just for you to fall asleep, have we? It's time we had lunch."

Gabriel adjusted his eyes after his attempt at forty winks. They were sitting with their backs resting against a tall mature oak tree in the middle of a sea of yellow

"Sorry, Naomi – it's such a beautiful day that I was taking in the air and the scent of the mustard seed."

"Well let's open the basket that mother has prepared. We have pork pie; there's a baked ham, fresh bread, a Bakewell pudding and some jellied pears. What more could we wish for, my Gabriel?"

"Well, something to slake my thirst after our walk to the Gospel Oak."

"It is a fine oak, too, Gabriel. Father says that Wesley preached under it over a hundred years since when he passed this way."

Naomi looked wistfully at Fenton, barely visible through the heat haze of the August midday sun.

"Just think, Gabriel – we might be sitting on the very spot that he stood all those years ago."

"Yes, Naomi, but I still have a thirst – my throat is as dry as a ...."

"Don't curse, Gabriel!!"

"I was not about to, my dear true one; for I could not think of anything as dry as my throat is this minute."

Naomi hastily passed a flagon of lemonade to her betrothed.

"Is there no ale?" asked Gabriel.

"No, mother says that you are not to escort me drunkenly home."

Gabriel's mind was reminded of another day five years previously when he and Naomi had first met. That day they had walked across fields from Linham Junction to Fenton having got off a train that had, by chance, stopped at the tiny station. That day when an adventure had nearly turned into a nightmare for Gabriel and only a five mile walk had saved his and Naomi's parents from the distressing possibility that their offspring had been lost. That day that had started their love for each other. That day when Gabriel had to promise Mayor Richard Eliott and his wife that he would never again lead their daughter into danger. That day when Gabriel had taken the blame entirely on himself for their childish escapade, for which Naomi had been truly grateful.

In a different time, over eighty years in the future, Ed Compton-Jones had been missed from afternoon registration at Fenton Central Junior School. It was ten past two and nobody had seen him for over an hour. Miss Sandbuck began questioning class 2Sb.

"Did anyone see Ed in the dining room?"

Several hands went up. Miss Sandbuck acknowledged Ed's best friend.

"Yes, Edward. Did you see him – he's usually with you?"

"No, Miss. I thought he'd gone home."

"Gone home? He never goes home at lunchtime. Why didn't you come and find me?"

"I don't know, Miss. I thought he was staying away from me because he didn't like me anymore."

As soon as she realised that no one had seen Ed since just before one o'clock, Miss Sandbuck quickly concluded her investigations with class 2Sb. She ran to the Head's office to notify her that he was missing.

Mrs Templeton got the office to phone home but without success as Ed's mum was not at home. It was immediately assumed that she was at work. Before they contacted the Hamsden number they had for Ed's mum, Mrs Templeton herself then tried his grandparents, only to discover they too were out. In her nine years as Head of Fenton Central Junior School, she had never 'lost' a child and it was in a state of mild panic and nervousness that she telephoned 'Curls and Twirls'. Jean Cooper answered.

"Hello, Curls and Twirls. Can I help you?"

"Oh, yes – is Mrs Compton-Jones there, please?"

"Hold the line, please. I'll just see if she's available. Who shall I say is calling?"

"It's the Head of her son's school and it's very urgent, please."

"Oh, I'm sorry; I'll get her at once."

By this time an anxious-looking secretary had joined her in her office as Valerie Templeton started pacing up and down, muttering to herself,

"Oh, come on, come on."

A voice came on the phone.

"Hello, Mrs Templeton – it's Mrs Compton-Jones here. What's Ed been up to?"

Mrs Templeton tried to keep the situation under control and her voice calm as she inquired whether Ed might possibly have gone to his grandparents for lunch, but when she received a negative reply in a panicky voice; she had no option but to inform Jenny that he was, alas, not now in school. Valerie Templeton had refused to use the word 'missing' and attempted to reassure Jenny that he couldn't have gone far, but the phone went dead after she heard a quavering voice say,

"I'm coming at once."

Jenny was on auto-pilot as she ran for her car and drove back to Fenton, where she arrived in record time and, with Sergeant Owen Hughes' familiar figure already in the Head's office when she arrived, her panic became almost impossible for her to bear. A cup of tea and the friendly police sergeant's reassuring Welsh accent did little to calm her mind which was fraught with the worst of possible nightmares.

"I've two men out already looking for him, Jenny, and they're scouring the town. He can't have gone far – he's bound to have been spotted with his school uniform on. Is there anywhere you can think of he might go?"

"Only home or his grandparent's house, but there wouldn't be anyone at either place. His grandad is at work at the station, as you know, Sergeant, and his granny is in Cambridge shopping for the day."

"We've already checked both your house and your parent's and there was no sign of him. I'll ring Fred now. There's nowhere else?"

"Only his dad, but he's in Hamsden at his car showroom. Surely Ed couldn't get there."

"You never know – you just never know these days."

When, after Owen Hughes had made both calls, and neither his dad nor his grandad had seen anything of Ed, Jenny finally broke down into floods of tears. Owen then told Jenny that both her father and Gary were already on their way to help in any way that they could, but she barely heard a word of what the burly policeman had said.

With their hunger and thirst satisfied, the young couple rested awhile in the warm afternoon sunshine. Betrothed and engaged to be married next year in the spring of 1895, they had both been brought up in God-fearing households and with Richard Eliott a lay Methodist preacher, any thoughts of intimacy from a different age were far from their minds. Thus, when Gabriel attempted to kiss his future wife, it prompted a stern reaction from Naomi as she backed away from his advance.

"Gabriel Thomas! What do you think you are doing? I'll have none of that behaviour from you."

Gabriel blushed deeply and brushed his hand through his long black hair.

"I apologise most sincerely, my dear one. It shall not happen again."

"It will, I hope, after the new lambs are born; but not until then, dearest one."

Gabriel smiled at Naomi's invitation for the future and said,

"I look forward to that day with honest heart and with all my being."

"Well said, Gabriel," said Naomi with an equally warm smile. "We must be patient, my love. God sees everything."

Naomi began to pack their picnic basket and soon she and Gabriel were walking back to Fenton via the path that they themselves had created that day through the sea of flowering mustard. They walked home hand in hand across further fields and down well-trodden country paths; contented young people without a care in the world and with their whole married future to look forward to with all the pleasures that would bring them.

The Eliotts lived in a cliff-top house adjacent to St Andrew's Church and it was far too big for the three of them – Naomi being Richard and Mary's only child. They had converted part of the *Fair View* to a boarding house for summer visitors and Naomi helped her mother with the cooking and cleaning. Their return from Gospel Oak had taken them into Fenton where the fields finished behind the beach just to the north of Fenton, and they then continued their walk along the beach until they reached the path that wound its way up the cliffs to Naomi's home. Gabriel had forgotten to mention to Ma that he had been invited to a late tea at *Fair View* that afternoon. Near the start of the cliff path they met a friend of Gabriel's mother, one Irene Brown, approaching from the direction of the Thomas' house. She called to Gabriel as she passed,

"Your mother was worried about you, Gabriel. She was expectin' you back an hour since for your tea."

"Your mother was worried about you, Ed. I don't think you should have been out of school today."

Ed found himself sitting on a wooden bench on the promenade and he looked up to see his dad standing over him.

"What have you been doing, son?"

"Er – nothing, Dad. I just went for a walk along the prom. What's the time?"

Gary sat down beside his son and put his arm round him.

"It's a quarter to four. Where *have* you been? Your mum is worried sick, Ed."

"Just walking."

Ed's replies had been automatic as he struggled to recall what he'd been doing. Where *had* he been? He could remember standing on the beach but what had happened to him next? Why did he say '*walking*'? His dad looked at his clothes.

"Walking – where? You look like you've been through a hedge backwards. What *have* you got on your clothes?"

Ed glanced down at his school trousers. They had flecks of yellow on them.

"I don't know, Dad," he replied and then he burst into tears.

"It's alright, son – you're not in trouble. We were just worried about you. Don't cry."

Ed's sobbing abated a little as his father continued to hug him. If only he could tell his dad that he wasn't crying because he thought he had been naughty but simply because he wanted to go back to wherever he'd just been. He had felt safe and warm there. Suddenly, he could hear his mum's voice calling in the distance.

"Oh, thank God – Gary's got him!"

14

A Walk in the Country

Amidst all the joy that replaced the nightmare in Ed's family that afternoon, it never really became clear where he had been for nearly three hours. Just glad to have him back safe and unharmed was enough to occupy their waking thoughts. For Mrs Templeton and the staff at Fenton Central Junior School, there *were* questions to ask but they were more concerned initially with the how rather than the why. She would organise a meeting for all staff the following lunchtime to discuss security arrangements in the school, including the obvious measure of shutting and bolting the main gate at certain times during the day. In addition, she would get estimates for securing other possible 'escape' routes as one old wag on the staff would put it. With extra patrols of staff at break and lunchtime, she thought that was as much as the school could do.

Jenny kept Ed off school the following day, the last one of the autumn term, and she also decided to take the morning off from work to stay with him. The local police and Sergeant Hughes, in particular, took no further involvement in the matter, preferring to leave it to Ed's family and school to offer Ed well-needed advice for his future behaviour. The following morning Jenny did eventually try to probe Ed in order to discover why he had walked out of school, and also where he been the previous afternoon, but without success. Reasons like: '*I was bored*' and '*he called me names*' seemed to be the mainstay of Ed's answers to the 'why'. '*Just walking on the beach*' was the *only* answer he had for the 'where'. When his mother pushed him on the matter, the tears would inevitably start again – tears that were probably born more out of frustration than as a mask for any mistruth. That frustration was due to the simple reason that even Ed himself had no idea where he had been.

Mixed with that frustration was the knowledge that he had lost most of an afternoon which, at the same time, was both a little scary and somewhat exciting.

By the end of that last Friday before Christmas, normality had more or less returned to Acacia Avenue and also to Fenton Central Junior School. Gary paid Jenny and Ed an unarranged visit at teatime at which Ed seemed to perk up for the first time since his walkabout. He ran straight to his dad when he arrived and threw his arms round him in an obvious display of affection. His mind had clearly moved on from the previous day.

"Dad, Dad – what are you buying me for my birthday and Christmas?"

Jenny stood in the hall and watched with relief on her face. He was back to normal! Even Gary's reply didn't seem to disturb his son's recovery.

"Maybe a compass, son, eh?"

"What's one of them?"

"Oh, just something that helps little boys not to get lost."

Ed looked slightly embarrassed and said,

"I don't want a compass, Dad."

"No, of course you don't. Dad was only joking. I've already got your birthday and Christmas present combined in one surprise. No Santa Claus this year, eh?"

"I hope I still get what I've asked for, though," replied Ed, and then after a slight sheepish pause, he continued, "I have been good most of the time, Dad, haven't I?"

"Of course you have, my love," interjected Jenny. "Of course you have."

A few minutes later with Ed now happily watching television, Jenny and Gary sat down for a chat in the kitchen over a cup of coffee. Important issues had to be discussed after the previous day's events. Gary had thought of a possible explanation for Ed's strange behaviour.

"You know what I think, Jen?"

"What?"

"I think it may be all our fault."

A quizzical look suddenly appeared on Jenny's face and with a frown, she said,

"How on earth can it be *our* fault? We do everything we can for that child – given the circumstances."

"Exactly," said Gary with some emphasis, "given the circumstances."

"What do you mean?"

"I mean it can't be easy for Ed having parents that don't live together, particularly with his sensitive nature as well."

"Oh," replied Jenny.

"Oh?"

"Oh, I hadn't thought of it like that, Gary, love. Are you thinking what I think you're thinking?"

"Which is?"

"That we should live together under one roof as a normal family."

"Maybe."

Gary reached across the table and held Jenny's hand. She did not pull it away.

"I miss you, Jen. Every time I go home after we go out, I miss you desperately until the next time I see you. You know what that means, don't you when someone can't bear to be apart from someone else?"

"Yes, I know, Gary, and …."

Jenny looked down and took Gary's other hand in hers.

"And it's the same for me."

Without either of them coercing the other, Gary and Jenny stood up as one and embraced passionately for the first time in more than six years.

With tear-stained face, Jenny pulled her head back from Gary's kiss and said,

"I love you, Gary."

"I love you, Jenny Wren."

"*I love you, Mummy and Daddy.*"

Neither of his parents knew how long their son had been standing in the kitchen and how much he had see and heard. At that moment in time, they didn't really care. When Ed extended his small arms and flung them round both Gary and Jenny in a loving embrace, they knew – they were a family again.

Ed got two surprises on his seventh birthday the following Wednesday. Firstly, Jenny told him that his daddy was going to live with them again and secondly, he received his first bicycle. He took the first surprise with a calmness that suggested to Jenny that he had heard more than she had thought the previous Friday. The realisation of what it would mean for his daily life had to compete with the immediacy of his second surprise, as he acknowledged the future change to his routine with nothing more than a, '*Ooh good, Mum*'. That more tangible surprise dominated his birthday afternoon. Though his feet could barely reach the pedals, he was soon out in Acacia Close, with stabilisers attached and his dad walking quickly behind him, holding the saddle and helping him steer a straight line. It took the arrival of Jenny's parents and Minor, together with a summons from his mum for tea, to get Ed to allow his dad to put the shiny green bicycle away in Jenny's shed for the day.

After his birthday tea, Ed and Minor repaired to the lounge to play, while Gary, Jenny and her parents remained in the kitchen chatting. Ann and Fred Compton were clearly overjoyed to hear that Gary was going to move in with their daughter some time early in the New Year. It brought tears to Jenny's mum's eyes, and with her old-fashioned values, there was only one question on her mind.

"So, when are you going to get remarried, then?"

"Oh, mother! One thing at a time. Gary and I have only just decided to try living as a family again or, indeed, for the first time. And anyway, it's for Ed's sake, not ours. You know we've sorted things out between ourselves."

"Yes," said Fred Compton, "we've seen it coming, Jenny, and we're really pleased for you both – and for Ed. I hope it's the right thing for you all – and Gary, son, welcome back."

Jenny's dad reached across the table and warmly shook his ex-son-in-law's hand. Jenny's mum kissed her daughter lightly on the cheek. Gary looked bewildered, but was clearly relieved that their news had been so well received. His mind was immediately drawn to the sad loss of his own father earlier that year. He felt a new chapter in his life had begun.

Christmas passed quietly for Jenny and Ed, with Gary joining them in the afternoon and evening, after lunch with his mother and some relations in Hamsden. Boxing Day brought unusually fine and mild weather and Ed's parents proposed some exercise outside with a country walk in the afternoon. Since Ed was keen to show his dad Peewit Hill Farm up close, Jenny rang Evelyn Morrison to see if it was alright for the three of them to pop over and use the farm tracks for a walk, ending up at the duck pond. Minor's mum was only too pleased to accommodate them, particularly to get Minor outside if they didn't mind him joining them.

Ed seemed more excited than normal with the news that his friend would come with them, Jenny realising, no doubt, that it was due in no small way to his desire to 'show off' his reunited family to his friend.

After Jenny had parked her Austin 1300 next to the farmhouse and Minor had joined the three of them, they set off down a farm track that Ed had not been down before. Minor assured everyone that it would eventually link with the one that led to the pond. Mrs Morrison had given Minor a large bag of bread and scraps for the ducks as well as a few carrots for Sunshine. The weather had remained fine with a clear blue sky overhead. With the trees bare of any leaves, it was easy to see further across the neighbouring fields in all directions. Five minutes into the walk, after cresting a small rise, they came upon a ploughed field which was empty except for one object in its very centre. Ed's dad was first to make comment.

"Mm – that's strange; just one tree for miles around and it's bang in the middle of a field. I bet it makes your dad's job hard when it comes to ploughing and seeding, eh, Minor?"

"Yep – he's always moaning about it and he wants to chop it down but he's not allowed to."

"Why, lad?" asked Gary. "It's on his land, isn't it?"

Minor looked at Ed's dad as though he should know better.

"It's the Gospel Oak and it's famous. Dad says it's been here over 200 years or more. You're not allowed to chop it down."

"What's famous about it?" queried Jenny.

"I dunno, but Dad says it is and he should know – he's always trying to find a way to get rid of it."

"Who says he can't get rid of it?" continued Gary.

"Dunno – just some important people, I think."

Ed had remained quiet while the other three had stopped to study the tree from a distance of about fifty yards. He had moved closer to his mother and had linked arms with her. Nobody seemed to notice this apparent request for comfort. Unbeknown to anyone, Ed's fleeting images of his other world had returned and he knew it had something to do with the tree – but what? His mother broke his thoughts.

"Are you alright, Ed – you look miles away?"

"Oh, what? Oh, yes, I'm fine. It's just boring looking at a tree, Mum – that's all," he lied.

"Yep, come on – which way do we go, Minor?" said Ed's dad.

"We just follow this track round to the other side of the big field and it joins up with the main track. It's not far."

Ed walked on the outside of the track keeping at least one of his parents between him and the Gospel Oak. It was too much effort to wrestle with forgotten memories on such a beautiful afternoon and even only a glimpse of the oak tree was promising to be a source of constant distraction to him.

"I swear that tree is following us," said Ed's dad after they had walked another hundred yards or so.

"Don't be daft, love," said Jenny. "How can it move? What a silly daddy."

"Yeah, silly Daddy," echoed Ed.

"It just seems to look the same as it did when we first saw it, Jen. I mean – we've walked at least half-way round the field and yet it still looks like it did to begin with. We should be seeing a different side of it by now."

Ed had again moved closer to his mother. Jenny pushed Gary playfully.

"It's your imagination, love. And stop it – you're frightening Ed."

"Sorry."

"Anyway, how could you prove it unless you had taken a photograph when we started, because I certainly can't remember what it looked like when we were back over there," said Jenny, pointing to a spot in the distance.

"I suppose you're right, my love. Just me being silly," said Gary finally.

They continued their walk and when Ed's dad next studied the orientation of the tree, his illusion had gone.

"I can see we're behind the tree now. It must have been a trick of the light."

Ahead they could see the main farm track joining from their right. The going got easier as they approached the junction and their path widened. The ground was hard after the dry autumn. Within a couple of minutes they were adjacent to Sunshine's paddock and the white pony ambled over for his treat. For some strange reason both the pony and Ed seemed nervous of each other and Sunshine would only take carrots from one of the other three.

"He doesn't like me," said Ed ruefully.

"Maybe it's your hair, Ed," said Minor with a grin.

"Oh don't say that, Minor," said Jenny. "You'll upset him."

"Stupid horse," said Ed as he threw his carrot through the fence and into the paddock.

"Pony," responded Minor. "He's a pony."

"Well, he's still stupid," and Ed walked to stand next to his dad who tried to offer some sympathy.

"Don't worry, son – horses can't distinguish colours, so don't listen to Minor."

Although he didn't show it, his dad's remark had made matters worse for Ed, because another thought had occurred to him. *'If it wasn't his hair that had made Sunshine nervous then what was it?'*

The duck pond was much more to Ed's liking – the ducks lacked any kind of sensitivity to the niceties of the source of their snacks and they gobbled up everything that was thrown into their pond without any inhibitions. The afternoon was getting colder and the sun suddenly disappeared behind some grey and threatening looking clouds. Jenny was anxious to get back to the farmhouse before the heavens opened up.

"Come on, it'll be dark soon. We'd better make tracks."

"Good pun, Jen," observed Gary.

By this time, Ed's mood had changed and he seemed happier as they followed the main track back to the farmhouse, only occasionally glancing to his right, but, to his relief, the Gospel Oak was hidden from view by the undulations of the fields.

Ed and his parents were invited in for tea, Mrs Morrison providing a vast spread of pies, both meat and mince, together with the obligatory leftover turkey sandwiches. With the boys treated to jelly and ice-cream to finish, everyone's hunger was satisfied after their physical exertions. Jenny allowed Gary to drive home with the farm track requiring tricky manoeuvres in daylight, let alone after dark and with rain steadily falling. Ed was already fast asleep by the time they reached the roundabout and it was an easy task for Jenny to persuade him to go to bed immediately they got back to Acacia Avenue. Gary stayed for an hour or so, leaving just before eight; his final remark being,

"I thoroughly enjoyed today, Jen. I felt like a real father at last."

"I did too – and you were, Gary. I think Ed enjoyed it as well. I just hope he hasn't eaten too much. He was certainly putting it away at the farm. I don't need nightmares tonight or I'll be calling you and you can come and pacify him."

"Do you want me to stay?"

Jenny looked uncomfortable. She knew that propriety wasn't really the issue as Gary was going to move in soon anyway, but somehow it still didn't seem right that Boxing Day evening. Maybe it was because she'd told Ed that it wouldn't be until January the 6th that stopped her from saying yes. She gave an apologetic look and replied,

"Better not, Gary. We'll start living together as a family when we agreed."

"O.K. – no problem. You're the boss."

After a quick hug and kiss on the doorstep, Gary left with a whispered,

"Love you, Jen."

Jenny returned her own testimony with a kiss blown from her hand.

15

Storm

By the time that Gary, Jenny and Ed had been living together as a family for a couple of months, there appeared to be a slight improvement in Ed's general demeanour in his day to day routine. He seemed happier at school and appeared to look forward to going each morning. He still hadn't had the growth spurt that his mother had expected and indeed, wanted, and whether the name-calling had stopped or not, he seemed to be riding above it, at least for the time being.

Ed *was* happier and there was no doubt that his new family situation was an important contributor to this. But it wasn't the only one. His dreams had continued on and off, but after a while they had become briefer and remained as just vague impressions. However, by the end of March, and despite their brevity and lack of clarity, he found himself still longing for them most nights. The new equanimity with all around him in his waking life was therefore also due to this warm anticipation of the dreams that allowed him to return to his other world, where he always felt respected and important, particularly after the occasional bad day.

As his dreams shortened, Ed found his mind returning to that day before Christmas, when he seemed to have had the power to enter his other world, simply by wishing that return to happen. More of that afternoon had come back to him, including the memory of standing on the beach and closing his eyes against the sun's rays while he concentrated his mind on his yearning. With the warm spring weather returning, a question kept coming back to him time after time. Could he enter his other world again without waiting for the randomness of dreams, just by wishing it to happen while he was awake?

As their rediscovered romance developed into something that both of them could cope with on a permanent basis, Gary and Jenny took less to evenings out together and more to evenings spent at home with Ed as a family. Indeed, when Gary suggested a romantic dinner at the Angel Inn in Clayton Ferrers, it was the first such occasion since New Year's Eve. Both Fred and Ann Compton would come and look after Ed for the evening on Saturday, April the 16th.

A chance remark by his granddad, soon after Jenny and Gary had left at seven, prompted Ed to try his experiment at waking time travel. He was watching television with his grandparents in the lounge.

"Now then, lad, when are you going to put on some weight? Isn't your mum feeding you enough?"

Ed managed a mumbled and somewhat embarrassed response but his grandad's words had hurt him. His recent equanimity with himself had suffered a setback and it was the catalyst he needed. He wanted to go there and then to his other more welcoming world – the world where people didn't make comments about his size or any other inadequacy and where he was liked just for what he was. That world where people didn't want to change him into something that they thought he should be. Ann Compton brought him out of his daydream, only to rub more salt into the wound, thus taking him further back to his unhappy self.

"Grandma will have to bring you some of her apple pies, Ed."

"I only like Mum's pies, Granny."

Ed's grandma looked a little put out by his innocent remark.

"Maybe, little Ed, but your grandma showed her how to make them in the first place when she was a girl so don't be so ungrateful. Granny is only trying to help you grow big and strong."

"I don't want to be big and strong."

"Of course you do, dear. Your mum may have to get something from the doctors for you."

That was enough for Ed.

"Oh, leave me alone! Why can't people leave me alone?"

Before either of his grandparents had a chance to say anything, Ed had stormed out of the room for his bedroom where he would lay sobbing for a few minutes. Ann Compton's mouth was still open when Ed shut his door with a bang. The noise jolted her and she made as if to go and comfort her grandson. Her husband smiled and said,

"Leave him be, love. It's all part of growing up. He'll put on weight when he's ready. I'll go and see him in a bit."

Ann Compton sat back in her chair with a touch of guilt for her remarks. That guilt would have been heightened all the more if she had been able to hear her grandson's misery upstairs, but the noise of the television drowned his crying.

When the tears abated, Ed sat up on his bed and almost immediately he knew what he wanted to do. He closed his eyes and, to no one in particular, he made his wish.

"Take me to the nice place."

The wedding was less than a month away and the early spring weather had kept Gabriel's mind off the prestigious event for the town. The fish were plentiful and the Rosalind Ann was out from dawn to dusk every day bar the Sabbath. His mind was thus fully occupied with the fishing, which did much to help calm his nerves for the big day. And a big day it was going to be. Mayor Richard Eliott was seeing to that. As well as his civic duties, he was the manager of the town's one and only financial institution – the East Shires bank. Such a prominent person insisted on nothing but the best for his only daughter and he was determined to make an impressive statement of his status in local society. The marriage between Naomi Ruth Eliott and Gabriel Wesley Thomas was to be a grand affair – or at least as grand as Fenton could stage. The service had been arranged to take place at St Andrew's Church with reception following in the adjoining hall, which doubled as part of the local elementary school. The event was all set for Saturday, April the 20th, in the year of our Lord, 1895.

Three weeks before Gabriel and Naomi's big day – on Saturday, March the 29th – an event was to take place that would provide an unfortunate distraction for their pre-marriage nerves. The storm began in earnest soon after the Rosalind Ann had reached a position a mile and a half offshore and adjacent to the mouth of the Wentham. The sail from their mooring at the South Quay had been brisk in the strengthening wind, but it was only a foretaste of what was to come. It was about as far as the forty-foot fishing smack ventured. With fifty-foot mast, thirteen-foot beam and nearly thirty-foot main boom, she could cope well with all but extreme wind and swell, having survived two wicked storms of gale force strength in her time. Signs were that the storm on the Saturday before Gabriel's big day was going to be more than just a little wicked.

Amos was at the tiller watching the end of the boom which began to veer heavily to port; Joshua had suddenly ceased laying the tackle and nets and Gabriel was minding the sails. They had to shout above the noise of the wind whistling through the ropes and canvas. The rain hammered loudly on the deck.

"Haul the mainsail, Master Gabriel! Tighten them ropes," cried old Amos from the stern.

"Keep her turnin', old man," called back Gabriel from the foot of the mast. Joshua added his own commands from the smack's side.

"Fast as you can both, my boys!"

The Rosalind Ann turned into the teeth of the gale; no chance of return to their mooring at the South Quay.

"Make for the Wentham!" shouted Gabriel. "We'll have to take shelter till she passes, old man."

Gabriel was suddenly blinded by spray and rain; lightning flashed behind closed eyelids. He saw the vision. He knew what he had to do. He let go of the rope and bounded as he best he could across the bucking deck to the stern. The boat was almost out of control, the boom swaying drunkenly from port to starboard and back. Amos was clinging on for dear life; hands frozen in a vice-like grip to the tiller. Joshua shouted from the pile of nets, now all aboard,

"Watch the main boom; she's loose!"

The Rosalind Ann pitched and rolled in the ten foot swell; the deck awash. Gabriel dived forward and pulled Amos from his hold, a fraction of a second before the boom snapped in two, its end smashing uncontrollably into the unattended tiller and missing the old man's skull by an inch. The four hundred pounds of solid oak finally broke free from its straps and hit the deck with a crash of splitting deck timbers. Gabriel and Amos rolled and sloshed around the deck in a blind embrace, born out of both relief and fear. Joshua scrambled over the wreckage of the boom.

"Whoa, my boys! God preserve you!"

"Get thee off me, young Gabriel!" shouted Amos, clearly no worse for his narrow escape. "Get me to the tiller!"

But there was no tiller to return to for old Amos that day; its long wooden arm broken at deck level. With no control over her rudder and a mainsail flapping violently in the gale, the Rosalind Ann was out of control and at the mercy of Mother Nature.

"Brace yourselves, my boys!" shouted Joshua as they clung to any solid and fixed part of the fishing smack they could find.

"Stay low and pray, lads!" cried Joshua above the storm. "Stay down!"

The fishing smack's sides creaked and groaned in objection to their treatment by the violent waves which now crashed over the deck with regular monotony. Gabriel tried to look skywards and prayed – prayed that they wouldn't go down. How far was the shore? Where had they been when the storm had suddenly prevented any visibility through its raging torrent? With their brains addled by the battering rain and wind, all sense of time was lost. The Rosalind Ann bobbed like a cork; sometimes up over the waves and sometimes through them, but the old smack remained upright with dignity. Suddenly, Joshua shouted from his position a few feet away from his two fellow fishermen,

"She's easin', boys!"

Gabriel shouted back,

"Stay down; brace yourselves!"

Suddenly, above the storm's rage, they heard the reassuring telltale sound of timbers scraping shingle.

"She's beaching!" cried Joshua; his voice now louder above the lull provided by their closeness to land. The Rosalind Ann gave one last lurch and rolled onto her side, like an exhausted beached whale with no more will to live or fight the sea. Gabriel and Amos were once again catapulted into an embrace against the deck's sides with Joshua joining them a few feet away. The groaning from the fishing smack's timbers stopped, to be replaced immediately by that emanating from Gabriel.

"Ah! My ankle! It's …!"

"Lie still," said his father. "Where's old Amos?"

"Here, Master Joshua. I'm not bound for me maker just yet, thanks to thy son, Gabriel. Nothin' that a drop of whisky won't cure. Me head's still on me shoulders. Thou saved me life, Gabriel."

The Rosalind shifted position a little as further waves from the advancing tide stretched out their foaming claws and tried to pull her back into a watery grave. Despite his exhaustion and damaged ankle, Gabriel spotted the danger.

"Out – we must get ashore!"

Joshua scrambled to Amos first and helped the old man to his feet from his dazed position on the deck. Stumbling over the debris, he managed to pull and steer Amos across the now horizontal side of the boat.

"Quick, Father – she's shifting!" shouted Gabriel. "I can't get out. My leg …!"

Amos collapsed in an undignified heap on the shingle while Joshua returned to half drag, half carry his son to safety, seconds before the Rosalind Ann lurched upright and slid once more into the water.

By the time the three fishermen had – by one means or another and aided or unaided – reached the safety of the shingle higher up the beach, the Rosalind Ann had begun to break up as she was battered by the tide against the land. Joshua sat with his head in his hands and cried out loud,

"She is no more – oh, God, she's gone!"

Gabriel sat beside his father and tried to comfort him, his ankle still throbbing with pain.

"We're safe, father. Thank the Lord, we're safe."

Sitting beside them, Amos was silent, all speech drained from him by an ordeal that would have defeated much younger and fitter men. Gabriel looked at the old man, huddled beside him, and then he remembered his vision. The old man's narrow escape had happened exactly as he had seen it. He shuddered inside, but he would say nothing, least of all to Amos or his father. His thoughts were disturbed as Joshua put his arm round his son and smiled grimly, his livelihood ruined.

"I'm sorry, son. We should not have taken to sea today. I'm sorry."

"I'm sorry, Ed. We were only trying to think of you. I'm sorry. What are you doing?"

"Hm? At least we're all ...."

"Why are you sitting on your bed with your eyes closed, Ed? Are you feeling sick, love?"

"What? Oh hi, Granny – no just thinking."

"Thinking? What about and who's we?"

Ed was quick with his reply.

"Oh, Mummy, Daddy and me – we're all a family again, Granny."

"Of course you are, dear. Now are you going to come down and have some supper before you go to bed?"

"Yes – what's the time?"

"It's half past eight, love. You've been up here on your own for over an hour. Granny's got some nice chocolate downstairs."

"When will Mummy and Daddy be home?"

"Oh, not till after you've gone to bed."

"Hope they don't get caught in the storm, Granny."

"What storm, dear? It's not raining. I've just been outside to the dustbin and it's dry. You silly thing – I bet you *were* asleep and dreaming, eh?"

"Yes, Granny."

"Now come down stairs and have some chocolate, but I don't think you ought to have so much now – you'll be having more dreams. Thunder and lightning, indeed!"

When, an hour later, the wind got up and Fenton-on-Sea was subjected to torrential rain, accompanied by thunder and lightning, even Ann Compton began to wonder if her grandson was gifted with the ability to tell the future. Her husband soon told her not to be so silly, as Ed had probably only been dreaming – and, in his opinion, dreams never came true anyway.

16
Guilty Feelings

In the days immediately following the storm and loss of the Rosalind Ann, Joshua Thomas received many offers of help from the local fishing community, including a substantial interest-free loan from Gabriel's future father-in-law in order for him to buy another boat and necessary fishing tackle. Though Joshua was very much against the idea, which he regarded as charity, Ma managed to make him see sense and, in the end, he gratefully accepted Richard Eliott's kind offer, agreeing to pay off the loan over a period of not more than two years. By the end of May, Joshua would be the proud owner of a brand new fishing smack, which would be quickly named the Richard Goodman, in honour of the Thomas' benefactor.

In the meantime, thoughts naturally turned to the young couple's wedding. Fortunately, Gabriel's ankle had only been badly bruised, and though without a boat, he, Joshua and Amos busied themselves as best they could, refurbishing and mending their remaining nets and tackle. Occasionally, they would be hired for the day by other fishermen to help work their boats; not only out of sympathy for their plight and loss, but also out of necessity as the fish were unusually plentiful that spring.

However, Gabriel had other thoughts that were unique to him. He couldn't get the 'vision' out of his mind. He knew that he had saved Amos' life that day and he also knew that it hadn't been the only 'vision' he had ever had. Always a dreamer in his youth, Gabriel used to imagine what it would be like to live in the future. After the latest vision, his mind had taken him back to one occasion when he had been twelve or thirteen – he couldn't remember which – when he had dreamt he was a little boy again. Though he had never been able to remember much else since, of one thing he was sure – he had been in a different age, with unusual sights and sounds pervading his dream. However, despite this, he still had two other less clear impressions of that time. He was sure that he had still been in Fenton and also, for some reason or other, he just didn't feel comfortable or happy in his environment of the future.

Together with her nervousness and pride for her son's wedding, one other thing constantly nagged Ma as the big day approached. She hadn't thought about it for some time, but the near tragic events of March the 29th had brought her other tragedy back to her, and at supper exactly a week before Gabriel's big day she let her emotions out.

"Oh, Joshua, how I wish Mary could see our Gabriel wed."

Joshua looked up from his bowl of broth.

"Now, now, Ma – don't you fret, lass. You know she can't be there. She can never leave the asylum."

"I know, but she should be there. She loved Gabriel so much until he was six and then …."

"Then she was taken by the insanity, Ma," said Joshua quietly. Gabriel said nothing – he had loved his elder sister deeply. Though she was eight years older than him, she had always seemed to understand him better than his parents when he had been five or six. He missed her as much as his mother did. He never understood what happened to her that day after a nightmare the night before seemed to send her mind into a raging oblivion.

"Father's right, Ma – she'll never be the Mary we all knew. T'would do no good for her and surely not for you or us."

"I know you're both right but when you're a mother it ain't the same, Gabriel. I brought her into this world and I …."

Ma broke down into tears – something she hadn't done for over a year. Joshua stood up and came round the kitchen table to comfort her but it would take a few hours that evening before she would come out of her melancholic state.

Soon, Gabriel himself would also get melancholic, but his state would not be caused by sad thoughts of family secrets of the past. His was to be self-induced, though due in no short way to a father concerned that his son should sleep well on the eve of his wedding day. By eleven on Friday, April the 19th, Gabriel had consumed, willingly or unwillingly, four substantial measures of whisky, a drink to which he was very much unaccustomed. Joshua was just about to refill his son's glass when Annie came into the kitchen from the parlour and interrupted her son's excess.

"Joshua! What *are* you doing? The lad has had enough. Do you want him to forget his lines tomorrow, for goodness sake?

"Sorry Annie, love – it's to help him sleep tonight."

"He his asleep. Just look at his eyes."

"I am tired, Ma," said Gabriel sheepishly. "I'm away to my bed now."

Gabriel didn't quite make it to his bed unaided, needing his father's support and firm pushing when he climbed the stairs. His sleep that night was not to be totally undisturbed, and the visions that he would 'see' in the small hours would leave him feeling very uneasy and with feelings of guilt on the morning of his wedding. He would remember only part of his dream and that only temporarily, too. He would not be able to understand where the guilty feelings had come from or why. In the end, he would put it down, at least partially, to Joshua's 'medicine' which had induced more than just sleep.

Ann Compton didn't mention her contretemps with Ed to her daughter when she and Gary had returned from their dinner out on the night of April the 16th, and despite her fears, Ed slept soundly that night and without any further dreams. It would be several more weeks before Ed would visit his second world; his last one hadn't given him as pleasant a feeling as usual on such trips and thus there was no motivation on his behalf to try to think his way there again for the time being, at least not during his waking hours. He had been left with the distinct impression that he had been involved in danger and near human tragedy.

April passed into May, and whether or not it was the normalcy of the new family situation, but Gary and Ed spent less time together at the weekend on pursuits by themselves. Generally, things were done together as a family, be it shopping or playing on the beach. Occasionally, if Jenny worked all day on a Saturday and Gary didn't, then he and Ed would take themselves off to the beach and for a spot of fishing off the pier; both of them seeming reluctant to return to the Wentham. Such a Saturday occurred on June the 4th when Gary didn't have to be at the showroom till the afternoon. With the weather warm and sunny when they woke, Jenny made a suggestion to Gary after the three of them had sat down for breakfast.

"Why don't you and Ed go out this morning? He's been looking a bit peaky this week. And with my dad at work all day, I don't think Mum is going to do anything with him by herself this afternoon when you take him to her house. She's had a bad cold all week."

Gary's face seemed to light up at the idea.

"O.K. – that sounds good. I was only going to clean the car, but that can wait till tomorrow. What do you say, young man?"

"Ooh yes, Dad. We haven't been out together for ages. Can we go to the pier?"

"Exactly what I had in mind, Ed."

"For fishing?" asked Ed. "Can we take the proper rods?"

"I don't see why not, son. One day, when you're a bit older, we'll have to hire a dinghy and I'll take you out past the end of the pier where the best mackerel are, eh?"

Something stirred in Ed's memory. He felt a coldness within. He didn't like boats – that was it, but why? At first, he tried to sound normal.

"Maybe, Dad, but I can't swim."

"No problem – we both have to wear life jackets."

"Oh, but I don't like boats anyway."

Neither Gary nor Jenny said anything more. Both knew their son's anxiety when presented with situations he hadn't met before. As far as they were concerned, his lack of stature was still causing him to be timid with anything new or demanding of physical participation. If asked, it would never occur to Ed to admit that his physical self-consciousness was a reason for his apparent reluctance. However, he wouldn't be able to give the real reason, simply because he just didn't know.

The beach was busy when Ed and his dad arrived, one or two of Ed's classmates being among its early occupants. As they made their way along the promenade to the pier, Ed heard the usual derogatory comments, despite being accompanied by his dad. Nobody said anything directly to him; nobody pointed a finger in his direction and backs were permanently to the promenade. They were more subtle than that. Said just loud enough for Ed to hear, but not too loud so that his dad would realise they were meant for his son, the comments ranged from,

'*There goes Shorty*', to '*he's got his dad with him for protection today*'.

Ed kept his head down until well out of sight of Jack Collison and his mates, praying that the end of the pier was going to be free of any more of his classmates. It was – being occupied only by a family of four; a mother, father and two children, one aged about four and the other just toddling on very unsteady legs. Ed relaxed immediately, fortunately not realising that the elder child – a boy – was three years younger than him, despite being more or less the same size.

"Here we are, son. This is where we fished last time," said Ed's dad, choosing a spot against the railings on the side of the pier opposite to the family. Mum seemed to be having difficulty in controlling the little girl while Dad was having equal problems attempting to help her elder brother use a crab line. In the end, as Ed and his dad got their lines ready, the toddler was taken by mother to a bench about ten yards away with the promise of a story and a bottle. With bottle in hand and teat in mouth, the little angel settled down beside her mother.

The fishing was slow and unproductive in terms of landing a living catch. Ed, however, did manage to hook some old twisted fishing line and what looked like the head and shoulders of a hollow plastic doll. He and his dad had better luck when they changed bait to tempt any unsuspecting crabs, catching three small 'throwaways' and two reasonably sized ones to be kept in a plastic bucket and taken home. After more than an hour, Ed began to get tired and a little bored. Gary, spotting, his son's waning enthusiasm pulled the lines up for the last time and turned to Ed and said,

"Time to go, I think, young man. Ice-cream?"

"Yes please, Dad."

By this time, the four-year-old boy had also got bored with fishing for crabs and wandered over to inspect Ed's catch.

"Wow – they're big ones," he exclaimed.

"And I caught them both," said Ed proudly.

The boy's sister toddled over to see what her brother was looking at. For no apparent reason, Ed turned and looked over the railings. Suddenly, in his mind, he 'saw' what was going to happen. The little girl was falling, tumbling head over heels and down into the water right below him. She hit the water with a splash and disappeared. He turned back. The toddler was still looking at the crabs in the bucket. He had to do something. He had to tell his dad or the little girl's parents. '*Oh please keep her away from the railings*!' He stood transfixed. He said and did nothing. The little girl bent over to get a closer look at the contents of the plastic bucket. Ed watched as she overbalanced and pitched forward at such an angle that her head went through the narrowest of gaps in the railings. Her mother screamed,

"No, Emily! No!"

Ed's dad made a grab for her, but he was too late – the rest of her tiny body had followed, like that of a cat that had tested the gap for size. Her body slipped through and she disappeared from view. The woman screamed again,

"Oh no! She's gone over. Do something, Pete – for God's sake do something!"

She was running round in a mad panic now. Pete, her husband seemed helpless. Gary reacted quickest and vaulted the railings without looking below, shouting as he did so,

"Dial 999! Get an ambulance."

But there was no need as a passer-by had already run to the pier office fifty yards away, screaming,

"Ambulance! Ambulance! Little girl in the water!"

Ed's mind was in turmoil. The little girl's father had at last come to life and he broke an emergency lifebelt free from its box, hurling it blindly over the side of the pier. The little boy clung to his mother, both of them crying uncontrollably, unable to move or look. Ed prayed, and after a few more seconds, eventually built up enough courage to look over the railings with Pete. He breathed his first sigh of relief. Pete shouted,

"He's got her! He's got her!"

Ed looked down to see his dad holding little Emily above the surface. Ignoring the lifebelt nearby, he swam frantically for the shore with his one free arm, hardly appearing to be encumbered by his small apparently lifeless bundle. Within a few grotesque strokes, Gary reached shallow water and was able to stand and run the last few yards to the beach where he quickly laid the little girl on her back and started mouth-to-mouth resuscitation, learnt from his fire service training. A St John's Ambulance man was sprinting down the beach from the promenade. Ed joined the little girl's parents and son for the dash back along the pier. An ambulance siren could suddenly be heard in the distance.

Gary stayed calm when the little girl didn't respond. The St John's Ambulance man shouted,

"Here, let me do that!"

Gary didn't move, ignoring the man's command. He bent down again, using the lightest pressure on the little girl's chest.

"Get out of the way, sir!"

As the man tugged roughly at Gary's shoulders, the miracle happened and Emily's eyelids fluttered. She coughed and a spurt of water bubbled from her mouth. Her eyes opened and she cried. Gary fell back onto the sand, exhausted. The St John's man took over, cradling the little girl in his arms and covering her shivering body with a blanket. Seconds later, her family arrived, and all three were immediately reduced to tears when little Emily held out her arms and cried,

"Mummy! Mummy!"

Ed went to sit beside his dad. He showed no emotion at the little girl's miraculous survival. He looked back at the end of the pier and thought: '*What if she had* ...?" Then he cried like the others.

Gabriel was quiet at breakfast on his wedding day.

"Too much whisky last night, my son," observed Ma.

"Nerves, I'll be bound," said Joshua.

"Neither," retorted Gabriel. "Just some bad dreams."

"What about, Gabriel?" asked Ma.

"Don't know, Ma – but it had to do with drowning."

"I expect you've still haven't got over the storm on the Rosalind Ann."

"No, it wasn't that, Ma. It was different. I weren't on a boat. It was like I was ...."

"What, son?" asked his dad, grinning. "Floatin' in the sea, eh? That's the whisky, my boy."

"No, father, not floating. It was like I was on a big rock looking down at the sea. I think someone was in the water and I ...."

"And, son?"

"And I couldn't save them and they drowned."

"Who was it, Gabriel?" asked Ma.

"Don't know, Ma – I can't remember. I'm not even sure now that there was someone there. It comes and goes, like I'm seeing it through a thick sea fog in November."

"Well let's hope it's gone by noon. You've a big day ahead today, my lad."

Later, when all the inevitable repercussions of the near tragedy had died down, Ed would realise just how much he had done wrong that day. Unlike before, with Mrs Morrison's horse, he began to feel real guilt at what he had failed to do. He could have stopped the little girl from falling. He wouldn't have needed to make a fuss or tell anyone that she was about to fall through an impossibly small gap in the railings. He could have stood in front of her until her parents came and picked her up or spotted the potential danger. There were lots of things he could have done, but he didn't. If it hadn't have been for his dad's instant and experienced reaction she would probably have died. What would he have done then? How would he have lived with himself? Though he wasn't facing questions like these, he still felt guilty. Should he tell someone – unburden himself of his 'problem'? In the end, he would continue to say nothing. He made himself one promise, however. If anything like it ever happened again, he would do something, no matter how dangerous it might be for him. After all, his dad had risked his own life to spare him a lifetime of irreconcilable guilt.

17

Good Times, Bad Times

They had gone to the Gospel Oak again. Three months wed and gloriously happy in each other's company, Naomi and Gabriel had walked the tracks and lanes to reach their favourite spot, surrounded again by the heady yellow crop of mustard seed. It was one of those hot and dry days at the end of July with summer at its height and the promise of bounteous harvests to come. With picnic basket at their side, the young husband and wife lay daydreaming, with backs resting against the mighty tree.

"You look tired, my love," observed Naomi, suddenly. "You were dreaming again last night, I think."

"Was I, dearest? I don't recall. Did I talk?"

"A little."

"And what did I say?"

"It was just stuff and nonsense. It sounded like you were having an argument with someone."

"Who?"

"I think you called him Jack."

"Jack? I know no one called Jack – except for ...."

"Who?"

"I was going to say old Jack Wilson who worked on the Rosalind Ann when I was little, but he died two years since. Did I say anything else?"

"Not that made sense – you just groaned and tossed and turned in your sleep."

"Oh."

Naomi placed a kiss on her husband's cheek and said,

"You have been dreaming a lot just recently. Is there anything troubling you? Aren't you happy?"

"No, I'm fine, Naomi. Just a bit concerned for the future."

"Why? What is there to worry about?"

"Oh, I just wish we could be in our new house instead of living with your mother and father at *Fair View*."

"And so we shall, my love – just as soon as it is completed. We are lucky that father has lent us some money to buy it. We will be in before the end of the year. Just be patient."

"What if you are suddenly with child?"

"Well, I'm not, and besides, if I were, we would still be moved before the child was born, so stop fretting and pass me the basket. Looking at the sun, it is time for lunch."

Gabriel kissed and embraced his wife.

"You make everything so easy, Naomi. Oh what joy the day I married you!"

The young couple kissed passionately until Naomi pulled away and exclaimed with a smile,

"Gabriel – calm your ardour! We must eat."

The sun was warm on their brows and despite moving slowly round the tree's girth to follow the shade, soporific sleep followed their ample meal, aided by a half-bottle of homemade wine. They lay side by side with nothing but a few bees and butterflies for company.

Jack Collison had annoyed Ed all morning on the last day of the summer term with his incessant teasing and baiting. It was if young Jack had decided that, because it would be another six weeks before he might see Ed again, he wanted to vent his jealousy for one last time – for that was what it was – jealousy, pure and simple. He was jealous of Ed's cleverness and powerful memory and it was born out of his own insecurity and fear of anything unusual or different from the norm. Ed's size and brain stood him apart from the norm in Jack Collison's eyes, and that continually annoyed him. Matters came to a head near the end of lunchtime with Ed and Minor in their special corner of the playground. Jack approached the friends with evil on his mind.

"Hey, titch, my five-year-old sister is bigger than you."

"Ignore him," whispered Minor.

"Are your mum and dad so poor they can't afford to feed you, eh?"

Jack Collison had placed himself between Ed and Minor and with hands on hip, he glared down into Ed's eyes. Ed turned to walk away.

"Oi, I'm talking to you, Shorty!"

"Go away, Jack, and leave him alone," said Minor.

"Why? Are you gonna' make me? Anyway, I can't understand why you like this freak."

That was the word that was going to get Ed into some painful trouble that day. He turned back, and with all his might, threw a fist at the unsuspecting bully's face. It hit him full on the nose, drawing blood. Jack Collison was more shocked than hurt and was stunned motionless for a few seconds. Then he made a grab for his assailant, and Ed, equally stunned by his own actions, was easily and quickly hurled to the ground, where the two boys wrestled and writhed until Jack inevitably gained the upper hand and sat squarely astride Ed's chest. With arms pinned down at his sides, Ed looked into the face of his nemesis, expecting the worst. Suddenly, the weight was lifted from his chest.

"Now then, Jack Collison – what *are* you doing?"

Ed narrowed his eyes against the sun. There stood Mr Osgerby with Jack held in his firm grip.

"Get up, young Ed. What is this all about?"

Neither boy said anything, but looking at Jack's nose, Mr Osgerby quickly drew his own initial conclusion and Ed was soon marched away to Mrs Templeton's office.

A small crowd of curious children had gathered by now, which was quickly dispersed by a couple of other staff, Miss Sandbuck included, who eventually took Jack to the sick room for repairs to his nose. No real damage was discovered, other than inevitably to Jack's pride.

With both boys interviewed separately by Mrs Templeton, she soon decided that it was six of one and half a dozen of the other and both miscreants would be held back for thirty minutes when school finished. She would talk to both mums when they came to collect their children, stressing particularly to Ed's that he must not react in future in such a violent way if provoked.

Naomi woke first, a particularly annoying fly attempting to investigate her left ear. She glanced at her husband, sleeping peacefully with arms folded across his chest, covered only by a loose cotton shirt, open almost to his stomach. She did not disturb him and turned to her small volume of poems by her beloved Shelley. Opening the leather-bound book randomly, she smiled as she read the first line,

> *'Thou who didst waken from his summer dreams*
> *The blue Mediterranean, where he lay ...,'*

Though she knew that they weren't in some far off exotic land, or lying next to the Mare Nostrum, the words gave her pleasure as she glanced once more at Gabriel.

Gabriel was indeed having *'summer dreams'* – dreams of another time, but not of another place and not as pleasant as the name would suggest.

It was the first day of the summer holidays when the weather in Fenton-on-Sea had been warm and sunny. It was Thursday, August the 4th and Minor Morrison had invited Ed to play at Peewit Hill Farm. After his fracas at school, Ed had done his best to avoid the places Jack Collison and his cronies were likely to frequent – the beach, the pier and even the town, though there he had, at least, the protection of the shops. He felt comfortable with Minor out on the farm. Surely there would be little chance that Jack would manage to find his way there.

Mrs Morrison had packed the boys a picnic lunch and plenty of orange squash for the increasingly hot day. As they got ready in the cool of the farmhouse kitchen, she had suggestions for them as to how they might spend the morning.

"Why don't you take Ed up Peewit Hill and show him the views of Fenton from there? On a clear day like today, you should be able to make out the beach. You can come back by the Gospel Oak field and the pond. I don't want any food bringing back, so give what you can't eat to the ducks."

"I'm not going up there if Dad's got the cows in the top field, Mum."

"He hasn't, dear. He and Ben moved them first thing this morning to the other side of the hill by the Wentham. You don't need to go anywhere near there."

"O.K, Mum. It's an easy walk for Ed, too."

Minor's slightly patronising remark did not go unnoticed by Ed. Fancy his best friend even making reference to his supposed lack of physical stamina. He would show him that a gentle climb was not a problem for him.

They set off at ten-thirty with Minor shouldering a small rucksack and Ed in charge of a specially shortened walking stick to clear, as Minor put it, '*any jungle from their path*'. With their floppy white hats as usual, they felt and looked like Victorian explorers on safari.

"I'll lead the way," said Minor as they entered the narrow track that led into the top field. Ed followed dutifully behind, swishing his stick at non-existent obstacles.

"Ouch – you hit me, Ed," exclaimed Minor, as one particularly careless swat landed a glancing blow on his thigh.

"Whoops! Sorry, Minor – just clearing the path."

"You do it from the front, stupid!"

"I said I'm sorry."

"When we get into the field you can lead and I'll tell you where to go."

"O.K."

They soon reached the low stile into the top field and scrambled over it, with a final jump needed onto the dry, cropped meadow.

"Right, you take over, Ed. Head for that gate over there," said Minor pointing into the distance. Ed squinted and could just make out their target. He soon found there was no need to keep accurate aim as the correct path had been clearly etched into the ground by countless herds of cows over the years on their way down from Peewit Hill.

They soon reached the gate, although Ed still managed to strike his friend again with his stick even though Minor had tried to stay well behind the lead explorer. This time there was no stile to aid their passage and both boys had to resort to climbing the gate. Minor completed the exercise with some ease, but Ed found difficulty. When he had reached a position with each leg astride the top of the gate, he moaned,

"I can't get over. I'm stuck!"

"Hold on – I'll pull you."

Minor reached up and dragged his friend roughly over the gate. They landed in a heap on the hard, dry ground. Minor let out a yelp of pain as Ed fell on top of him.

"Aargh! My arm!"

The boys rolled apart and Minor sat up clutching his left elbow, rubbing his numbed funny bone in almost mock anguish.

"Ooh, it hurts!"

"It's only your funny bone," said Ed with a grin, as he could tell Minor's pain would be only temporary.

"You should have it. It's not funny."

Ed helped his friend to his feet and with Minor still rubbing frantically, they started their gentle climb. After a few yards, when his elbow had eventually returned to normal, Minor switched positions and led the way. With nothing to think about but concentrating on keeping up with his friend, Ed's mind suddenly started to wander. Blurred images flitted in and out of his mind. He knew what was happening and in a flash the 'vision' came to him. He could see the future again. He stopped dead in his tracks. Minor carried on for several more paces until he turned round to find Ed motionless and with a grim look on his face.

"Come on, Ed – keep up."

Ed didn't move.

"What's the matter?"

Silence. Minor walked back to his friend.

"You look bad, Ed."

Minor attempted to pull Ed forward. He came out of his trance.

"What? Oh, I just felt a bit hot. I'm alright."

The vision had gone, but not the memory. They walked on together side by side.

The climb was not as difficult as Ed thought it was going to be and they reached the top of the hill in another twenty minutes. The views were magnificent. Ed's feeling of dread seemed to have disappeared. He made a 360 degree turn.

"Wow!" exclaimed Ed. "You can see the pier and the river is so close."

"Yes – the top field goes right down to it."

"There are lots of people fishing," observed Ed wistfully.

"We have our own path over there that goes to the best place. Dad showed me once. Everyone can use it to get to the Gospel Oak, if they like."

Ed looked to where Minor was pointing to the right of the river meadow. Three small figures were approaching in the distance. He shuddered. He was brought back to reality by Minor.

"I'm hungry and thirsty. Let's have our picnic."

For the next half an hour, Ed and Minor lay on Peewit Hill and consumed their lunch. Soon, however, Ed was anxious to be moving and Minor led them down the hill, heading for the river path. At the foot of the hill the path split left and right.

"If you go down there you'd get to the river. That's the path we saw from the top. We go right," said Minor.

Ed said nothing – his sense of foreboding had returned and after a few strides, he suddenly turned to his friend and shouted,

"Run! Find somewhere to hide!"

Minor looked at Ed in astonishment.

"Why?"

But Ed had already started running towards the Gospel Oak field and he clearly wasn't going to give any explanations. Minor had no choice but to follow and then he realised what had sent his friend into a blind panic. Ahead, and to the right, the same three figures Ed had seen from the hill were running across the meadow in their direction. He recognised one – Jack Collison. Three against two was no match and he doubled his speed to catch his friend up at the entrance to the field.

Their luck was in. The field had not been harvested and the wheat stood straight and strong. Ed had already disappeared from view amongst its tall stalks. Minor dived in and, keeping low, he scrambled to where his friend was – a good fifty yards into the field. They crouched down. Voices could be heard close by.

"That was Shorty. I'm gonna' get him."

"They went in there. He's got Minor with him."

"Come on. This way."

Ed and Minor crouched lower, Ed's breathing became pronounced and jerky. Minor tried to say something, but Ed put a hand over his mouth. They waited. They heard the swish and crackle of the corn being broken. It got louder. Jack and his mates were close. Suddenly, Ed and Minor heard Greg Patterson's voice.

"Oh, leave them, Jack. I'm thirsty and your dad said we shouldn't go too far from the river. Let's go back and see if he's got any fish yet."

The violent swishing stopped; Jack and the third member of the revenge committee seemed to be agreeing. A gentler swishing began as the voices got fainter. Ed held Minor down as he was about to put his head above the corn. They waited. Soon, nothing could be heard other than the buzzing of bees and the gentlest of murmurs from the tops of the corn swaying in the gentle breeze. Ed raised his head. At first, he was disorientated, but after spotting the Gospel Oak, he turned to look in the opposite direction. His nemesis, accompanied by Greg Patterson and a third unknown boy, was back on the path and heading back to the river. They had gone, and Ed immediately sat down in relief, squashing any remaining food in Minor's rucksack.

"Here, watch it! I hadn't had my apple pie yet," exclaimed Minor.

"Sorry – I was just checking they had gone."

"They were after you, Ed – for Jack's bloody nose."

"I suppose so."

"Are you alright? How did you know they were there? I didn't see them when you scarpered."

Ed didn't say anything at first. They had started to make their way back to the path at the edge of the field. When Minor asked again, Ed said quietly,

"I just knew."

Minor shrugged his shoulders and said,

"Well, it's just as well you did."

Ed was quiet for most of the way until they reached the duck pond, only occasionally making comments or replying to Minor's questions. The preoccupation with his own thoughts was a direct result of something else he had seen in his vision. Something that, if it came to pass, would force him to honour that promise he'd made to himself a few days after the near tragedy with little Emily on the pier.

Minor eventually put his friend's moodiness down to tiredness after his exertions on the trek up Peewit Hill and the mad dash for cover when he had spotted Jack and his cronies. By half past one, he had given up trying to cheer him up. Even he was feeling a little bored after feeding the ducks and geese.

"What time's your mum coming to pick you up?" he asked pointedly.

"When she gets back from work – I think she said about three."

"We'd better get back then."

"O.K.," said Ed, and, for almost the first time in over an hour, a hint of a smile appeared on his face He was going home – to his mum and safety."

On the walk back up the main farm track, he thought about what had happened that day. He hadn't enjoyed himself, and nowhere seemed to be safe for him anymore. It had been a bad day. He longed for his other world where he always felt happy and he got the impression that the people liked him. How could he get there again, even for just a short while? He was apprehensive of trying to think his way there again. He'd managed to explain his absence from school the last time by pleading ignorance, but would he be able to do it again? Another question kept trying to raise itself in his mind, but he quickly shunned the temptation it was attempting to offer him. He just daren't let it become a concrete idea or proposal. By the time he and Minor had reached the farm, the thought had evaporated from his mind, at least for the time being.

Later that evening as he lay in bed, Ed began to realise that, at the tender age of seven and three quarters, he had reached a crossroads in his life. He knew he was going to make a decision about his future, and he also 'knew' that it involved some momentous event of which he was to be an integral part.

Finally, with her husband snoring and muttering in his sleep, Naomi woke her husband up. He was not best pleased.

"Huh? What ...?"

"Wake up, my beloved," said Naomi soothingly. "You have been talking again."

Gabriel opened his eyes. His brow was running with perspiration.

"Huh?"

"I said, you were saying things, Gabriel."

Gabriel wiped his brow on the sleeve of his shirt.

"Oh, I must have been dreaming. What did I say?"

"Nothing this time that made any sense. You just kept groaning as if the dream was a bad one."

"I don't know, my love, what it was about – but wherever I was, it was not a nice place. I'm glad I'm back here with you, dearest."

Gabriel stood up and shook himself down. He glanced north at the big hill by the Wentham. He quickly looked away as he felt a cold sensation grip his body.

"Come on, I ready to go home, Naomi."

Gabriel might have added something like, '*I don't want to go back to the other place,*' but he didn't.

18

Fulfilling the Promise

Ed would not see either Jack or Greg for the next four weeks of the summer holidays. He began to relax a little, Minor having found out that Jack had gone on holiday to North Wales with Greg and his parents. The unknown boy that they'd seen near the Gospel Oak turned out to be Greg's cousin from Aberystwyth, with whom they were all staying for most of the remainder of the school holidays.

Mrs Morrison often brought Minor over to Fenton during the rest of August, the two boys playing happily on the beach and the pier's amusements, whenever Jenny or Gary could take them. Ed had some news for his friend when he came over on the last Saturday afternoon of the month, just ten days before they were due back for their third year at Fenton Central Junior School. Ed's mum was driving them through town to the beach.

"The fair is coming to town."

"When?" asked Minor.

"Next weekend," said Jenny, as Minor looked interested.

"Are you going, Ed?"

"Yes – Dad's taking me Friday teatime after work. Do you wanna' come? Mum, can Minor come?"

"I should think so. You'll have to ask your mum when she picks you up later, Minor. Ed can ask his dad when he gets in from work, but I'm sure it'll be alright. What do you say, Minor?"

"Oh, yes please, Mrs Compton-Jones. I've never been to a fair before. Dad says that they used to hold one in the Gospel Oak field in olden times."

"Did they?" said Jenny. Ed said nothing; it was the first time for a few days he'd been reminded of the day earlier in the month when he and Minor had cowered from Jack Collison and Greg Patterson in the very same field.

"Where will it be held?" queried Minor. Jenny glanced in her rear-view mirror as she turned at the bottom of Steep Hill and onto the promenade.

"Ed? Are you asleep? Tell Minor where it's going to be."

"Oh – on the playing fields where we played cricket once. Do you remember? It's at the back of Acacia Avenue and we can walk there from our house."

The new house was ready by the end of October, at least a month earlier than expected and Gabriel and Naomi moved in with much help from Joshua, Amos and Naomi's father. The day was wet and tiring with the young couple not really able to relax until well after dark. Finally they were on their own in their new parlour, devoid of furniture apart from two old upright chairs, a large mahogany table and a dresser, kindly donated by Naomi's mother. Two oil lamps burned brightly in the centre of the table.

"Well, dearest – here we are under our own roof at last. Let us hope that you are able to sleep better. You have had some disturbed nights just lately," said Naomi.

"Just worried by the move and our new freedom, I think. With God's grace I shall find rest here."

"I pray you do, else it's separate beds for us both."

Gabriel smiled. He longed for dream-free nights again. Some of his visions had been confusing and filled with impending doom and danger. Every time he woke after a bad night, he could only recall tiny portions of his dream and within minutes, they had evaporated, leaving him with a sense of frustration and worry. Gabriel sighed and said,

"I shall take a glass or two tonight – to make me sleep, dear."

"I do wish you wouldn't. It makes you sweat and I swear the dreams are worse when you do."

Naomi paused.

"I sometimes think that you are …."

Gabriel knew what his wife was about to say. She had hinted at it once before after being disturbed by her husband's moaning. He finished her thoughts.

"That I am going mad?"

Naomi said nothing, her silence saying it all.

"That I'm going to be like Mary?"

"Oh, no! Heaven forbid, Gabriel. I didn't mean that."

"My father says that his great uncle was put in the asylum when he was forty. It may be in the family."

"But you are only three and twenty, my love," said Naomi. "You are far too full of life and level-headed. You told me that your Mary was always in books and spouting strange sayings to you."

Gabriel clasped his hands behind his head and relaxed.

"You are right, no doubt, my love. These humours – for that is all they are – will pass, I'm sure. A lot has happened this year; enough for any man to bear – from losing the Rosalind Ann, and facing my maker, to wedding the most beautiful woman in the world. How can I go mad with you as my companion, confidante and lover?"

"Oh, how I love you, my Gabriel. Promise you'll never leave me."

"Oh, that you should think I would!" replied Gabriel. "I love you with all of my mind, body and spirit."

In the end, Gabriel didn't reach for the whisky bottle that night and he slept peacefully in Naomi's arms, undisturbed till morning. His bad dreams would leave him for a while, all thoughts of madness vanishing temporarily, at least, like the autumn mist burnt off by the morning sun.

The fair rolled into town on Thursday, September the 1st and Jenny and Ed strolled up to the recreation ground just before teatime to look at what would be on offer over the weekend. Despite the sprawling new housing development, of which Acacia Avenue was a part, the town planners had preserved the sizeable play facility for the increasing local population. Covering an area of more than two football pitches, it had long been one of the few such areas in Fenton-on-Sea and seemed to get more use in the winter months when the beach attractions were closed.

Ed and his mum made the short walk via a second alley from Acacia Avenue, which extended into a purpose-built tarmac path that followed the northern boundary of the housing estate. Even before they had reached the rec, Ed was getting excited.

"Wow! It looks much bigger than last year, Mum."

"Yes, dear, I think it's a different one. They've got rides and dodgems."

"Can I go on them? I'm nearly eight."

"Probably – it depends what Daddy says. He may have to come on them with you. You know I'm at work in Hamsden until six tomorrow."

The path turned right and suddenly they were there. The fair was still only about half complete; some of the fairground workers were clearly having difficulty fixing the various tented amusements to the rock hard ground. It looked like the static rides were already operational as some of the staff were trying them out and making last minute safety checks.

"There's a train, Mum!" said Ed, excitedly.

"It looks fast and it goes very high, dear. I don't think you'll be allowed on that on your own. It's like a small roller coaster."

Ed ran forward to the *Runaway Train* and, ignoring the odd warning from the staff to keep back, he read the sign:

'UNDER-EIGHTS TO BE ACCOMPANIED
BY AN ADULT'

He was quickly back with his mum, apparently deaf to some obvious catcalls about his possible age.

"You have to be eight to ride on your own, Mum."

Jenny smiled to herself. Even if the sign had said that under-fives had to be accompanied, her son might still have struggled to satisfy the requirement for an unaccompanied ride.

"Oh well – your dad will have to go on with you. There looks like two seats in each carriage, but you must fasten the safety harness and hold onto Daddy – do you understand, Ed?"

"Yes, Mum."

Ed looked back at the *Runaway Train*. It had started another test run, and as it swept round the oval track – that in one place reached nearly twenty feet above the ground – Ed suddenly had his 'vision'. He stared at the train as it reached its highest point, and as it swung violently right on its clockwise circuit, he gasped in wonder. It just didn't seem possible that it could stay fixed to the rails at such a speed. Then he froze and glanced anxiously to his left, concentrating his eyes on a spot on the bone dry, concrete-hard ground. Then his mind went blank. His mum was still talking to him.

"Come on, Ed – what are you looking at?"

"Oh, nothing, Mum."

"Are you still sure you want to go on it?"

"Maybe, Mum."

An irritated member of the fairground staff then approached and asked them to move further back while the ride was being tested. They moved away to inspect what other amusements were already completed. The dodgems didn't seem to interest Ed so much as the roller coaster train ride had; it was clearly the main attraction of the fair this year. After a brief tour of the other amusements, Ed and Jenny made their way home where, later that day – no matter how hard he tried – Ed could not recall what he had 'seen'.

The following day, Gary picked Ed up from his grandma's at four, having managed to leave the showroom early. They were back at Acacia Avenue just before Mrs Morrison brought Minor at half past. Ed was clearly excited when Minor and his mum walked in. Gary was upstairs attempting to get washed and changed with his son impatient to be off to the fair.

"We are going on the train, Minor. I've been waiting all day."

"Me, too."

"Dad! Minor's here!"

Ed's dad called down from the bathroom,

"I won't be a minute or two."

With Ed urging him to be quick and jumping up and down with excitement, Gary was down in seconds and after saying goodbye to Evelyn Morrison, they headed for the rec, with both boys' pockets bulging with coins of the lowest denomination. The late afternoon was cooler than of late and a gentle sea breeze had sprung up, fluttering the flags and pennants that they could just see above the roof tops. They had hardly entered the alley when Ed's mood suddenly seemed to change. He didn't actually stop walking but it was soon clear to his dad that something was wrong.

"Are you alright, son?"

Minor looked at his friend as Gary asked his question. Ed's face was pale and his eyes seemed to have glazed over. His dad came over and knelt down in front of him.

"What's up, Ed? Do you feel sick?"

"No, I ...."

"What?"

Ed shook his head and lifted his eyes to look at his dad who was still kneeling holding both his son's arms.

"No, I'm O.K. I've just bit a bit if a headache. It's going now."

"I'm not surprised, son. You've been like a whirling dervish for the last twenty minutes. You've just got too excited, that's all."

"What's a whirring dish, Mr Compton-Jones?" asked Minor.

"A whirling dervish, Minor, is someone who goes wild and runs around madly – a bit like Ed here a few minutes ago."

"Oh," said Minor, and he tried to pronounce the name again – failing miserably.

"You were closer the first time, Minor!" said Gary. "Come on, let's get going. It looks busy already, boys."

Minor saw him first, walking with his mother and younger sister. He didn't say anything to Ed, who was tugging his dad's arm to get him to go to a shooting gallery with rifles. Behind the targets were several enormous teddy bears and assorted cuddly toys of all shapes and sizes. One huge white teddy had obviously caught Ed's eye and had temporarily become a bigger priority than a ride on the *Runaway Train*. After a pause,

Minor followed his friend and as he did so, he saw Jack Collison out of the corner of his eye take his sister onto a small carousel of ponies, located roughly half-way between the shooting gallery and the *Runaway Train*.

By the time Minor had caught up with Ed and his dad, Gary was already taking his first shot. Ed was urging him on.

"The big white one, Dad. I want the white teddy."

Minor looked up at the enormous cuddly toy. It was at least as big as Ed himself. Gary fired his gun. He missed the targets. He reloaded and missed again. Whether it was just to prevent tears or it was his pride that kept him going, in the end it cost Ed's dad nearly three pounds to acquire the teddy bear, which was probably more than it would have cost to buy. Ed was ecstatic as he held the white bear in his arms. From the front, hardly anything could be seen of Ed himself, apart from a pair of arms and his trainers. Gary had to carry the teddy bear under his arm so that his son could see where he was walking. They headed for the train and then Ed saw him too. He quickly changed position and walked behind his dad, trying to use him as a shield. Jack with his sister and mother had left the carousel and were already negotiating a ride on the *Runaway Train* ahead. Ed tried to dawdle.

"Come on, son. Don't you want to go on the train?"

Ed peered from behind his dad. Jack Collison, though still seven, had convinced the attendant he was old enough to ride by himself. He was already in a carriage with no one sitting beside him. The rest of the carriages were full and the train began to move. Ed relaxed and he joined his dad and Minor in the short queue for the next trip. Jack Collison's mother and sister had moved a few yards away to watch him. The train was already heading to its highest point and was quickly lost to sight as it followed the sharp right-hand curve on its first circuit. It would reach its maximum speed and g-force on its second and third laps.

Ed's headache returned and with it his vision. He knew what he had to do. There was no point telling anyone. It had to be him and him alone. Without saying a word, he grabbed the white teddy bear from under his dad's arm. Gary had had it loosely gripped and he was caught off guard as it came away in Ed's hands with ease. Without stopping to offer any explanation, he ran to the spot he'd seen in his vision. He turned to face the ride, holding the teddy bear in front of him. Gary shouted,

"Ed! Come back! What are you doing?"

A few spectators glanced Ed's way and smiled.

"He's letting his furry friend get the best view," one said, with a smile. Gary started to walk towards his son.

Fifteen feet above them, Jack Collison was being clever. He had waited until his carriage was out of sight of his mum and had released his harness. He was now deliberately sliding from side to side in the carriage, trying to follow the motion of the train.

From below, the train suddenly came back into view. It was close to its maximum speed as it shot past the entry platform and started to rise to the sharp right-hand curve. Gary was still a few yards away as someone beside him screamed,

"The door's open!"

Gary glanced upwards and in a split second, the horror unfolded. Whether or not the door to Jack's carriage had been properly secured, wolud never be known, as his body was suddenly flung violently out of the carriage and into the air right on the apex of the curve. Gary watched in excruciatingly slow motion as Jack was hurled skywards, somersaulting once before heading inevitably for the hard ground. But he didn't hit the ground – his screams were suddenly muffled by white fur and thick cotton padding. Gary screamed,

"Ed! Oh, God, Ed!"

Ed was flung backwards as Jack Collison landed full on the teddy bear. Gary heard the sickening thud as his son's head hit the rock hard ground. Jack Collison bounced once and rolled off the white teddy bear. His scream became a low moan. Ed lay motionless under his teddy. Mrs Collison ran forward in horror, only just realising that it had been her son that had performed the aerial acrobatics. Spectators shouted,

"Get an ambulance! Fetch a doctor."

Gary was the first to his son. He knelt down. It looked bad. Ed had still not moved; blood seeped from behind his head which lay at an odd angle. A lady grabbed Minor and hauled him away. Mrs Collison was held by a member of staff as she clutched her daughter to her side. Jack was still moaning and holding his stomach. A doctor emerged running through the gathering crowd.

"Let me through!"

He went straight to Ed. Jack was on his side and attempting to get up. The doctor had ignored him. He could read the signs – the boy was not seriously hurt. The little black-haired one was, though. He felt for a pulse in his neck.

Within seconds, two St John's Ambulance men arrived and, seeing the doctor, went straight to Jack Collison, who was now clutching his arm and still trying to stand.

"Lay still, son. It looks like you've broken your arm."

"Oh, thank God," said Mrs Collison as the doctor ushered Gary back. Minor ran forward and hugged his legs.

"What's happened to Ed," he said quietly. Gary did not reply; his mind was in turmoil. It was like déjà vu, but this time it was bad – very bad. It looked like his son could be ....

An age seemed to pass before sirens could be heard as an ambulance entered the rec from the South Road entrance. The doctor, now aided by a nurse, rose to his feet.

"Clear a path – let the paramedics through, please!"

The little magpie was not quite dead, but he would not be flying for some time. With a fractured skull and broken neck, it was a miracle that Ed Compton-Jones was still breathing when the paramedics got him to Hamsden County Hospital, his injuries being too severe for treatment at the local cottage one in Fenton-on-Sea. He was rushed immediately to intensive care where the doctors and nurses fought to save his young life. He did not regain consciousness that night as Jenny and Gary took it in turns to sit by his beside, and by Saturday morning, it was clear that he was not going to come out of his coma for some time. The consultants were starting to warn his parents of possible brain damage that was often inevitable in cases like his. Only time would tell what kind of damage had been caused to his head and whether his cervical fracture would mean that some part of his body would be permanently paralysed.

Jack Collison sustained a double fracture to his left arm, two cracked ribs and severely injured pride. He stayed in hospital for four days. His accident, caused entirely by bravado and stupidity, and not by any mechanical failure that the investigators could find, would be the beginning of a change in his character. The investigation would eventually conclude that he had opened the carriage door, either by accident or design. Though all Jack Collison's family were to be eternally grateful that Ed and his teddy bear had broken their son's fall, his fortuitous position was accepted as a complete and utter stroke of good fortune that, combined with a cruel twist of fate, caused an innocent boy to sustain such life-threatening or life-changing injuries. Other bystanders remembered the suggestion made by one of their number that the little boy had taken the teddy bear to get a better view, and thus, nothing much more was said on the matter. Like most members of the immediate families, their thoughts and prayers were with little Ed. When he eventually sat down and remembered what his son had done, Gary would begin to think otherwise, but that would not occur for some time, his mind being completely wrapped up in his son's fight for survival for the foreseeable future. Minor, however, was fairly convinced that his best friend's actions had indeed been deliberate, but he would say nothing; fear of ridicule permanently preserving his silence.

Ed had fulfilled his promise to himself, but only with such immense cost to himself. If there was enough left of his mind to be able to realise it, he would feel released from his earlier guilt and, medical science allowing, he would one day start a new conscience-free and happy life.

19

A Family Curse

December the 22nd, 1895 proved to be a day of double celebration for Gabriel Thomas. Not only was it his twenty-fourth birthday, but his wife of eight months also had important news for him when he got in from a day's fishing on the Richard Goodman. He'd hardly had time to remove his damp and pungent clothes and wash before she pushed him into the parlour. They sat either side of the big mahogany table. Expecting a surprise birthday gift, he smiled in excited anticipation as Naomi started to speak.

"You are four and twenty today, my love."

Gabriel nodded knowingly and began to reply.

"I know, Naomi, and what have ...?"

"Shh, Gabriel. I have something to tell you."

"What, beloved?"

"I am with child."

Gabriel's jaw dropped. Had he heard her right?

"You are with ...?"

"Yes, Gabriel – God willing, we will have an addition to our home some time early next summer."

Gabriel reached across the highly polished table and grasped both Naomi's hands in his.

"Oh, this is the best birthday present that any man could wish for. How long have you known? I have noticed no change in you."

"As a woman, I had read the signs for nearly a month, but Doctor Entwhistle confirmed it only this afternoon. He predicts that I shall be delivered of child towards the end of May."

Gabriel got to his feet and pulled his wife to hers. They embraced each other for a few seconds before, suddenly, Gabriel released his grip, almost as though he thought he was crushing their unborn child. He looked at her belly and though it was concealed under layers of cotton dress and petticoats, he observed,

"Now I think I can see the beginnings of the fruit of my seed. How stupid of me not to have known. I am sorry I did not enquire after your condition earlier, my love."

"Are you happy, Gabriel?"

"Oh, yes – it is the second most important day of my life."

"And the first?"

"The day you said you would marry me."

After a birthday supper of freshly cooked mackerel and a Bakewell pudding with home made custard, Gabriel proposed a small liquid celebration for the notable occasion.

"Join me in a glass or two of whisky, my dear?"

"Oh no, Gabriel – it would not be right for me in my condition and for you neither, I think. For, apart from ale to quench your thirst, you have not taken a drink for six months or more and thank the Lord, your dreams have been infrequent, too."

But Gabriel would take some whisky that night. His euphoria would overcome any feelings of apprehension at what the liquid might do to his mind, and he would ignore his wife's pleadings, insistent though they would be. Three large glasses proved to be enough to send him to bed well before ten, fearless and unsuspecting of what the hours of sleep might bring him.

It was not an unpleasant sensation. He couldn't see but he felt warm, soft fur upon his face. Was he hiding from someone or something? Why did he feel he was drowning in a sea of white? Voices shouting – screaming. He didn't like it. He was afraid. He awoke to reality. He was in a cold sweat, holding his head and screaming for all he was worth.

"Aargh! My head! Oh, my head!"

Naomi was out of bed in a flash and quickly lit the bedside oil lamp. She turned back to her husband. He was sitting bolt upright with a look of sheer agony and pain engraved on his death-white face.

Oh, Gabriel, what is the matter?"

Gabriel did not move, his body gripped by pain. Naomi wrung her hands in panic. She moved to hug him, but he flopped back onto the pillows crying,

"It's my head; it throbs! It throbs!"

Then his mouth closed and he lay there, once more racked with pain; as limp and white as a sheet. Naomi felt his forehead. It was cold. She listened to his breathing which, though shallow, seemed regular. It calmed her panic a little. But what should she do? Was it just a bad nightmare? Why had he clutched at his head and why had it appeared to hurt him so much? She paced the room. Should she call her mother – or the doctor? There didn't seem to be anything physically wrong with him, however. She studied his face – his eyes suddenly looked heavy, and as she watched anxiously, they closed in sleep. She breathed a sigh of relief. He seemed to be breathing normally again. It was over.

But it wasn't over. Gabriel, though possessing of all the accepted human signs of sleep, was living a waking nightmare, unable to move or speak. His mind was functioning, but not his body. After Naomi climbed back into bed and lay quietly beside her husband in the darkness, Gabriel's eyelids would regularly flutter open – the only physical movement his comatose state would allow him. In the morning, Naomi's panic would return when her husband resisted all her attempts to get him to move from his rigid horizontal position. When, in addition, she discovered the bed sheets wet with bodily fluids, she screamed in sheer terror.

Naomi's scream reverberated throughout the house but there was no one to hear; no one came. Naomi tried to calm herself and for ten or more minutes she tried everything practical she could think of to raise her husband. Wet compresses and needle pricks all failed. She sobbed at the sight of Gabriel's staring, glazed eyes. He looked awake, but wasn't. She was desperate as she finally tried lifting his head for him to take a drink of water, but his lips remained tightly closed and unresponsive. She fell to her knees at his bedside.

"Oh, please help me! I pray thee, O Lord, bring my beloved back to me."

She mouthed the Lord's Prayer, but it was no use. Her husband was in another world. She ran out of the bedroom and downstairs. She would fetch her mother. She would know what to do.

Fortunately, *Fair View* was only a hundred yards along the cliff path and she ran like the wind, sobbing as she fled to her mother's arms. She didn't knock and burst into the kitchen where Mary Eliott was clearing away after breakfast. Her father had already left for work at the bank. Naomi's mother turned around, some crockery in hand.

"Oh, you startled me, Naomi. Whatever is wrong, child?"

Naomi ran to her mother and threw her sobbing body into her arms. A plate shattered on the stone floor.

"Naomi! What ever has happened?"

"Oh, mother, it's Gabriel – he is sick!"

Mary Eliott put her arms on her daughter's shoulders as she tried to keep her quivering body from fainting.

"Sick? What did he eat last night?"

Naomi looked deep into her mother's eyes.

"Oh, mother – he is more than just sick like that. If it were not for his open eyes and shallow breathing, I would swear that he was dead. He has been like it for hours after he woke from one of his nightmares. And, Mother, he held his head in such agony that I just cannot describe the look on his face."

"Dead? Oh, don't talk nonsense, girl."

"Oh, Mama, you must come now. You will see. He does not move, but just lies in his bed staring at me with no expression on his face."

Naomi's mother put down her cloth. She now could see from her daughter's face that Gabriel's illness was way beyond anything simple like an upset stomach.

"Gabriel must have had a fit, my love. We must fetch Doctor Entwhistle at once. Go back home and stay with him. I will send for him straightaway and I'll fetch Annie on the way. Do not leave his side until I get there and if he moves violently, do not restrain him – you hear?"

Naomi did not reply as she had already left her mother's kitchen. Once outside, she had barely broken into a trot when a voice called from behind her.

"Naomi! Where is your husband?"

St Andrew's Church bells had just finished striking nine times. She turned round – it was Joshua Thomas. He could tell from his daughter-in-law's face that something was gravely wrong. He'd seen that look before on Ma's face – many years ago when Gabriel had been only six. He just somehow sensed he knew what it meant. Naomi shook her head and no further words were exchanged as she and Joshua ran together to be at Gabriel's bedside.

Mrs Eliott returned with Dr Entwhistle less than ten minutes after Naomi and Joshua. Annie was on her way, having gone to inform Amos that there would be no fishing that day. From Mary's description, she too knew what the signs could mean. She had, however, said nothing to Naomi's mother, keeping her suspicions to herself.

Though Winstanley Entwhistle had seen many fits and seizures in his thirty years as a family medical practitioner, he had never seen anything quite like the condition that he would observe that morning. After Naomi's mother had escorted him in to the bedroom, she went to stand beside her daughter who was sitting on the bed, holding Gabriel's hand. Joshua was standing erectly at the foot of the bed with his chin cupped in one hand, supported by the other. He was staring intently at his son's face, as though trying to remember something. He did not move when Dr Entwhistle first entered the bedroom, or when the doctor spoke to Naomi.

"Well, what have we here, Naomi?"

Naomi raised her eyebrows and looked at Gabriel's face as if to say: '*Well, can't you see for yourself?*', but she remained silent until the doctor then asked,

"When did this first happen, Naomi?"

"Last night in bed. He woke from a bad nightmare, and sat up clutching his head and screaming in pain. After he fell back on the bed, I thought he had gone back to sleep because he then closed his eyes. When I awoke this morning, I found him as you see him now – eyes wide open and unable to move or respond to me. He is incontinent, too."

Suddenly, as Naomi finished speaking, there was a noise behind them and Gabriel's dad turned to see Ma standing in the doorway. She immediately linked arms with her husband who seemed to be shaking his head in resignation. Naomi seemed exhausted after her explanation. She stood up and clung to her mother.

After Dr Entwhistle took some time walking round the bed looking at Gabriel from several different positions, he sat on the bed and started his examination. He was thorough, from peering through a glass into Gabriel's eyes to testing his reflexes by tapping his legs with a small hammer. He felt pulses, checked breathing and poked about in his ears with a long metal tube. Finally, he clapped his hands sharply in front of Gabriel's face and when his eyelids didn't even register a flicker, he sighed,

"Well, there's not much I can do I'm afraid. In my opinion he's had a severe seizure of the brain. He has reached a comatose state where his brain has ceased to function. Whether this paralysis is temporary or not, I really do not know, but in cases like this, the situation is often only reversed slowly over an extended period of time."

Naomi burst into tears and buried her head in her mother's arms. Annie then spoke for the first time.

"Are you sure there's nothing you can do?"

"Well, I can give him something for any pain he might be experiencing, but rest is the only answer. He will need constant care, day and night. He will need to be fed liquids through a rubber tube which I will give you. Things like clear soups and tea are good. I will show you how to use it. His body will continue to function internally, but his arms and legs and so on will not move till his brain recovers from the shock of the fit. I am sorry, Naomi."

"He will recover, though, won't he?" said Naomi.

"God willing, my dear. He is in His hands now."

Joshua and Annie clung tighter to each other as the doctor gave Naomi a small bottle of pale green liquid. After a few minutes explaining to her in more detail about Gabriel's care, Dr Entwhistle left, saying he would check in on a daily basis. He would also arrange for a nurse to help with washing and general care.

Naomi's mother and Gabriel's parents spent some time organising shift arrangements for Gabriel's care before Joshua and Annie left their son with Naomi and her mother. Ma would return later to relieve Mary Eliott. Gabriel's parent's original nightmare had been replaced by one equally as frightening. But, unlike their daughter, their son didn't appear to be mad. However, to all intents and purposes, he wasn't alive either. It was going to be a hard Christmas for them all, made all the more heart-rending when, on Christmas Day, Naomi told everyone of her pregnancy.

Contrary to what Dr Entwhistle had said, Gabriel would quickly undergo a sudden, rapid and somewhat frightening transformation. It was just before lunch on Boxing Day when the remarkable change in Gabriel's condition occurred. As usual, Naomi had prepared some thin chicken soup for her husband and was just about to force the feeding tube between his lips when, suddenly, his mouth opened unexpectedly on its own. She nearly dropped the tube and jug in surprise and though there was no one else to hear her, she cried out in surprise.

"Oh God, Gabriel, my love!"

Gabriel's mouth closed. She leant forward, rubber tube held tightly. This time she really did let go of all the feeding apparatus as she put both hands to her mouth in shock. Her husband's mouth had not only opened, it had started to move as well. Her astonishment was all but complete when, with a glazed stare, Gabriel started to mumble something.

"*I want to go home, Mum.*"

Though the actual words were bad enough, both in their total unexpectedness and context, their intonation finally concluded Naomi's bolt from the blue. Her husband had spoken with the voice of a child.

"*I don't like it here. My head hurts. I want to go home.*"

She leant over the bed and stroked Gabriel's forehead.

"There, there, my love. You are home."

"*Where's Daddy?*"

Naomi was at a loss to know what to do or how to answer her husband's question. She tried to remain calm and respond as normally as she could, ignoring the childlike quality of his voice.

"He's at home with Annie, dearest one."

Though Gabriel's first question could possess an acceptable interpretation, if not relevancy, given his age, his next one could not.

"*Where's Jack? Is he …?*"

Naomi was getting worried. This was not her husband's voice. It was that of a small boy. Nevertheless, she continued to try to humour him by answering normally. His eyes still had not moved.

"Who is Jack, Gabriel?"

"*Oh, Mum – you know – Jack Collison.*"

Naomi knew she had to make pretence of being acquainted with her husband's unknown friend – she had seen the frustration suddenly appear in his eyes when she had queried his identity.

"Oh, yes – Jack. I know. He is fine, love."

Suddenly, Gabriel's body started to twitch. Up until then, he had not moved a muscle and had spoken his meaningless words with a fixed stare. Now, he was obviously trying to sit up. Naomi bent over and helped him into a more comfortable position. She nearly fainted when Gabriel reached up with both arms to hug her. She smelt the unmistakable odour of bodily fluid. She held his arms and looked into his eyes which had started to focus properly again and, for the first time, he looked back into her eyes. There was life there, but it was not her husband's life. The eyes showed fear and concern. Naomi knew what the look meant. Her husband did not recognise her.

"You're not my mum. I want Mum."

Gabriel released his grip on Naomi's arms and flopped back on the bed. He started to cry.

"I want to go home! Where are my mum and dad?"

Naomi walked to the end of the bed, and for a minute or two, she tried to study her husband carefully. All his physical attributes seemed to have returned. She watched as he rolled from side to side, occasionally assuming a foetal position under the bed covers. The sobbing continued but he did not speak. She had to tell someone. Dr Entwhistle was due that afternoon, but when? Should she wait till he arrived?

"Get this machine off me!"

The childlike voice was still there and she saw the anger and frustration on her husband's face. Naomi made for the door. She couldn't take any more of her husband's wild and incomprehensible ramblings. What machine?

"I want some chicken nuggets."

Naomi looked back. Gabriel's eyes were wild and rolling in their sockets. She turned and ran out of the bedroom.

Dr Entwhistle came. He said and did little, other than to prescribe a strong opiate sleeping draught which Naomi managed to force down Gabriel's throat, aided by the doctor's strong-armed assistance. Gabriel resisted terribly, scratching at and attempting to bite Dr Entwhistle's hands and arms. Annie and Joshua came too and when they did, Naomi said,

"Here they are, dearest – your mother and father are here to see you."

He barely looked their way before he screamed,

"*Go away – they're not my mum and dad!*"

When Joshua and Ma heard their son's voice, they knew. They did not approach their son, remaining silent, as they had done several times before, by the bedroom door. They watched Gabriel for more than half an hour, as his wild and frenzied look began to fade into drug-induced sleep. They knew. They'd seen that look on their son's face elsewhere. He had gone just like Mary. Naomi would be left with a fatherless child.

Naomi's parents came later that day, too, as did Amos the following morning. They did not see Gabriel at his worst; he moaned but, thankfully, moved little, as regular doses of the drug kept him under control. Hardly anyone said anything, their silence confirming what they all were inevitably thinking. Gabriel looked like he had gone mad.

Days became weeks as Gabriel remained artificially controlled by the sedative. Occasionally, he would come to, thrashing about in his bed. At other times, too, he would rant and rave in his childlike voice. It often took Naomi all her strength to administer enough of the liquid sleeping draught to calm him. Her condition had become a concern for Dr Entwhistle and when he made one of his routine calls at the beginning of March, he could see that Naomi's health had started to suffer and that two other lives were now at risk – hers and her unborn child's. She was weak and tired. He put his hand on her arm and said,

"My dear Naomi, I think you should prepare yourself for the worst. Gabriel is not going to recover. Your burden is too much for you to bear with your child due in less than three months. We must make other arrangements for your husband."

Naomi knew that this day would come. She had known for a long time.

"Arrangements?"

"Yes, my dear. There is a better place for him, where he can be looked after by trained nurses, so you can get on with you life. You have a child to think of."

"What place?"

Dr Entwhistle smiled, sympathetically. Though she had asked the question, Naomi already knew what place the doctor was referring to. No one ever talked about *that* place and Dr Entwhistle was no exception. His meaning had been silently communicated. Gabriel would be taken to the asylum.

"*I want to go home!*"

Gabriel had woken and was screaming from his bed behind them. They turned to see him trying to get up, but he was too weak and fell back limply. More of the sedative was quickly administered by Dr Entwhistle.

After ten more agonising minutes, the 'arrangements' had been made. Dr Entwhistle would draft the necessary letters to the Bethlehem Asylum near Canford that afternoon. As soon as the good doctor had gone, Naomi collapsed in tears on the bed. Her life with Gabriel was at an end.

20
Miracle

After a week, Ed was moved to a specialist hospital in Cambridge. The doctors and nurses at Hamsden had stabilised his condition as best they could, given their facilities. He had continued in a deep coma, which required twenty-four monitoring, though a life support machine had only been needed during the first day after his accident. Thankfully, the consultants had found that his body was able to function more or less unaided by artificial means and, apart from a feeding tube together with heart and brain monitors, his care was very much one of watching and waiting. Of course, prayer might prove to be his biggest hope. Medical science had done its best for little Ed Compton-Jones.

Gary and Jenny made the one hundred and twenty mile round trip nearly every day in order to be with their son, watching for any movement. They thanked God that all his vital signs had become normal. That part of his brain, at least, was undamaged. Until other parts were stimulated into action, there was nothing they could do but pray that his condition would not be permanent and that he would regain full use of his paralysed body.

Summer slid away into autumn almost unnoticed and they began to take it in turns to make the long journey to Cambridge and back, reducing their individual visits to just one or two per week. Their son had become the full focus in their daily life as they sacrificed all other interests, with even work just a time-filler between visits. At home together, their relationship deepened as they clung to each other for support, as if afraid that they might lose each other as well.

Just when they had resigned themselves to months, if not years, without seeing even an infinitesimal change in their son's condition, they received a phone call one Friday evening at the end of October. Jenny answered as Gary was taking a shower after work.

"Hello?"

"Is that Jenny?"

"Yes."

"Oh, hi, Jenny – it's Nurse Collins."

Jenny's heart started to pound.

"Oh yes?"

"Can you and your husband come over tonight?"

Jenny's voice quavered.

"Ye-es."

"Good; Ed's brain waves have changed slightly. We think it might be helpful if you could provide an additional stimulus by talking to him."

"Does that mean he's …?"

"Dr Franklin doesn't know what it means yet, I'm afraid, Jenny, but I know you said you'd like to be kept informed of any change in his condition, no matter how small. You can stay overnight, if you wish."

Jenny's heart was racing.

"We'll be there as soon as we can."

"Good – ask for me when you get here.

"O.K. – bye."

Jenny put the phone down and looked at her watch. It was ten past six. She did the calculation – with luck, they could be there by a quarter to eight. She ran upstairs to tell Gary. This was the first bit of news, good or bad, that they'd had for weeks.

Cambridge's Allington Hospital was a twelve-storey modern building, occupying a purpose-built site two miles from the city centre on the northern ring road. It had gained an international reputation as a leading centre for trauma and coma care. Gary broke a few speed limits to be driving through the main entrance at just after seven-thirty. Ed was on the ninth floor in a private room, adjacent to the main desk.

It had started earlier that day and he was the only one that knew it, too. Unbeknown to all the doctors and nurses, Ed's mind had started to function and the power of thought had returned. There were no outward physical signs of this development and, at first, only mixed flashes of memory entered his dormant brain. By the time his parents reached his bedside, even his staring eyes were able to focus on his surroundings, though physical movement was still impossible. Gary and Jenny had only been in his room a few minutes when Ed's mum gave a squeal of delight.

"His eyes moved – I'm sure of it, Gary!"

Gary looked hard at his son's face for a few seconds.

"There's nothing there, love. You must have imagined it. Dr Franklin said the changes in the brain patterns were small and that we shouldn't expect too much."

"I'm sure his pupils seemed to twinkle and dilate."

"I expect that can happen involuntarily or it may have been a trick of the light. We're both tired, Jen."

But it hadn't been a trick of the light and Ed had recognised his parent's voices. His mind was programming their conversation and trying to piece together his life, held together by the random images that were rattling the door to his brain. Visions of the 'other place' mingled with them and gave him a warm feeling of contentment. Memories of what he had seen and done that first day of September were filtering through. He had used his power for good and his job was done.

Despite continuing to talk to Ed and sharing memories of good times with him until well after midnight, neither Jenny nor Gary saw any further change in his condition that night, perceived or otherwise, and by morning they were resigned to a further period of waiting and praying. It had been a false dawn. According to Dr Franklin, his brain activity had shown a marked increase, but no one, save for Ed himself, could know what the meaning of that activity was. Ed *was* on the road to recovery which, though not yet physical, was leading him a direction he'd always dreamed of going – which was definitely not where his family wanted him to be.

Despite the bitter disappointment and frustration of their visit on the 27th of October, it would transpire that, subsequently, Jenny and Gary had little time to wait before the 'false dawn' became the real one that they had so desperately prayed for. Exactly one week later, and just after lunch on Thursday, November the 3rd, Jenny received the phone call while she was at work. This time, the message was simple. Her son had shown signs of movement.

With people anxious and willing to cover them in their respective places of work, Ed's parents were at his bedside before three o'clock. Dr Franklin was there to greet them in person at the nurse's station.

"Jenny, Gary; this is good news at last, I think. Ed has started to move. We just hope that your presence here will give him that extra push to bring him completely out of his coma."

Jenny had hardly waited for the consultant to finish speaking as she was already on her way to her son's room, to be closely followed by Gary. Dr Franklin tried to urge some caution as they left him by the main desk.

"Please take your time and don't expect too much when you see him."

He quickly caught up to find both of them leaning over Ed's bed, each with one of his hands in theirs. Jenny was already talking to him.

"Come on Ed, love. Please wake up. Mummy and Daddy are here now."

"Yeah, come on, old son – you've been a bit lazy these last couple of months. I bet you're missing school. They're certainly missing you," joked Gary.

Gary's had been deliberately provocative and his words had an immediate and startling effect. School, and the teasing and name-calling that Ed had often associated with it, galvanised him immediately into action, both physical and verbal.

"Ugh! I don't like it there."

Jenny burst into tears and went to hug her son till Dr Franklin and Gary held her back. Ed raised one arm in acknowledgement. The doctor said,

"Careful, Jenny – he'll be weak. Give him space and let him talk."

"Oh hi, Mum. Where am I?"

Jenny couldn't say a word and Gary leant forward.

"In hospital, son."

"What's the time?"

"It's half past three, my love," said Jenny at last.

"How's Jack? Is he alright?"

Then they knew that their son was going to make it. Dr Franklin nodded to Jenny.

"His memory seems O.K. Try asking him a few more obvious things he should know, like names and so on."

Gary took over as Jenny seemed unable to continue. She sat in a chair and held her head in her hands.

"Who is Jack, son?"

"Jack Collison, Dad – I hate him. He bullies me but I got my own back when I punched him in the nose, didn't I, Dad?"

"Yes, son. Now, do you remember where you live?"

By this time, a nurse had propped Ed up on some pillows; he was moving his hands as he talked. He put his left to this chin as though struggling to recall the answer.

"Hmm – by the seaside?"

"Good," said Gary. "What was the last thing you remember doing?"

This seemed easier for Ed.

"I was at the fair with you, Dad, wasn't I? And er, er – someone else, I think."

"What were you doing at the fair?" continued his dad.

"Watching the train and Jack …."

Ed moved his hand to the back of his head, now free of bandages and back with a full cover of black hair.

"Jack was flying through the air and …."

"And?" asked Jenny, suddenly.

"Nothing. I can't remember anything else. It's all black," he lied.

"That really is pretty good, you know. Most people don't recall anywhere nearly as much as that, particularly after an accident as bad and traumatic as your son's," whispered Dr Franklin to Jenny. He turned to Ed and asked,

"What's your name, son?"

"Edward Compton-Jones."

"How old are you?"

"Twenty-fo ..., oh no, I mean seven."

"When's you birthday, Edward?"

"December the 22nd, and I don't like being called Edward – I'm just Ed."

Neither his parents nor Dr Franklin paid any heed to Ed's apparent initial mistake with his age, and as Jenny and Gary hugged each other in sheer relief, even Dr Matthew Franklin could not hide his joy and astonishment at his patient's amazing and sudden revival. He found it absolutely remarkable how much the little boy could remember. Indeed, it was nothing short of a miracle.

Ed's incredible recovery continued apace and by the end of November he was moved to Fenton Cottage Hospital for convalescence and physiotherapy. His memory had got stronger day by day and, apart from a few isolated incidents, including the last few seconds before Jack had hit him, his brain seemed back to normal. His body was weak and his muscles needed strengthening before he would be allowed home, but his nurses and doctors thought Christmas was not an unreasonable target to aim for.

21

Gospel Oak

The 'arrangements' took a little longer than Dr Entwhistle thought they would, giving Naomi some precious extra days with her beloved Gabriel. The harsh reality had begun to set in, but there was still part of her that wished the present situation could continue, despite the difficulties it imposed on her with his care. His ravings has continued unabated, little of which made any sense to her and with his childish voice continuing, it was clear that his mind had gone. However, a couple of apparently unrelated words kept recurring in his mumblings, and one day at the beginning of April – after his usual morning feed – Naomi became a little clearer as to their possible meaning. Gabriel hadn't spoken that day and she was slightly unprepared when he said,

"I want to go the big tree with Minor."

She'd heard the words 'tree' and 'minor' a few times before, but never in the same sentence and never with a request to visit said tree with anyone, if, indeed, 'minor' was a person, or just an occupation. She sat on the bed, and as Gabriel started to dose off, she repeated the words to herself.

"Tree, minor, tree, minor"

What did they mean? Then a partial explanation came to her, and she couldn't believe how stupid she had been. Her husband must have been talking about the Gospel Oak – it was the only 'big' tree she knew. But what did 'minor' mean? After a few minutes she gave up on trying to find a possible explanation. She was certain there were no miners in Gabriel's or her family. One thing was certain, though, and no matter how hard it was going to be, she would have to help him satisfy his wish – he wanted to go to the Gospel Oak. In some strange way, she wanted to go there, too. It had been a favourite spot, both in their courting days and after they were wed as well. It also brought back memories of her husband having one or two less than pleasant dreams under its spreading branches. But it was their special place – the place where Gabriel had first tried to kiss her and where she had accepted his offer of marriage.

When, later that day, Naomi mentioned her husband's request to her mother, she was less than encouraging or supportive with her reply. They were sitting on Gabriel's bed watching him sleep after a strong dose of sedative.

"Oh, what nonsense, my dear. His mind has gone and you mustn't place too much emphasis on what he says. You know that Dr Entwhistle said he would just ramble at times."

"I know, but it makes some sense to me. We always used to like to go to the big tree, as he called it. And, besides, *I* want to go back just one more time before he leaves me forever."

"How will you get him there? He cannot walk – you will need help. Have you thought of that? It just seems it would be too difficult for you, especially with the child due in less than two months now."

"I shall ask Gabriel's father what to do. I'm sure he will help."

"You have no transport, Naomi."

"I'm sure that Joshua had the use of a horse and cart to take fish to market in Hamsden before the Beach Station was opened. Gabriel told me. I can take him in that."

"He will fall off or he may become wild and thrash about. It just seems pointless if it is only to satisfy a whim, whether his or yours."

Naomi looked her mother directly in the eyes and said sternly,

"Mama – I *am* going to do it. If I have to strap him to a chair and tie the chair to the cart, I will do it – I must do it."

"Then do it you must, but don't say I didn't warn you when it turns into a nightmare for you."

"What could be more of a nightmare than what I am enduring now? Even if my beloved Gabriel were to die as a consequence of my actions, I should not blame myself. I'd rather the good Lord took him than he should spend the rest of his days in the asylum. That's how I truly feel, Mama."

"So be it, and I'm sure your father will do everything to help in whatever way he can."

When he was informed of his daughter's suggestion, Mayor Richard Eliott was far more accommodating of the idea than his wife had been initially. There was no need, he said, to get Joshua to find transport. Naomi would have use of one of the mayoral horse and carriages. When word got out of her unusual plan, people rallied round in support. Amos and Joshua agreed to help carry Gabriel if necessary and when Dr Entwhistle said she could borrow a wheelchair and that he would provide a nurse for his care on the journey, Naomi knew that her husband's request would be met.

The eccentric outing was finally set for April the 7th, two days before Gabriel was due to be taken to the Bethlehem Asylum outside Canford. Joshua and Amos arrived at nine-thirty to prepare him for the journey out to Gospel Oak and, judging by the raised voices that Mary Eliott could hear as she went to open her daughter's front door, the choice of route was obviously causing some argument. Amos seemed to be winning it.

"And I tell thee it'll be best to follow the road to the Wentham and take the river path until it reaches Peewit Hill. There's a track somewhere there that leads right to the Gospel Oak."

Naomi's mother smiled as she opened the door to greet the two men.

"I think Amos here might be right. I believe my husband spoke to Ted, the carriage driver, yesterday about times and I'm sure he said much the same thing."

"Oh, good morning, Mary," said Joshua. "At least the weather is fine. It is a beautiful spring morning and, given Ted Purley is driving, I must concede the argument. He knows all the tracks for miles around and there isn't a better man with horses."

"Good – he is due at ten. You'd better both come up to see Naomi and Gabriel."

Naomi's mother glanced at the heavy leather straps that Joshua was holding and her mind was taken back to her namesake – Gabriel's sister. She had needed much restraining. Hopefully, with the powerful sedative, Gabriel would not require such ruthless handling. Joshua noticed Mary's look and said, reassuringly,

"Don't worry, Mary. They're just for keeping the wheelchair from sliding about in the carriage."

Naomi and Mary had dressed Gabriel as best they could in a fine woollen brown suit with an open-necked pale blue shirt. With his long, fine jet-black hair brushed back from his forehead, he looked as good as he had done for some time. His father was obviously impressed.

"Well now, here's a fine looking gentleman."

Immediately, Naomi started to cry.

"He is," she sobbed. "And he always will be."

Joshua put his arm round his daughter-in-law. She was dressed in one of her best Sunday dresses – all pale yellow and blue, like the sun against a mid-summer sky.

"Hush now – don't fret, lass. You both look a picture."

They had propped Gabriel up on some pillows and he was shoeless, his feet covered with thick woollen socks. He looked peaceful and calm, apart from his usual rolling eyes and a not-so-usual twitch from his left arm. The wheelchair stood at the side of the bed. There was an awkward pause for a few minutes while the women made some last minute checks for the journey. The silence was finally broken when the nurse arrived just as St Andrew's Church sounded the three-quarter hour.

"Are you ready, Naomi," said Gabriel's father. "Shall we get him into the chair?"

"Yes – I think we have everything. I gave him a stronger than normal measure of sedative not half an hour since."

Joshua and Amos lifted Gabriel with ease, his clothes flopping at the sides of his emaciated body. Though Naomi knew how much weight her husband had lost, she still put a hand to her mouth when she saw them put him in the chair. Then, despite what he had said, Joshua quickly slipped and tightened one of the leather straps round his son's body – though more for ease of carrying the chair than for restraint.

Gabriel was silent and quiet when the men carried him downstairs and placed the chair carefully on the path outside. No one saw the brief smile that flickered on his face, though. He hadn't smiled in over three months. It lasted but a second. The clip-clop of hooves could soon be heard in the distance.

"That will be Ted," said Mary Eliott. "It's nearly ten."

When it came into view they all could see it was a sizeable carriage, pulled by two horses, though its trappings almost forced Naomi to her knees in despair.

"Oh no, Mama! Father has sent the hearse."

"It is the best one in Fenton and perfect for transporting a wheelchair, love," said her mother.

"Mary's right, lass," said Joshua. "It'll make it so much easier. You mustn't think of it like that. After all, Ted's not dressed for a funeral. He has just left some ribbons on the harnesses, that's all."

Naomi seemed to recover her composure. She quickly decided that it wasn't going to spoil her and Gabriel's outing.

"I suppose you're right, father-in-law – it's for the best."

"Let's get everyone aboard who's a-coming," said Ted.

There was just enough room – Naomi and Amos next to Ted upfront and Joshua and the nurse either side of Gabriel on the flat bed of the hearse behind. It was the strangest sight to behold – a cross between a wedding carriage and a king on his mobile throne. Several neighbours had come out of their houses to gaze at the unusual scene.

The road to the River Wentham was flat and sloped gently from the town of Fenton, following the cliff as it made its way down to the river estuary. In contrast, the river path to the meadows beneath Peewit Hill had a well-trodden surface, having been used by countless horses that had pulled the river barges for more than a hundred years. Though it was not much more than a couple of miles from the main road to Peewit Hill, the going proved painfully slow, as Ted Purdey fought to keep the carriage from getting stuck in the deep ruts. Nurse Ellen seemed more concerned with Naomi and her condition than Gabriel. Fortunately, the early spring weather had been dry and the surface was hard. Occasionally, they had to divert into a meadow in order to avoid particularly rough ground. Gabriel's chair had been strapped securely to both sides of the carriage and it followed its undulating movement. However, the strong sedation kept him quiet with his head resting on his chest. The sun was warm and Naomi had to keep her wide-brimmed hat on to keep cool and the mid-morning sun off her neck. They nearly missed the track near Peewit Hill until Joshua shouted from the rear.

"That's the turning, Ted!"

For all his local knowledge, Ted Purdey had never ridden or driven horses along the river path and he bowed to Joshua's instruction, turning the horses quickly left, necessitating both Joshua and Ellen to combine their efforts to prevent the chair from toppling over.

"Are you sure this is right, Joshua," called Ted after they had gone about hundred yards down the side track. "I don't see any trees ahead."

"Yes – the field is on the other side of the hill. It's not far now."

The track, though narrower than the river path, was much flatter and even and they made good progress. A few minutes later and they had reached their destination.

"That's it, Ted," said Naomi. "It's the tree in the middle of the field ahead."

Immediately, Ted knew there was going to be a problem.

"We can't go in there. The carriage won't make it. It's too rough, I'm afraid."

"Well, we can't push the wheelchair," said Joshua.

Naomi nudged Amos awake.

"Come on, Amos, you have a job to do."

"You mean …?"

"Yes, Joshua – we must carry him there."

"No, child – *you* must not carry anything. Amos and I will do it. It's not far."

Naomi shaded her eyes from the sun. The Gospel Oak stood tall and handsome, freshly painted in the bright green of early spring.

Like a scene from a jungle expedition, the tribal procession set off for the majestic tree, standing isolated and lonely in the middle of the immaculately ploughed field. Ted remained with the horses to feed and water them, while Ellen and Naomi walked beside Gabriel's bearers. The ploughed field proved harder to cross than they'd thought as Joshua and Amos fought to keep their footing in the deep rich soil. Twice they had to put Gabriel down while they reorganised their grip on the chair. Finally, when they reached the tree and the welcome shade it provided, they placed the wheelchair so that Gabriel faced Peewit Hill and the river. Naomi had gone very quiet, as if she had suddenly concluded that the arduous journey had been a mistake and that she was regretting the decision to bring her husband. She wandered over to Joshua and whispered in his ear. He nodded and turned to Amos and Ellen.

"Ellen, Amos – we must leave Naomi and Gabriel now for a while. We will go back to the carriage and wait."

Ellen started to protest.

"But Dr Entwhistle said I must …."

"Please, nurse – we will leave Gabriel strapped in his chair. Come, we will go."

Ellen nodded and not another word was spoken as the three of them left Naomi and Gabriel alone together in their special place. Naomi watched as they walked in single file down a furrow towards the horses and carriage. They had only gone about fifty yards when she heard the wheelchair creak behind her.

"Please release me from these straps, Naomi."

Naomi froze. She daren't turn round. It had not been a child's voice. It was her husband's own.

"Please, my love. Why am I in this chair?"

Still she did not move as she steeled herself to turn round. Surely she was hallucinating – it was the sun; her condition; memories of their special place.

"For pity's sake, Naomi – set me free!"

She slowly turned, hardly daring to look.

"Come on, my beloved."

There, feet in front of her, sat her husband – her Gabriel – smiling and with arms outstretched towards her. She didn't know what to do. Should she shout for someone? Suddenly, Gabriel made it easier for her.

"My nightmare is over, Naomi. The pain is gone from my head and I am back forever from that other terrible place."

Naomi knelt down and held her husband's hands. She kissed them.

"Oh, my Gabriel – God has worked a miracle. Praise the Lord."

"So, are you going to release me?"

Naomi walked round to the back of the chair and carefully undid the leather strap.

"Thank you, my love. Now help me to stand."

"Gabriel, you shouldn't try. You will fall."

"Help me, please."

She helped him, but he could only remain upright for a few seconds; just enough time for him to plant a kiss on Naomi's lips before he collapsed back into the chair.

"How long have I been asleep? You are full with child."

"It has been more than three months, my love."

"*Keep away from him, Naomi.*"

Naomi did not turn round. It was the sound of Joshua shouting and the crunch of footsteps returning on the ploughed field.

"We have company, Naomi," said Gabriel as he peered from behind her dress.

"*Oh, lass, what are you doing?*"

"Why, father – she is merely helping me."

"Gabriel?"

"*I'll sedate him, Mr Thomas.*"

"No, Ellen," said Naomi, as she turned with arms raised to prevent the advancing nurse. "Not this time; not ever. My husband is back."

"But ...."

Joshua fell to his knees in front of his son.

"Gabriel?"

"Yes, father – Naomi speaks the truth. I am whole again and I can see."

"Oh, praise be to God!"

"Now I want to go home. I am tired and hungry. Please take me home."

Gabriel's father looked up into his son's eyes.

"But when did this all happen?"

"I do not know, father. Who can tell? Maybe I saw things before I understood them. Maybe I understood them before I saw them, but I could not speak about them until just now."

Naomi moved to stand in front of Gabriel's father.

"No more talking now, my own true love – I am taking you home."

22

Another Curse

Jack Collison and his parents only visited Ed once when he was in Fenton Cottage Hospital. Though he seemed a little embarrassed over his stupid actions, Jack never really apologised to Ed for causing him such severe and life-threatening injuries. As far as he was concerned, Ed had just been unlucky to be standing where he was. Of course, his parents would constantly remind him that if it hadn't been for Ed and his teddy bear, he himself would probably have suffered equally serious injuries and, indeed, might not have survived the accident.

For himself, Ed had not been surprised at Jack's attitude toward him and the accident. He had not done his good deed out of any sympathy for the bully, but merely to prove to himself that he could use his special power for good, whether the recipient of the act was thankful or not. It had been a kind of final act before he made his attempt at permanency in his 'other' world. Ed knew he didn't belong in Jack's world or, sadly, his parents. He had had much time to think about his future – or his past – while in hospital and his mind was made up. At the earliest and most convenient opportunity he would try to engineer his way back to the place where he felt content and he was respected for what he was. That opportunity was to present itself a week after his release from hospital. He didn't want to deliberately cause his mum and dad grief, but his Uncle Eddie had disappeared – or so they said – so why shouldn't he, particularly if his disappearance could be believed to be the result of a tragic accident? That way, he hoped, his family might eventually be able to come to terms with it, apportioning blame to nobody, least of all themselves.

At teatime, two days before his birthday, Ed prepared the ground for his departure. His mum and dad had been discussing what he would like to do as a special treat on the day that they thought he would never see.

"We could go and see Town play on Saturday, Ed," said Gary.

"That's two days after my birthday, Dad."

"What about going to the cinema in Hamsden?" suggested Ed's mum.

"What's on?"

"I don't know, dear – we could check," replied Jenny. "We'd like you to do what you want, love. It's an extra special day this year."

"There is something I really would like to do."

"What?" asked Ed's dad.

"Fishing."

"Fishing? It's a bit cold for fishing, son."

"You once said that the fish didn't know what time of year it was – and also that when the water was colder they were easier to catch."

"Did I?" said Ed's dad. "There's only one problem, though."

"What?" asked Jenny.

"The pier's closed till Easter."

"I don't want to fish off the pier, Dad. I want to go back to where we fished in the Wentham – where you took me in the Jaguar."

"Oh, I see," said Ed's dad, thoughtfully. "Why there?"

"Because that's what I want to do. You said it was my special day and I could do what I wanted to do. Please, Dad."

"Are you sure you feel strong enough, love?" asked Jenny.

"Yes, Mum – I want to get out doing things again. I've been in hospital for ages."

"Nearly four months, Ed," said Gary. "And if that's what you really want to do then that's what we'll do, old son."

"I do, Dad. I really do."

Thursday, December the 22nd turned out to be an unusually mild day with only a gentle breeze for Ed to contend with. By the time he and his dad were ready to set off, even the sun had decided to honour his special day. After the half hour drive down the winding lanes, they were at their chosen spot by just after eleven o'clock. The wind has picked up a little and the Wentham was running fast.

The fish obviously knew it was Ed's birthday, as they caught three nice trout within the first hour, causing Gary to remark,

"This was a brilliant idea of yours, son. You must have known they would bite today."

"They knew it was my birthday, Dad," joked Ed.

By this time, Gary had allowed Ed to hold the small rod on his own and the last fish, though netted by his dad, had been the first one that he could claim he had caught unaided. With lunchtime approaching, Gary said,

"I'll go and get our lunch from the car, Ed. Will you be alright holding the rod till I get back?"

"Yes – no problem, Dad."

"If you get a bite, shout me and don't try and land it on your own – alright?"

"Yes, Dad."

Ed took the rod from his father and said,

"Take your time."

Gary would never read any significance into his son's last words, for that was what they were to become – the last words he would ever hear his son speak. He simply nodded to Ed and set off for the car which was parked about a hundred yards away. Ed waited until his dad had opened the Jaguar's boot so that he was partially hidden from his sight. He made his move, taking off his yellow anorak and holding it, together with the rod, in two hands in front of him. He closed his eyes and uttered his plea.

"Take me to the nice place."

As soon as he had finished speaking, he threw both his anorak and the rod into the fast-moving river. It had to work now.

The clip-clop of horse's hooves greeted his ears. He was sitting at the front of an open carriage and he felt happy and warm. This was his reality now and he was back from his unpleasant sojourn in the future. Naomi was next to him and was gently holding his hand.

"Soon we shall be three, my love. I am due in less than two months now."

"We will have to think of a name," said Gabriel.

"We must wait to see what God provides us with. What do you want – a boy or a girl?"

"A boy, Naomi."

They would never find a body. A few day's later, Ed's yellow anorak and the remains of his fishing rod would be washed up further downstream. The inevitable conclusion would be reached – Ed Compton-Jones had slipped or overbalanced and fallen into the swollen river and then been swept out to sea. He had – they would say – obviously taken off his anorak in a vain attempt to swim to shore. His little body had not been strong enough to withstand the tidal pull of the river and he had drowned.

Initially, Gary would blame himself for leaving his son unattended, but Jenny's love for her husband would be strong enough for them both to somehow manage to survive the tragedy and remain as a couple. It had been a tragic accident and little Ed was at peace at last. In the forthcoming days, Jenny would console herself in the knowledge that Ed had joined his Uncle Eddie in a far, far better place.

23

Two Little Magpies

Naomi would be delivered of a son on June the 2nd, 1896 and, after much discussion, the proud parents would name him Edward Joshua Thomas. He would have his mother's deep blue eyes, but his father's jet black hair.

Eighteen months after the tragic loss of their son, Gary and Jennifer would be delivered of a beautiful baby girl, who they would name Maggie in memory of their first little magpie.

> *One for sorrow,*
> *Two for joy,*
> *Three for a girl,*
> *Four for a boy,*
> *Five for silver,*
> *Six for gold,*
> *And seven for a secret never to be told.*

THE END

www.ingramcontent.com/pod-product-compliance
Lightning Source LLC
Chambersburg PA
CBHW020831260626
47169CB00003B/929